HER
IMM
A

TASTE ME

USA TODAY BESTSELLING AUTHOR

J.R. THORN

To those who like 'em thick, this one is for you.

... I'm talking about large books, pervert.

Just kidding, large dicks too!

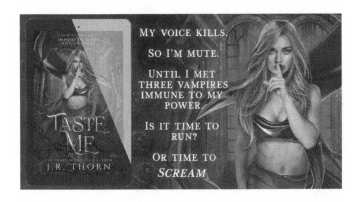

One word could kill them all.

That's what I was warned about after the first accident when I killed my family's allies. My powers manifested too young.
Powers I never asked for.
I can connect with the realm of the dead. My medium?

My voice.

And so I don't talk. Ever. Not to anyone—except my sister, of course. She's the only reason I'm not utterly insane after a lifetime spent hiding.

In the darkness.
In silence.

Under a shroud of loneliness with only the dead for company.
Until I meet them.

Jasper.
Kornelius.
Zyran.

Three sinfully gorgeous vampires without a House who I
don't trust.
Because my words didn't kill them when they came
for me.
My time spent hiding is over, because now all of the
Houses know about me.

And I can choose to run... or I can scream.

Taste Me is a spicy standalone romance with obsessively
protective mates. These psychotic vampires will guide
Ishara on a road of self-acceptance and forgiveness, but
not before breaking down her emotional walls. There will
be biting. There will be darkness. And there will be
blood. Reader discretion is advised.

Trigger Warning

This is a dark paranormal reverse harem romance, meaning you might want to be aware of some of the fucked-up shit that goes on in this story before you la-di-da on in.

Like breath play. Blood play. Knife play, to name a few.

There are three brothers who intimately share their mate at the same time. They do not interact with each other, but sharing requires a certain level of comfort between the triplets when it comes to bedroom play. If that makes you uncomfortable, do not read this book!

I would also be remiss if I didn't mention self-destructive love interests who turn psychotic and murderous. Actually, spoiler-not-spoiler, murder happens in chapter one.

There's orgasm denial, to the point that it's not fun, y'all. There is a safe word and it's not respected—which is one of the most heinous of all sex-play crimes and I have to mention it before you open this book. There's apologizing and groveling, but I'm still mad about it. (If I'm mad, I don't even want to guess how readers might feel, so, in the TW this goes!)

Finally, there is depression, trauma, and self-harm. If

any of these things trigger you or have a potential to bring you to a dark place, close this book and find a new read that makes you happy.

If you choose to stay, know that there is always a happy ending in my books.

And orgasms. Lots and lots of orgasms.

XOXO

Jen

An Introduction from Ishara Doyle

Over fifty years ago, a portal opened in Portland, Oregon. It wasn't the first, nor would it be the last. But it was the first to appear on an open highway filled with mortals.

As one could imagine, chaos ensued. Magic overtook our world and changed all humans within it, leaving no one untouched.

In response, Houses formed in an attempt to regulate the surge of supernaturals and magic—but power is a disease.

I know that better than anyone.

It corrupts. Infects.

It brings *death*.

Or the Great Sacrifice, as the Houses call it. But that's just a fancy name for genocide.

One I'm more intimate with than most.

Because I'm a Death Witch and I can still hear their screams. If it weren't for my sister's voice in my head, I would have gone mad long ago.

Fallon Doyle. We're everything to each other.

And this world wasn't built for us. We're too powerful.

We were born without a House, leaving us without protection against those who fear power.

Or want it for themselves.

I'm not one for politics. My sister became queen, not me.

But I live in this world just like all the unfortunate souls trapped on this plane. Except for the prior Gold and Garnet King, Vesperus, who managed to find a way out with his Goddess Queen.

I can't be too sour. His fated mate, Nyx, the Goddess of Night, was the driving force to break the forced-mate spell on my twin. One that kept her mate-bonded and subservient to a monster.

A spell I couldn't break myself, leaving Fallon to be a tortured prisoner to a fake, power-hungry mate for three terribly long years, four if I'm including her imprisonment with Kaspian while still bonded to that bastard.

Four years of guilt on my conscience that will never go away.

Four years of the voices from the death plane to invade my dreams without support or reprieve. Because my sister wasn't there to save me from madness when it came knocking on my door.

Even when my sister survived the execution of her fake mate and eventually ascended as Queen of Gold and Garnet, I didn't feel safe.

Because the spell that nearly destroyed her is still a threat.

Because that same horror could happen again. I was proof of that.

Fallon thinks I killed them all.

I *know* I did.

But somehow... I think the nightmare isn't over yet.

The Houses
House of Gold and Garnet
House of Blood and Beryl
House of Air and Amethyst
House of Earth and Emerald
House of Spirit and Sapphire
House of Death and Diamond
House of Fire and Fluorite
House of Sea and Serpentine

No Man's Land
No Man's Circus - Portland, Oregon

Supernatural Syndicates
New York City

Manhattan - The Wards - Shifters
Brooklyn - The Roses - Fae
Staten Island - The Outcast Coven - Witches
Queens - The Divine - Angels & Demons
Bronx - Clan Tepes - Vampires

Chapter 1

Issy

My heart thunders in my chest as I stare at the only exit to my little cottage in the middle of nowhere.

I watch as it bows against the weight of the male's fist behind it.

Fuck. Fuck.

Fuck!

The incessant male beating against the door clearly isn't going to go away. I clutch my new book to my chest as I pace across the plush chocolate rug that Ayla chose for our living room. The echo of the screams that sound as I tread back and forth tells me that whoever made them is dead.

Ayla doesn't know I hate the rugs, or the furnishings, or any of the decor she chose that are antiques—meaning they all exude the screams of the dead when I'm near them.

I hate anything that reminds me of what I am.

And I hate Dominique Andrias, my date who has somehow found out where I live.

The urge to shout at him to go away sticks in my throat, but I can't utter a word.

Because as much of a horrible date Dominique was, he doesn't deserve to die.

And unluckily for him, he has no idea that my words kill. I'm a Death Witch and that's my power.

Or my curse, if I'm being honest with myself.

Issy? my sister asks, her soft tone venturing into my mind like the gentle breeze it is, banishing the screams all around me just from the power of her voice.

She doesn't know the calming effect her mind has on me, or the depths of my suffering. I didn't start hearing the screams until my powers manifested, and after that, it was easy to keep the burden to myself.

Lately, though, it's tempting to tell her my secret.

All the more reason I need to shut her out until I can fix it.

She likely felt my panic and is just checking on me, but I don't want to distract her.

She's finally happy.

Finally with mates who treat her like the queen she is. Quite literally.

She wound up with multiple fated mates, one of them being the King of Gold and Garnet. I'm not particularly jealous of the king part—she can keep all the politics and drama that come with that position—but I wish I knew what it felt like to be safe.

Protected.

Adored.

"Come on, bitch. Open the door!" Dominique shouts as the door cracks under another blow. "I know you stole the book of shadow spells!"

My eyes widen. Is that the book he thinks I took? The title was better translated to "Death's Whispers," which interests me a great deal, given my problem. But not many can read ancient witch script, much less translate it properly.

When I don't answer, the beating at the door goes silent.

But I very much doubt that Dominique has given up. He's likely circling the property now, looking for another way in.

There isn't one. This is supposed to be a safe place and under the protection of the Dukes of Lapland. So he'll be back at the door, or breaking in a window if he's desperate enough.

Either way, that gives me time.

Issy? my sister says again, this time more urgent. *Do I need to arrange a portal spell? Nolan can be there in less than—*

Fallon, I'm fine, really, I assure her. I know I'm going to have to give her something or she's just going to make this worse. *I just... my ex-date is here and he's mad that I stole a book.*

Fallon goes silent in my head while I sort through the potion shelf Ayla set up. She usually leaves the "book learning," as she calls it, to me and likes to experiment with the potion recipes I give her.

I circle my fingers around a bottle of purple liquid when Fallon finds her voice, drowning out the screams that would

3

normally follow. *I'm not sure what shocks me more. That you went on a date, or that you didn't ask me for money.* Again.

I snort as I place my new book in a glass box. It's temperature-controlled and designed to keep ancient texts in prime condition. A few hours drying out and I suspect I'll be able to open it without damaging it.

Ayla suggested that I get out more, I say, wrinkling my nose at the idea.

In my opinion, I've been *getting out* plenty. After a lifetime of being imprisoned in my family's basement, I've been wandering the forest, learning about the types of flowers that grow here, and I even took up gardening.

I much prefer an isolated hobby after a lifetime of seclusion. Maybe I'm damaged. Maybe I'm traumatized.

Or maybe I just don't like people.

Regardless, after a lifetime of being too dangerous to be around others, I'm used to being by myself. My nerves can hardly take too much social interaction, although Ayla doesn't bother me. I quite enjoy her company.

My new hobby is something that she benefits from, too. I learned how to grow some of the rarer flowers for her potions and I'm particularly proud of my Middlemist Reds. They remind me of my favorite flower, the rose.

And my favorite thing about gardening is that it's free from death screams. Nature and flowers are the essence of life, untouched by lost souls.

However, the screams still find a way to reach me the moment I touch something that's man-made. My own cottage has generations of screams within it, some of them from the Great Sacrifice.

Even here, I can't escape.

I need a spell to silence them once and for all, for my own sanity.

I can't keep relying on Fallon. I'm not the only person in her life anymore.

And I refuse to be a burden.

So, when Ayla mentioned Lapland's spell book curator as my test subject, my head somehow bobbed up and down in agreement.

Because books are my weakness, and Ayla knows it.

And what excuse do you have for turning to thievery *instead of asking your twin for some blood vials? Hmm?*

A grin purses at my lips. *Would your mates approve of you abusing your position just to buy your sister some old books?*

She returns my earlier snort with one of her own. She somehow manages to make the sound come off more regal than mine. *Knowing you, it's a rare book, one worth at least a vial of the blood from Kaspian himself. Which I can get you, you know. If you'd just* ask.

Walking around with a vial of king's blood sounds like a terrible idea, but I don't say as much to my sister. She's just trying to look out for me.

Well, I don't need to ask because I got this. I'm just borrowing the book, anyway. And I'm going to use a memory potion on him. So don't worry about me, okay? I ask my sister. Then I add, *I expect you're busy anyhow. Tell me I'm wrong.*

One of my sister's giggles is music to my ears, and proof that I'm right. Because that giggle came from one of her mates trying to get her attention. She's probably in bed with one or more of them.

That's what I thought. You have many duties as queen. One of the most pressing seems to be beating the record for most orgasms in a day.

Hey! she shouts, but there is a grin to her words. *Don't tell that to Nox or Bane. They'll make it their life mission to fabricate some ridiculous number and then half kill me to meet it.*

I can practically see her dirty-blonde locks bouncing around her face as her eyes glitter with happiness.

Her phantoms are definitely my favorite of her mates.

She managed a brief visit once with her phantoms as her protectors, and her happiness had kept me going when my nightmares threatened to take me under. I loved how Nox and Bane hung on her every word and clearly adored her.

At least Fallon found her happily-ever-after. She deserves it.

I'm the one who failed her. Before all this, she agreed to mate a monster in order to protect me.

It resulted in her being buried alive for sport, all while under an obedience spell.

For three years.

I'm glad you have them, I say, my words turning somber. *Now quit worrying about me and go back to your mates, okay? I can handle a pissed-off bookkeeper.*

She sighs in my head, and I can definitely envision her wistful smile. *Fine, but if you need something,* please *tell me, okay? And not because I'm Queen of Gold and Garnet. Because I'm your* sister, *Issy. And I love you.*

Heat pricks at my eyes, and feels an awful lot like tears. *I love you, too, Fallon.*

I shut my mind off from her before she can feel the wave of pain that follows that statement. Because it's my love for her that demands my isolation.

The screams rush into my head the moment Fallon's presence is gone. No matter how much I brace myself, it still startles me.

The haunting sounds are more like nails against metal than anything else. It grates on my nerves and makes me tighten my grip on the bottle causing it.

The purple liquid comes from a living creature—likely some sort of shifter that Ayla killed.

Fallon could help me silence this torment, but I refuse to indulge the need to engage her mind again.

She needs to live her happily-ever-after.

Not be constantly worrying about me and leaving her mates behind just because I'm in trouble. Even she has to realize the time has finally come for us to build our own lives.

And I will build my own. With my own blood.

And my own screams.

Quite literally.

My gaze lingers on the bottled screams on the weapons shelf, a shelf indented into the wall for protection. The potion is a deadly magical grenade I had experimented on for Ayla.

My own power terrifies me.

Swirls of gold and satin red wisps flutter inside the fragile glass container. It's lethal if opened or broken, which is why it's on the top shelf inside the wall itself.

Walking past it, I decide my memory-altering potion will do the trick. Dominique isn't anything like the evil souls I have faced in my twenty-three years.

Plus, I don't need a bottle with deadly screams. My whispers are just as fatal.

All it would take is a few gentle words and he'd be dead.

This is for Fallon.

A memory flashes through my mind. The only time I ever intentionally used my voice to kill is seared into my brain and likes to revisit my waking moments every chance possible.

Shoving it away, I return to the living room and wait patiently at the front door. I uncork the bottle and am careful not to sniff the contents as I hold it away from my face.

I place my hand on the handle and wait for Dominique to return.

It takes longer than I like and I frown, hoping he didn't mess up my garden, or else I'm going to do worse than a memory-altering potion.

When a knock sounds, I swing the door open and shove the potion's contents in the intruder's face.

Only it's not Dominique Andrias.

It's a male I've never seen before, but at the same time, I know exactly who he is.

Because my stomach clenches.

My entire world shatters and the breath rushes out of me in a silent gush of air.

Not a sound, or a gasp, or else I would kill this perfect creature.

Mine. The word forms in my head with such solidity that it scares me.

The world seems a little bit brighter, even in the soft dusk of sunset in Lapland, suggesting my pupils have blown wide.

His do the same until the potion takes effect, leaving him with a dazed sense of confusion.

Now I'm really in trouble.

Because I just threw a memory-altering potion at my fated mate.

Chapter 2

Issy

The male with a sinfully kissable jawline blinks at me a few times.

It takes me a moment to realize his pupils have shrunk. His eyes are incredibly dark, like a starless night where even the dead finally sleep.

He's so beautiful.

So perfect.

Entirely mine.

Fate magic is extremely powerful. After watching it destroy my sister and build her back up again, I'm both hopeful and afraid of what my own experiences might be like.

I already know the dark side of it, having been subjected to the same spell as my sister and forced into a bond that fate didn't approve of.

Until I killed him, anyway.

This connection, though, is the real deal. Burning desire unlike anything I've ever felt crawls through my veins, pleasantly warming me when I'm more accustomed to the ever-present chill of the death plane.

I knew if I ever encountered my fated mate, it would hit like a death stone.

But I didn't expect the impact to be so distracting and all-consuming.

So *alluring*.

Because all I want to do is climb this man like a tree even when I have no idea who he is or why he's here.

My thighs clench and my lungs struggle to take in air because I need this male's kiss like I need oxygen.

Logically, I know I need to keep my distance.

My body seems to have other ideas in mind.

Taking a deep, shuddering breath, I ignore the urge to reach out to my twin.

I need to focus, so I opt for my second-favorite habit to center myself, which is mentally reciting the translation of the word "death" in as many languages as I know.

Which is a lot.

Mortem.

Morte.

Dood.

Kuolema.

死

موت

...

I go through each word, slowly calming myself enough to think straight.

Only to be enveloped in pure silence, the first I've experienced in a very long time.

And that's when I realize that the screams have stopped.

Is it because I emptied the bottle's contents? I wonder as I open my palm to stare at the object.

There's still a little smear of purple left behind on the glass. It should be enough to link me to the soul on the death plane that offers me its torment.

"Those screams are power. Poor female. You can't even appreciate what you have. You're too weak. Too fragile. Too sweet. Let me take your burden, my new mate..."

The unwanted flashback hits my mind again, making me flinch.

Daithi O'Neely was the one to trap Fallon with her tormentor. His dark magic betrothed her to a monster, but Daithi wasn't Fallon's tormentor; he was mine.

Because he took *me* as his mate.

Without my permission. Without my consent.

Without a care as to what would happen to me when he pushed me into a state of unconsciousness and trapped me in my own mind.

But the body remembers what happened to it. My soul might have been inside a cage, but my mind and my flesh felt every touch and invasion.

He stuck me in a freezer and stuffed me with tubes. That was the only way to keep me subdued enough to make sure he was safe while he stole my power.

And my body seems intent on informing me of every horror I missed in my spiritual absence.

Daithi talked to me while I was unconscious and frozen.

While he petted me like a trophy.

While he thought I wouldn't remember what he'd said and done as he'd forced a fake mate bond on me to steal my magic.

While he violated me.

"What has your eyes so haunted?" the man before me asks, banishing the nightmares just like he banished the screams as he cups my face.

I lean into his touch, my body reacting on instinct to my fated mate.

A jolt of *wrongness* lurches through my body.

I only ever knew that sensation from one male.

Daithi O'Neely.

I flinch away, but he catches my hands in response.

"You're terrified. Is someone trying to hurt you?" Anger flares in his dark eyes. "I'll rip them to shreds. I'll..." His words trail off as if he forgot why he so viciously wants to protect me.

Or why he's even here.

I'm not sure what impact a memory-altering potion is going to have on someone who just met their fated mate, but it seems this male is struggling with it.

He shakes his head as if to clear it but doesn't release me, leaving my knuckles crunching under his iron grip.

My heart thunders in my chest as I debate what the hell I'm going to do.

Why does he feel like dark magic?

Why does he feel like Daithi?

While I've fantasized about finding a true fated mate of my own, this isn't at all how I imagined it going.

I have no idea who this man is, other than that he

showed up at my cottage, unannounced, when Dominique had been beating down my door.

Dominique...

He definitely should have been back by now.

I shove into my fated mate, forcing him to give way. He gives me space, but he's not letting me out of his sight. He follows me as I hurry around the cottage.

Normally, this would be the best part of my day.

Or my night, as it were.

The forest comes alive in the dark and it's my favorite time to explore. That's when the animals venture out, when the dusk flowers bloom, and when I can forget who I am, just for a little while.

Except now, my carefully tended garden is trampled and has a body on top of it.

My nails bite into my skin as I clench my fists.

Really?!

So, my fated mate is a mercenary for hire, somehow connected to Daithi O'Neely, and Dominique had clearly pissed someone off.

Or I was the target before I took the mercenary off guard. Meaning Dominique was in the wrong place at the wrong time.

"Do you realize you have a dead bear shifter in your garden?" the male behind me unhelpfully provides.

I didn't realize Dominique was a bear shifter. That explains his burly appearance. But it's useless information, otherwise.

Except to suggest that my fated mate is a terrifying force. One that can kill a bear shifter without breaking a sweat.

Whirling on the mercenary, I glower my best death glare—which is pretty damn good—while I decide what in the spirits I'm going to do with this male.

While he smells like Daithi, he so far hasn't presented further threat.

Likely because of the potion I doused him with.

Depending on what kind of supernatural he is, the memory-altering potion could wear off rather quickly. Especially if he has rapid healing powers.

I really hope you're not a vampire, I think as I grab him by the wrist and drag him back toward the cottage.

The impact of his skin on mine should be intoxicating, and it is, but I can feel the repulsive magic that ruined my family's lives lingering underneath.

I need this male to be cooperative and stupid for a while longer, because if Daithi's magic is still alive, then the threat of him is still out there.

The threat to Fallon is still out there.

And that's something I can't tolerate.

"Are you taking me in for tea?" he teases as I shove him into a chair. "I hope not, because I spotted some poisonous blooms in that garden of yours."

I give him a raised brow. Most people would be more interested in the dead body in my garden, but he has a good eye if he picked up on the contents in the dying light of Lapland's forest.

He drums his fingers on the chair's arm, then continues as if to fill the silence. "While the Middlemist Reds you have are the first I've ever seen, those are the only non-fatal blooms you seem to grow. The form of nightshade you have on hand could potentially be mistaken as a raspberry, which may be the point." His dark eyes sparkle with mischief. He might not remember who he is, the events from the past few days, or why he's so attracted to me, but he doesn't seem to care. Instead, he's charming me and he knows it. "I wouldn't want you to give me the wrong one."

Hmm, a mercenary who knows his flora. Intriguing.

He knows his poisons, I correct myself.

Meaning I definitely shouldn't be attracted to his knowledge of ways to kill someone.

Or flowers. Especially his knowledge of flowers.

He simply grins at me from his chair and I realize I've been staring at him.

Unable to respond verbally, I point my finger at him and mouth the word *stay.*

He throws up his hands and gives me a disarming, toothy grin, one that suggests he's either indeed a vampire or a shifter with sharp teeth.

Either way, I don't have much time before he remembers why he's here. If he's as powerful as he seems to be, he'll retrieve his memories within the hour.

The very real possibility that this mercenary is here to kill me brings the chill back to my skin.

Or worse, *use* me.

Is an ally to the patriarchs still alive? I wonder. I killed them all, freeing my sister and myself in the process.

Daithi was one of them.

And his magic was somehow on this male.

Are you here to kill me?

Even though I direct my thoughts at him, he doesn't seem to hear them.

It's a suspicion I should immediately share with Fallon, but I made it a point this far not to burden her.

If I ran to her with all my problems, what kind of life could I ever hope to build for myself?

Luckily, my mental wall is still in place and she can't hear the stray thought. If she had, she would have made good on her threat to have her angel mate, Nolan, portal over and save the day.

Which means making things worse, because no one understands dark magic better than I do. And tackling it with brute force only works when one knows an appropriate counterspell.

In this case, I have no idea what kind of spell, or combination of spells, is at work. Any attempt to kill this male could blow up in my face.

Including using my necromancy, especially since he has Daithi's magic on him.

Completely unaware—or at least unconcerned—of my plotting, the male's gaze dips, clearly taking in my figure while I debate what to do with him.

Even if he can't remember that we're fate-bonded or that he's likely here to kill me, he's surely feeling the magic that makes him want to do other things to me.

The fate bond won't be complete until we consummate it, and I know the desire is only going to grow more powerful until we reject each other.

Right now, rejection seems to be the last thing on this male's mind as he appreciates every line and curve of my body, making me feel immediately vulnerable and naked even though I'm clothed.

Well, sort of clothed.

I'm wearing my dress from my date, one that Ayla picked out for me, and I gravely regret wearing it. It's too tight, too revealing, and too short.

All things this mercenary appears to appreciate as he tilts his head, seeming to admire every slice of skin available to his view.

Snapping my fingers at him, he manages to look up.

If he keeps looking at me like he's going to eat me, I might just let him, and I can't have that.

Because when I felt his hand on my skin, it felt like Daithi's.

The repulsion of his memory makes me shiver.

But the sensation of Daithi's magic is diminishing as if it's simply a strange echo on this male, suggesting that it might wear off if I give it time.

Perhaps it's only temporary—Daithi's magic tried to find me, but it can't sustain itself forever.

Stop trying to rationalize sleeping with him, I chide myself.

"Sorry," he whispers, practically purring his words. "It seems that I have this overwhelming desire to taste you and I'm trying to understand why I haven't yet." He grins once more, this time not hiding his interest in *tasting me* as his fangs appear again. "Do you feel it, too?"

I give him one more glare for good measure—as if to say, *Absolutely not,* even when my body is saying, *Absolutely yes*—and then hurry to my bedroom to find my emergency phone powered by magic before I do something stupid.

Ayla is off tracking down a lead for a project the Dukes of Lapland gave us, so I can't ask her for advice.

But she gave me a number to call in the event that I need to talk to the dukes without her.

It isn't a number I ever intended to use, but the safest way to deal with this situation is to treat this male like a rogue mercenary.

He appeared out of nowhere, killed a bookkeeper, and ruined my flowerbed.

I'm just the queen's sister trying to live a quiet life, an insignificant mute witch with a penchant for languages.

Yes, I like this plan, I decide.

Giving the mercenary to the dukes would eventually get back to my sister, but it would buy me the time I'd need to do some research.

I could get some blood from him once he's in lockup and—

Why not explore this connection before you push it away? my mind interrupts. *You don't have to sleep with him. You could just have a taste. Surely he'd give you a little blood if you simply asked.*

I don't like that train of thought. It's one planted by fate itself and it knows how to speak to my innermost desires.

I've lived a life of solitude—by design, not by choice.

And this male is making me feel things I've never felt before.

As always, I override emotion with logic. I prefer books, knowledge, and facts to whims of the heart.

Or whims of alluring magic, as it were.

Fact number 1: My fated mate is a skilled killer.

Fact number 2: He has Daithi's magic on him.

Fact number 3: Daithi O'Neely tried to use me and I killed him for it.

Logical conclusion: Daithi's magic has found a way to repay the favor.

Which means I need to reject this male before I do something stupid, like sleep with him and make the bond permanent. It might be exactly what Daithi's magic wants me to do.

Like all the patriarchs of the Outcast Coven of Necromancer Witches, Daithi wanted a mate so he could steal her magic. If his magic found a way to live on, then it would be compelled to complete that mission, even if it meant doing so through a new host.

Because while I wasn't necessarily more powerful than Fallon, I was far more deadly.

This mercenary might just be a very prettily packaged potion designed to ultimately kill me.

Like nightshade tea.

But he silences the screams, my inner voice supplies once I enter my bedroom. The dead seem to find me as I rummage through my things, rattling around in my brain and scrambling it until I'm dizzy.

Isn't this everything you've been looking for?

I tighten my lips as I weigh the risks. My dream was to finally silence the dead.

Whether or not this male has Daithi's magic on him, he's my fated mate.

I can't know if it's even real. If Daithi has somehow created a new spell to ensnare me even after death, or if his magic latched onto my true fated mate as a carrier.

Regardless, my fated mate seems to possess the ability I've searched for all my life.

To give me peace.

And the more I think about it, the more I want to run back into the living room and taste him.

I definitely need to get him away from me before this urge gets worse, I think as I find the phone and punch in the number.

I hold it to my ear and wait. Magic hums to life inside the device. Technology was lost during the formation of the Houses, but magic replaced most advances with alternatives. And in many ways, it made it better, because this particular phone can translate my thoughts into words, allowing me to make calls without speaking—or killing anyone.

The phone begins to ring, and after five seconds a male answers.

"Is that tea ready yet?" the voice asks.

My eyes widen. Because the male who just answered is my fated mate currently sitting in my living room. I hear his echo from the phone rumble through the house, confirming he's the one speaking to me.

It's very unlikely that he's a duke, because the dukes are already mated.

Which suggests that this male works for them and knows them personally. Enough to be trusted with a carrier phone.

Enough to be protected.

Meaning I have to deal with this alone—and quickly, before fate or Daithi's magic takes me under.

Shit.

Chapter 3

Jasper

T he delectable female in the next room is most definitely playing games with me.

All I want to do is *taste her*. My fangs throb for a bite, my throat parched for blood.

No, not just any blood.

Her blood.

Something inside of me knows that her blood is the solution to everything. Her crimson gift is the answer to my burning questions.

Except... I can't seem to remember those questions right now.

Shaking my head, I rub my temple. "Are you going to speak?" I ask.

She has been mute thus far. I'm not sure if the little witchling is too stunned to talk or if it's something she's simply incapable of. But she's using a phone, suggesting she can communicate somehow.

Her lack of speech isn't a defect or an absence of power. I sensed her perfection in every way.

And her strength.

Fuck. I just need a taste.

An automated voice responds, disappointing me.

"I'm mute, mercenary. But this device translates my thoughts into words. This voice is automated for me to communicate." A moment of silence stretches out before the witchling continues in the half-garbled robotic voice that probably doesn't sound like the *real* her at all. "Do you care to tell me why you have the duke's phone?"

I roll that question around in my brain, but my thoughts feel sluggish and tired.

Frowning, I try to remember who the duke is.

I try to remember... anything.

Fear spikes in my chest when I realize nothing is coming to the surface.

Not who the duke is.

Not who I am, either.

Well, this isn't good.

"I'm afraid I can't answer that," I respond vaguely. The witchling wants to know why I have the *duke's* phone. I don't know the answer to that, but I have a feeling that's a temporary problem.

My head itches on the inside and I know my brain is healing itself from some sort of damage.

Did this little witchling cast a spell on me?

Perhaps that explains my raging hard-on and my desire to fuck her, to taste her, and to worship every inch of her.

Even if I can't remember who I am, I instinctively know that I am not the romantic type. One-night stands are more my thing.

I don't just want her for a night.

I want to *keep* her.

And while my attraction to this little witchling is powerful, it feels intense and compulsory.

Like a spell.

I should resist it. My existence could be in danger.

Not my *life*, because I'm not alive in the first place. I'm a vampire with necromancy hybrid magic.

I was born this way, I recall.

No, not just a vampire. A *master* vampire.

The itching inside my head ramps up as the memories start to return.

I was born with a gift, which qualified me for master vampire status.

The gift to kill anything I touch.

It's one I had to learn to control, of course. And it's one that very few know about, or else I'd be a threat to the stability of the Houses. So I rarely use it.

And when I do, I injure the body to make it look like my victim was killed by other means.

Like the bear shifter outside... I recall cutting his throat after he was already dead.

Frowning, I look down to where I stained my suit when I'd been startled. His death had an unpredicted side effect, one where I heard his soul *scream*.

That was new. I never *heard* the dead.

Glancing at the hall where the witchling went, I suspect she had something to do with that.

Hmm, some memories are returning. That's a good sign.

But not all the memories surface right away.

Darker histories of those times I couldn't control my death touch linger somewhere under the heavy netting of the witchling's spell. I selfishly allow them to remain there, a part of me recognizing that it's a burden I have dealt with all my life.

I lost those important to me.

I killed them and guilt festered inside my soul—but for the first time, it's out of reach. Grief that often consumes me is momentarily quelled.

Maybe that's a good thing.

A little reprieve won't hurt.

I'm a vampire of opportunity, if my broken memory serves. This is one like any other to help me refocus.

I may stay a little while and see what else this little witchling can do for me.

I know she's dangerous, but that only excites me more.

I do love a challenge.

A click on the other end of the phone informs me that the witchling hung up the call.

So, she can dish out silence but can't take it.

Noted.

She storms into the room a moment later, holding a knife.

My cock throbs at the sight of her in a shimmery, two-part dress that hugs her curves. It leaves her abdomen bare, enticing me to dip my tongue into her adorable belly button.

And then go lower...

She snaps her fingers, once again demanding my attention on her face, not her delicious assets.

Fine by me.

She has a striking face, one that could cause wars if word got out about her. Because I suspect she's powerful, too, or else I wouldn't be sitting in her chair with my dick saluting.

Because memory or no, I know I have never seen her before.

She's a treasure kept hidden from the world, and the apprehension and fear in her silver eyes tell me all I need to know.

She was betrayed once before and she isn't going to let it happen again.

The chair creaks as I lean back into it, sprawling my legs and making no attempt to hide what the sight of her does to me.

I'm wearing a suit, but the bulge in my pants is quite obvious. Her gaze dips to it and she clenches the dagger until her knuckles turn white.

Her skin is beautifully pale, like white petals of a Death Bloom, but her cheeks flush with warmth as she tracks her gaze up my body. My suit is unbuttoned, so she can see how my white dress shirt hugs my chest.

She looks like she wants to rip it open.

Yes. She absolutely feels this connection between us.

That's useful information. It means the seductive part of this spell either wasn't intentional or is something else entirely.

She's resistant to it, evident from the worthless blade in her hand.

All she's doing is turning me on. Blood play is my favorite type of bedroom activity.

"If I wanted to hurt you, you'd already be dead by now," I say with a flourish of my hand.

She doesn't know it, but this very hand could take her life with a simple touch.

I already touched her once, and it was *incredible*. Killing her is off the table.

But she doesn't have to know that.

She doesn't seem very impressed by my threat. The glimmer in her eyes seems to say, *And if I wanted to hurt* you, *you'd be dead, too.*

Clearly, we've gotten off on the wrong foot.

Sighing, I ease to my feet. The witchling backs up a step and brandishes the blade at me. I resist the urge to show her ways I could turn the danger of a blade into a mixture of pleasure and pain.

Something I suspect a little witchling like this might appreciate.

That requires her trust, of course. Knife play is an exercise in submission, obedience, and faith in one's bed partner.

There have been more than a few females foolish enough to trust me with a blade—or my teeth. I haven't always been as careful as I should have been.

But with this female, I vow to take my time. To earn her trust and prove my worthiness to paint her skin red.

Because my touch can do more than take life. It can give it, too.

Something I do even more rarely than its counterpart, considering the toll it takes on me.

"We seem to be at an impasse, darling. I merely meant to say that I mean you no harm."

She glowers at me, then pointedly looks at the blood on my suit.

Right, I *did* kill the bear shifter, even if I don't remember why.

Plucking a handkerchief from my chest pocket, I dab at the spot. There's something hard in my pocket, but it's too buried for me to retrieve to see what it is.

"Ah, yes, I'm sure it would frighten you that I killed someone on your property," I say, hoping I can assuage her fears. "Although, I'm sure I have a good reason, even if I can't remember it. My memory seems to be a bit *fuzzy* at the moment, you see," I say conversationally, but I return her pointed look with one of my own.

Because you cast a spell, little one.

She analyzes me with that intense silver stare of hers. I love being the center of her attention.

She lowers the blade, which proves I've earned a sliver of her trust. She doesn't seem pleased with me, but she believes that I don't intend to hurt her.

At least, not without a little pleasure mixed in.

She clutches the blade, clearly not trusting me enough to go without a weapon. But I suspect she has another purpose for the dagger.

She's powerful. She doesn't need a weapon any more than I do.

The energy radiating from her is intense and intoxicating.

It's also very *familiar*.

She's not a vampire. While vampires typically have heartbeats, they are... calmer. What gives her away is the adrenaline coursing through her veins. Her heart is racing and I can count every pump of blood.

But she is a witch and clearly familiar with death magic.

A necromancer, perhaps? But she feels different from any necromancers I've met.

I'm intrigued by her energy signature as she leaves the room, presumably expecting me to follow.

I do.

While I pocket my soiled handkerchief, she guides me to an office of sorts.

It's more like a witch's lair with spell books, ingredients, and potions that imbue the place with mint. It's a chaotic system of papers and various items that makes my fingers itch to start cleaning and sorting.

I'm notoriously organized.

A few more memories trickle back into my mind, informing me of the book in my pocket buried underneath my stash of handkerchiefs.

It's a list of names, one of which is Ishara Doyle. There are notes next to the name of a mute witch living in a cottage in the middle of nowhere.

"It's close to the dukes' headquarters, so it shouldn't be too much trouble. She's alone, and as long as you approach her by surprise, she poses no threat. The reward, though, will be the information you've been seeking for a very, very long time."

The voice of the male who ordered the hit makes my brain itch in all the wrong ways. For some reason, there had been a desperation to his words as if he wanted me to find what I was looking for even more than I did.

Which was odd, something I intended to investigate.

After Ishara's death.

He hadn't told me her power—said that wasn't necessary to know if I did my job right.

But I don't like this memory and I shut it off before it can go any further. It has to do with the guilt that claws behind the netting.

And the list of names? It's a secret collection not approved by the dukes that this witchling mentioned.

A swallow works down my throat because I have the sinking feeling that I *am* here to harm her.

She has something to do with my dark past, whether she realizes it or not.

She has her back to me—another show of trust I don't deserve—as she fumbles through her books.

"What are you looking for?" I ask, edging around her shoulder.

She freezes when my chest presses against her back. I can't help but initiate contact.

Something is drawing me to her and it's only getting stronger. Her spell clearly was one that only altered my memories. It didn't cause this attraction that seems to be going both ways.

Because it's an outside force.

Making her my...

Fated mate.

Yes, that must be what she is.

The realization makes me possessive as I sweep my fingers over her shoulders.

She shivers at the touch but doesn't recoil from me this time.

She hit me with a spell, I recall, and it was the first moment I met her.

Which must have altered my reaction to a fated-mate bond.

Perhaps I was here to kill her, but that was yesterday's desire. Whatever price her death would have paid, her life holds so much more value.

I'm not opposed to a fated match. Not if it feels like this.

Not if it's to you, Ishara Doyle.

I run my fingers across her throat, feeling her swallow.

And when this night is done, you're going to scream for me, little witchling.

Because you're mine.

Mine for life.

Mine until death.

And even then... I'll bring you right back so we can do it all over again.

Chapter 4

Issy

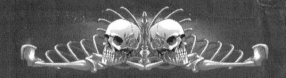

T error winds through me as the male runs his fingers over my throat. It's as if he knows my power resides in my voice.

And he's daring me to use it.

I feel the possession in his touch that indents my skin. The warmth from his chest against my back bleeds into me, chasing away a lifetime of chills.

He's a vampire. He's not supposed to be this warm.

But he's something else, too. There's another power that runs through his veins that amplifies what he is.

That makes him a perfect match for me.

Perhaps he is my true fated mate.

His fingers don't seem to hold Daithi's magic anymore, but I still sense the dark magic hiding underneath the surface.

It's as though he's suppressed it somehow, making his touch the magical experience fate intended it to be.

I'm starting to lean into the idea that Daithi's magic

found him and is behaving like a parasite, burrowing itself into my fated mate to make use of the connection.

Meaning it could burn out, if given enough time. It is already safe to be touched by him.

Or maybe I'm rooting it out simply by my presence. I never got along very well with Daithi.

Rationalizing with your heart instead of your mind, once again, my mind chides.

My left hand clutches the dagger I mean to cut him with to collect the blood I need. Blood that can tell me vital information.

Such as the extent of Daithi's magic. Its origins and its objective.

My right palm is poised over the inscription of the spell I need to say out loud to complete the task.

Most spells require a recitation, which is why I often pass them on to Ayla or Fallon for execution.

It won't work with my phone device, either. If magic could be transmitted through it, then the automated voice would kill just as much as my real voice does, which entirely defeats the purpose.

"That's an interesting book," the male whispers in my ear, making me shiver. "Wonderful penmanship."

It's as if he knows I wrote this book myself as he continues to pet and praise.

His body flattens further against mine, molding himself to my curves and allowing me to feel the full length of his arousal on my spine.

Because this male is much taller than I am and he dwarfs me with his presence.

I enjoy being in his shadow, even if I should be wary of him.

But this is a fated-mate connection, a real one. I'm sure of that now.

He continues to run his fingers down my throat and over my collarbone. He seems unconcerned by the blade I'm gripping for dear life.

I can't respond to him, not verbally, anyway, so I nod my head in agreement.

It *is* an interesting text, because it's from one of my unique adaptations. And after a lifetime of isolation with little else to do other than transcribe books into new formats and languages, I would hope I wasn't half bad at it.

A few books in this room are from my personal collection, but this one is because of Nox, one of my sister's mates. He actually sent me a chemistry textbook, but I adapted it into a spell book for more appropriate use—something I like to do with books of knowledge.

Everything is a little bit magical, if just given a chance.

Just like Nox. He's a phantom specializing in poisons, but he turned out to be part of an antidote to Fallon's misery.

I've been in search of an antidote to my own for as long as I can remember.

My analytical brain had time to develop during my years of isolation. Perhaps the pursuit of knowledge was an escape of sorts, but now it's a facet of who I am.

I take one of the male's hands and guide it down my skin. It's an indulgence to let him brush over my breasts, but my goal is to show him the spell I'm working on.

Because he's going to have to help me perform it.

This is your chance to prove you're not here to hurt me, I think.

His breath is hot against my cheek as he leans into me. I leave his fingers on the spell as I withdraw my hand, allowing him to read the lines.

"I'm sorry, witchling. I can't read this language."

I frown, forgetting that not everyone has my vast language capacity.

No worries. That'll just require another spell.

I go on my tiptoes to reach one of the bottles on the top shelf. It presses my ass into him, a movement that elicits an enticing growl from my potential mate.

A part of me wants to stay like this and let his hands roam until he frees me from my clothes. An urgency to complete this bond threatens to consume me, which is exactly why I need to perform this spell.

If he's an innocent caught up in Daithi's magic, I will protect him.

If he's complicit...

Then he dies.

I don't allow my heart to twist its way out of that reality. There's no rationalizing against the simple facts.

Despite the way the thought of his death makes me feel, I will never allow any form of the patriarchs who hurt Fallon, who hurt me, to persist.

"Careful, witchling," he says, using that cute pet name for me again. When I ease down onto the flats of my feet, he wraps his arms around my middle. He buries his nose in my neck and inhales, sending a shiver of excitement down my spine. "You're teasing me, and you really shouldn't tease a vampire that wants you."

While his words make my breath catch, it's the little fact he let slip that makes me freeze.

He knows he's a vampire.

He *remembers*.

Fresh urgency makes me uncork the bottle with my teeth, and then I spill the contents onto the page.

Nox will have to forgive me for desecrating his textbook once again.

The mercenary holding me captive hums in my ear as the words change. "Ah, do you wish me to read this, little witchling?"

I nod again and then take his left palm, opening it up. I tap the point of my dagger to his skin.

His throaty sounds turn into a delicious growl, rumbling against my back.

"Are you casting a spell or seducing me, darling? Because fuck if I'm not turned on right now."

I try not to tremble as I hold the blade in place. I don't have much practice with weapons, but Bane taught me a few things when Fallon visited with her phantoms.

I liked them a lot, so I indulged Bane in a few lessons that I really didn't need.

Not with a voice like mine.

But as we had all learned, there was a possibility that my voice could be suppressed. Only the patriarchs had ever learned how to do that, but if anyone else did, I would need more than just my voice.

Luckily, they're all dead, I think to myself, my lips flattening into a thin line.

Because with Daithi's magic floating around in the cosmos, I'm not so sure anymore.

I dig the blade into the mercenary's skin when he remains silent.

He growls at me again but doesn't move. "This is a spell that reads blood, little witchling. What are you hoping to learn from mine?" He knows I can't answer by now, so I assume the question is rhetorical. He presses a light kiss to my throat as he seems to ponder his own answers to that question.

Oh, spirits...

Dizziness washes over me as fated magic doubles down, demanding that I throw my spell books off this table and give in to the delicious heat at my back.

His whisper keeps me pinned. "You want to know if I'm really your fated mate?"

In so many words, yes, that's exactly what I want to know.

Not just that, but also if he is working with the Outcast Coven.

If he should live or die.

His left hand stays still where I hold the blade. He has tough skin, because it hasn't broken yet.

But his right hand has left the spell book and is now dancing up my arm.

He slowly closes his fist around my throat. "I can hear when your heartbeat increases, witchling. You like it when I do this."

Spirits. Yes, I do, because I like the challenge against my voice.

I want a mate who can stand up against it, even if I know no one really can.

Not even this male. Not even if he might be a master vampire over a thousand years old.

No one can survive against my voice in its pure, unadulterated form.

Not my parents.

Not my clan's allies that I unintentionally killed.

Not my own sister. I can never tell her how much I love her. Not out loud. Not in the way I really want to.

And if this male truly is my fated mate, I want to be able to tell him my story.

Tell him my name.

Tell him what I want and how I want it.

Spirits, I hope this is real.

Heat pricks at the edges of my eyes and I refuse to let the tears come. I refuse to admit how badly I want a happily-ever-after of my own.

"I'm going to say the spell, witchling," he said, relaxing his grip on me. "I can smell your fear, and I promise you I never want you to fear me."

He presses a kiss to my cheek, as if assuring me that everything is going to be okay.

Then he says the words and my magic reacts.

I pull magic from the death plane. My voice is my medium, but I'm a witch just like any other. I react to the magic of nature, life, and death.

The words activate with every ingredient in this room.

The mugwort. The strips of bark and the rabbit pelts I have hanging out to dry.

When he reaches the last verse, I press the blade hard enough for dark, red blood to pool at the tip.

It seeps up the metal and I wait.

I wait.

I pray.

His blood touches my fingertips and sends me into his memory.

Closing my eyes, I throw my head back against his shoulder and drink it all in.

A man appears.

A book and a list of names.

My name.

Ishara Doyle.

"Thank you for responding to my call, Jasper Justi. I've heard a great deal about you."

Jasper Justi.

That's this male's name.

The voice on the other end of the memory continues.

"This is off the books, yes? Good. We don't want the dukes to know of this one."

"It's close to the dukes' headquarters, so it shouldn't be too much trouble."

An exchange is going on. I hold my breath as I watch the moment unfold.

"The reward, though, will be the information you've been seeking for a very, very long time."

What are they talking about?

The male takes Jasper's hand... and that's when the exchange occurs.

He's a mercenary. Of course I know what this is.

It's an order for a kill.

And this is the moment Daithi's magic bleeds into his flesh and tells him my exact location.

He's complicit.

Spirits...

I let the tears flow as I open my mouth and force myself to speak.

"Jasper Justi, I reject you."

Chapter 5

Jasper

I don't know what the witchling saw in my blood to immediately reject me.

But I do know that I'm dying.

Not just figuratively because she rejected me. No, this is what dying definitely feels like.

It's something *other* that slams into me the moment her words wrap around my soul and *squeeze*.

This is her magic.

It's powerful, incredible.

Magnificently deadly.

I've terribly underestimated this little thing. My entire body hardens at the impact of her words as it sends me stumbling back. I fall to one knee as I clutch my chest and rip apart my shirt.

Black spots sprinkle my vision as agony rakes through my veins.

It's in my blood.

Her magic works fast, but I recognize it because it's so similar to mine.

I just need to counteract it.

I dig my nails across my skin as I scream and draw crimson, trying to get to the fractured part of me that this little witchling so easily destroyed.

Rejected.

The pain of a fated-mate rejection is only compounding the effect, but I didn't *allow* her to reject me.

She didn't get to know me.

She didn't give me a chance to tell her.

So I'll show you, little witchling.

I refuse to die. I refuse to lose my fated mate, not once I finally found her.

Fate led you to me.

You're mine.

You underestimate me if you think a little death is going to stop me, darling.

I growl as shove my nails into my skin, digging until I finally touch my heart.

It's frozen under my touch, which would normally be concerning even for a vampire.

But I'm a hybrid, and that makes me unique. I'm an immortal intertwined with the magic of death and necromancy.

I was born this way, without a heartbeat, but with a soul. And even if my heart doesn't contract, it's still a vault for blood.

And magic.

I tap into my gift. She can bring a soul to death's door, but so can I.

And I can reverse the pull into the afterlife just as easily as I can enforce it.

She locks onto my gaze as she watches me struggle on the precipice of life and death.

She's dropped her useless dagger and now her fingers clutch the edge of the table. Her knuckles are white as she waits, frozen, to watch me die.

Or watch me overcome.

Fear and fascination are a beautiful concoction in her silver gaze. I see the moment when she doubts I'll succumb.

Because I growl—it's a sound infused with a demand, with my *power*, and it makes the room's temperature plummet.

Frost crinkles on pages of open books and sends them curling. Her eyelashes are dusted with ice, framing her silver gaze in frozen lace.

She doesn't shiver. She doesn't seem bothered at all by the cold.

Because this is a communion with the death plane. I can't travel there, but my body itself is a lighthouse on the shore of souls.

It calls them to me and bridges the two worlds.

I don't pretend to understand how the magic works, or why it makes my touch call forth death—or banish it.

Instinct is what guides me, and right now my instinct is telling me to bring this little witch to heel.

"What *are* you?" she breathes.

Her words still impact me and threaten to splinter my heart in two.

I survive it only because I'm understanding the effect better now.

She has no control over her gift at all. Her voice itself seems to be linked to the death plane.

It's entirely different from how my power works. While I'm a lighthouse, she's a *medium*.

It's not something she can turn on or off, but it's something I could potentially temper.

My heart is still in my hand as I clutch it, willing it back together. "I'm like you, little witchling," I say.

Just a little more.

The death plane is resisting my call, as if it doesn't know if it should listen to me or to this witch.

She's its child, whereas I'm simply a friend.

"Are you an ally of the patriarchs?" she asks, her words slicing through me.

She rejected me.

She's killing me.

I hiss as the double-bladed sword wrenches through my soul. "I need you to stop talking," I tell her.

She seems to finally find her confidence as she pushes off of the table. She wraps her fingers around my throat and shoves me against the wall.

A shelf of potions digs into my spine, sending the bottles rattling against my back. Some fall off and break, warming the room.

A fire starts in the corner, but she ignores it as she stands on her tiptoes to keep me pinned.

Normally, such a petite thing wouldn't be a match against me, but I'm struggling not to tip over into the death plane permanently, so I allow her little tantrum.

"And *I* need you to answer my question," she says, her silver eyes reflecting the flames building in the room.

If her voice doesn't kill me, the fire might. I'm susceptible to it after being scarred by demonfire, and I don't want to relive that experience again.

Releasing my heart, blood drips down my chest as I hold on to her wrist. Instant relief fills me as her magic intermingles with mine.

Her words might have rejected me, and her voice might be deadly, but her *body* is life itself.

Finding my lifeline, I bring her closer. She squeaks with surprise as I press as much of her skin to mine as I can.

"These clothes are a bother," I tell her, using my teeth to shred the strip at her shoulder.

"I-I rejected you," she protests, but she shivers when I push my thigh between her legs.

She could step away.

She could use the thousand potions and a variety of spells to dismantle me if she really wanted to. Her power is incredible, but I recognize her strength as a witch, too.

More than just her voice is deadly.

Her mind is a weapon, too.

"You did," I confirmed, grazing my lips over hers.

I don't truly kiss her, not in the way I want to.

It's a test, and she passes beautifully when her mouth parts, opening to mine.

Something inside of me is dampening the effects of her voice, as well as her rejection.

It could be the impact of the connection we share to the death plane, or something I don't yet understand.

51

I'm not one to question things when they turn in my favor. I'm a man of opportunity, after all.

"Then why does it feel like I didn't?" she asks, her frosty eyelashes fluttering when I apply more pressure with my thigh.

The dampness spreading out over my pants proves that she still wants me.

Flames roar up all around us, but neither of us seems to care.

I'd burn alive with this witch if she wished it.

And with my history, that's saying something.

"Because we're fated, little witchling," I say.

A swallow works down her throat as she holds on to me. "We are," she agrees.

Testing her limits, I slip her other sleeve off, revealing her pale, plump breasts and rosy peaks.

She allows me to look.

Fuck.

She's perfect in every way.

My fangs ache and I want to bite.

As if she senses my desire to devour her, she backs away. Her jaw clenches, as do her fists. "Or maybe the bond won't break because of Daithi O'Neely's magic."

The slice of her words hit harder without her flesh to ground me.

I growl as the healing wound along my chest begins to open again.

Daithi O'Neely...

I roll that name around in my brain, but that memory is buried underneath that netting I don't wish to disturb.

The flames crawl up the walls, providing a sense of urgency for us to resolve this standoff soon.

Because death will only permit being toyed with for so long.

For her, though, I risk it.

A fresh scream rips from my throat as I tear open old wounds, revealing scars and blood.

Revealing the truth.

I stare at her as it all comes back. Not just what she hid from me, but what these patriarchs of hers had hidden from me, too.

Leaving me with only one possible choice, because I know we can't complete this bond. Not when someone like Daithi O'Neely is pulling the strings.

"Ishara Doyle, I reject you, too."

Chapter 6

Issy

My chest feels as if it ripped open when Jasper rejected me.

It should make me feel relieved, but the rejection isn't both ways. Even though I said the words, my rejection didn't seem to be effective. Daithi's magic wouldn't allow me a choice.

But it allowed *him*.

I hate this!

It feels so wrong. Rage wells up inside my soul until there's only one outlet for it to go.

Something I rarely ever got to do under threat of severe punishment from my now-dead father.

I scream.

The sound shatters the air and immediately quenches the fires that had climbed to the ceiling.

Smoke billows through the window that broke from my outburst.

Actually, everything that's made of glass broke from my outburst.

What ingredients and potions didn't burn from the fire are now blistering across wood and tile.

A secondary burst sounds when the bottle holding my screams explodes, sending my hair flinging across my face.

The vampire seems to handle my voice better now. It's something that both terrifies me and thrills me.

Another slice of agony rips through my chest, wishing he'd take his words of rejection back.

Because it *hurts*.

"I'm sorry, Ishara," he says as if he knows exactly the pain he's caused me. "But I remember everything now. You deserve to know everything I do." He slowly moves to his torn suit on the floor, one of the few things that appear to have been spared from the fire and splattering of potions. He extracts a handkerchief and presses it against his brow. "We need to slow this down, little witchling."

My lower lip trembles and I force it to go stiff. "You mean, you don't *want* to reject me?"

He flinches when I speak and I don't stop him when he reaches out and rests a hand on my shoulder. The gesture suggests he has an easier time with the deadly effects of my voice when he touches me.

And I like the excuse to feel his hands on my skin.

He picks up his suit again and strips it with his teeth, then begins to wrap it around my chest. "I don't, darling. Trust me."

How does this make any sense?

While the words are meant to break a fated-mate bond, the pull still remains.

Physical connection would repair the damage that's been done, but I'm not sure if that's really what I want now that I know Daithi's magic is involved.

That he accepted it.

But did he know what he was accepting? It was just a handshake. Maybe he wasn't aware.

He appreciates my breasts before he covers them up, then tucks the fabric against my rib cage.

His gaze flicks up to meet mine. "But you may wish to walk away once you learn the truth." He keeps his hand on my shoulder when he straightens.

His touch is helping the pain of his prior rejection. Nullifying it, in a way.

From my understanding of fated bonds, this isn't how it works at all. That should be all the proof I need that Daithi's magic is interfering, but it doesn't feel that simple.

I am a unique breed of witch.

And this male is clearly a unique type of vampire.

Together, we would be a fated pair unlike the world has ever seen. Maybe the rules don't apply to us as they should.

It doesn't change the facts, my logical brain argues.

Such as he's a mercenary and I am his target.

"I already know you are here to assassinate me," I tell him, not hiding the bite to my tone. "And that you have my tormentor's magic in your veins." I step closer, unafraid to tilt my chin to look up at him. "You rejected me after I said his name. Does that have something to do with your newfound truths?"

Perhaps he didn't know if he was accepting Daithi's magic, but he did *respond to the name.*

A strange sort of pain enters his eyes. "Something like that." He sighs and sweeps his gaze over the ruined room. "I *was* here to assassinate you, but obviously I am not going through with that anymore. I was told lies about who and what you are. I have no reason to kill you anymore."

"You don't?" I hedge. Because as far as I'm concerned, the fated bond is the only reason he hasn't tried to kill me. "You're a mercenary, as you say. Payment is all a mercenary cares about, so the only thing that's really changed is that you clearly want to fuck me."

Wanting to get into my pants doesn't qualify as a pious reason to show mercy.

His nostrils flare as if I'm testing his patience. "I'm a rogue mercenary because I don't believe in the structure of the Houses, witchling. I use my own moral compass. From the information I was given, you were a witch unable to control her power. Unchecked power only causes problems in this fucked-up world."

I raise an eyebrow. "I *can't* control my power," I point out. I've never been able to use my voice without summoning the deadly forces behind it, not once it fully manifested.

And it killed my family's allies in the process, starting a chain of events that led to misery after misery for my twin and me.

He tilts his head, causing his brown hair to fall into his eyes. "No, but you control *yourself*. And that is admirable."

58

"So, a vampire with a moral compass." I scoff. "Conveniently, that allows you to kill people, to judge when the death knell should ring and when it should remain silent." I lean in closer. "It sounds like you're just looking for a reason to get your dick hard."

He growls in return, sending chills over my arms. "You don't know me, witchling."

"And you don't know me," I retort.

He was willing to kill me on second-hand information. He clearly has a lot to learn if he truly intends to be a moral force in this "fucked-up world," as he called it.

He nods. "I don't."

"You don't," I agree. "So, what now, vigilante vampire?"

He sighs. "You don't deserve to die. That much is clear. Knowing what I know now, it's better if you stay hidden. The best thing would be to leave you and never return, for your own sake. But I'm afraid I *can't* leave you, witchling. If I don't report back tonight with proof of your demise, another mercenary will be sent in my place and I will be presumed dead."

"You expect me to run?" I challenge him.

He gives me a seductive smirk. "I expect you're not one to run from your problems, no. You face them, fearless and unstoppable."

He's not wrong.

"I'm not one to run," I agree. "But you don't need to protect me. I can take care of myself."

His fingers dance across my shoulder. I know it's to stabilize him against the effects of my voice, but I hope it's more than that, too.

I dare to hope he still wants this connection between us like I do.

I rejected him because I saw him accept Daithi's magic. I thought he was complicit in the insanity that was the patriarchs.

But I sense there's so much more at play.

And I'm eager to learn more about Jasper Justi, a vampire without a beating heart.

A vampire who shares a connection to the death plane, just like I do. His growl called forth the chill of souls, and while part of that might have been borrowed from me, it was only because we share this brand of death magic.

"I'm going to protect you, even if it's from yourself," he says, his words going low and husky. He grins again, showing off his lengthened fangs. It gives him a dangerous edge, one that I want to explore. "So why don't you be a good little witchling and show me to your bedroom, where I can keep an eye on you?"

Spirits. This vampire is going to be the death of me.

I'm not sure if this truce can last long if he intends to share a bed, but I'm too tired to fight him on it.

The pain of his rejection isn't fully going away, but I'm learning to manage it. Perhaps because it's not as effective as it should be with Daithi's dark magic interfering.

Or if it's because he keeps touching me.

I rub my sternum as I take the bathroom first, the ache slowly returning without him nearby.

But I do need a shower.

We're both bloody and covered in covens know what. Hundreds of vials exploded in my study, and the winds that had been kicked up sent all sorts of witchy ingredients into my hair, as well as ash from various objects that had burned.

Ayla is going to kill me.

That's a bridge I'll cross when I get to it. A burned study is the least of our problems if Daithi's magic has somehow gotten a foothold in my life.

I don't know how Jasper plays into all of this, but I intend to find out.

For now, he says he wants to protect me and I believe him. If he wanted me dead, he would have killed me already.

And if he wanted to use a fate bond to control me, he wouldn't have rejected me.

And perhaps he knew that rejection was the only thing that would convince me he *wasn't* a threat.

The irony.

Frowning, because I don't like this *at all*, I snatch up a comb and start yanking it through my blonde strands.

Who are you, Jasper Justi?

While I don't know much, I know he's a cocky-ass vampire mercenary, one who's arrogant enough to go rogue and think it wouldn't catch up to him.

And it didn't take me long to realize he was young. Infantile, by vampire standards.

He couldn't be much older than my twenty-three years.

It was trickier to figure that part out, but it was his memories that gave him away.

Or lack of memories, as it were. The spell I'd used on him allowed me a glimpse into his past. I'd been seeking something specific, but his entire life had briefly flashed before my eyes.

If it had been hundreds of years, the spell would have taken longer to sort through more recent memories. The past is like a weight, one that holds down everything in the present and makes it difficult for ancient supernaturals to cope with things like change or threats. It also makes memory spells more complicated.

But this one had been a breeze.

A vampire in his twenties or thirties, I decide as I pluck twigs and roots out of my hair. *A master vampire with a connection to the death plane. That's who you chose for me, mistress of fate?*

I don't often speak to the powers of fate, or the spirits, or anything greater than myself. As with everything in my life, I find solace in facts and knowledge.

But this is bigger than me, and I'm going to have to accept that.

You met your fated mate?! my sister shouts in my head.

Faltering, I drop the comb and it clatters to the floor.

Shit. Apparently, I was broadcasting that thought a little too loudly.

"Are you okay in there?" Jasper asks.

I know he still needs my touch to withstand my voice, so I knock twice on the door in response.

"I'll take that as a yes, but don't blame me if I rush in when you're naked the next time I hear something drop."

Heat climbs up my cheeks as I pick up the comb and try not to imagine that scenario playing out.

Because the way he looked at me suggested he wanted to taste.

To bite.

To *devour*.

And I very much wanted that, too.

Is someone there? my sister asks. She can't usually hear what I'm hearing, but she can sense when I'm distracted. *Please tell me what's going on, Issy. I mean it.*

Sighing, I slide down the wall and flick the teeth of the comb with my nail. *Promise not to be angry.*

While my voice is deadly, Fallon is by far a more powerful witch than me.

She can control her powers—until she can't. Her magic broke apart everything the patriarchs had built when she embraced her true potential.

A moment of silence lingers, suggesting she's still working on said control.

And promise you're not going to ask Nolan for a portal potion, I add.

I can practically hear her roll her eyes. *I won't if I don't have a reason to, Issy. Are you in danger?*

I don't know. Probably. I found my fated mate, I tell her, opting for the blunt truth. She heard my stray thought anyway. Might as well come out with it. *My voice doesn't kill him, and rejecting him doesn't work, either. At least,* my *rejection doesn't work.* His *worked on* me.

She blew out a breath. *Gods. That's loaded. But seriously, he can survive your voice? Then why did you reject him? That's amazing.*

It's a good question. *You're not going to like the answer.*

Issy.

I fumble with the comb until one of the teeth breaks off. I can't inform her that he has Daithi's magic in his veins. She will most definitely portal over if I tell her that.

But I have to give her something believable, or else she's not going to let this go.

He has necromancy magic, like us. He's not a warlock, though. He's a vampire, but he's also something else. I haven't quite figured that part out.

She huffs. *Isn't that a good thing? Wait. Does that mean you can* talk *talk to him?*

I cringe. *Only when he's physically touching me, I think. His power seems to work through touch and he's able to counteract my voice that way.*

Oh, Gods, Issy! That's amazing! I'm so happy for you!

She's about to gush and plan a fucking wedding unless I stop this, so I add one more truth. *He killed my date, Fallon.*

He what? You mean the ex-*date who was beating down your door earlier and not leaving you alone? Sounds like he deserved it. You should ask your hot new vampire hybrid about it instead of jumping to conclusions and doing something silly, like* rejecting *him.*

Launching to my feet, I practically growl as I yank the

shower faucet to the "on" position and set it to scalding hot.

I can't believe you, Fallon. You're siding with a killer? Just because you have a vampire mate doesn't mean you're the expert in overprotective immortal men.

Ishara, she says, using my full first name. She only does that when she's being serious. *You think I'm making this about me? I'm not. This has nothing to do with me.*

Damn right it doesn't. So why don't you just leave me alone?

Another moment of silence stretches out, and I almost wonder if she gave me my wish.

But that's not my sister. We never argue.

Ever.

And she knows me better than I know myself.

Which is why she'll never abandon me, even if I push her away.

I love you, Issy. I trust you to know what's right, but I also know you're hurt and scared. I can feel it, remember? We're twins. We look out for each other. And I know you're just pushing me away because you don't want me to get hurt. You're hiding something, and that's okay. I'm here for you when you're ready to talk about it, but do me a favor and play this thing out, okay? You're not one to run. Please don't start now.

The tears are coming and I strip and step into the shower before they can fall from my face.

I know she's right, and I hate it.

Promise me you'll sleep on it, she continues, knowing I'm still listening, *and promise me you'll talk to him tomorrow. Gods, you get to* talk *to him, Issy. Just give that a day. If you still decide to go through with this rejection, okay, but do. Not. Run.*

My chest constricts as I allow the emotion to seep through it.

Jasper's rejection is tearing me up inside, but so is his hope for our future.

And there, right in the middle of it all, is Daithi's magic just waiting for me to step into its trap.

Fallon doesn't know how right she is. I want to run from it and never look back. It's the first time in my life I have ever felt that sensation.

Because I killed Daithi O'Neely, but even death wasn't enough to keep him away.

That's what terrifies me most of all. Death was supposed to be my safe place.

When I was in the dark and alone, I always had my voice to protect me. I hated the screams of the dead tormenting my every moment, but I also grew to rely on them.

They protected me.

Now... now I don't know who to trust or what to believe, or if I can even protect myself with my voice like I always have, and that terrifies me.

But Fallon is my twin, and even if she doesn't know the full situation, she knows exactly what it is I need to hear.

I promise, Fallon, I tell her as I squeeze my eyes shut.

I promise I won't run.

Chapter 7

Kornelius

*E*verything's dead.

I stare at the screen, stunned, with dread winding my stomach into knots.

The magic-powered drone is showing me far more destruction than I expected if Ishara Doyle screamed.

The trees are already turning brown. Even in the dull moonlight, I can see the agonized curls of the leaves and the wilting of branches. Animals, large and small, lie unmoving along the various forest paths.

And for the unfortunate Gold and Garnet citizens within the blast zone, they lie forever asleep in their beds.

While my necromancy magic was being used to contain the power, it wasn't enough to save the edge of the city of Lapland from Ishara Doyle's scream—not when Jasper was apparently her amplifier.

Which doesn't make any sense. Or maybe it does, given that Daithi's magic is tied to the witch.

And I'd shared that connection with Zyran just last week. And he passed it on to Jasper. Although Jasper had no idea who Zyran was because of the memory alterations. But that's a temporary issue.

Daithi had shown me how to transfer my power with a specific set of instructions.

"Contain any fallout, should your brother fail."

It should have been me, I think with a growl.

But my power made it too dangerous for me to take on such a job alone. Just one death could send my power into overdrive.

The kind of death that a witch like Ishara Doyle was capable of would make me implode.

Still, I'd challenged Daithi over who should send the witch's soul to the death plane when it was time. Now that he was dead, we ironically had a better means to control her.

Not that we gave Jasper the mute collar we had developed—he didn't need it and it would be too risky for that kind of magic to fall into Gold and Garnet's hands.

Because it could control us, too.

Although, now I regret my decision as I stare at the destruction on the screen. I admired my brother the mercenary, the one who survived every day, but could he have survived *this*?

My memories remind me why Jasper was left behind —not because of his strength but because of his usefulness.

"Do you think the patriarchs framed Jasper Justi for your murder for fun? He's our link to the insides of Gold and Garnet. It was immensely good fortune that Ishara Doyle chose to retreat to Lapland. He's destined for this sort of job."

"It's why he lives at all. Don't forget that we control death—not you strange collection of necromancy-vampire hybrids. You're abominations and are only still alive because you're useful. Don't forget your place."

His order was simple enough. Kill the witch, then Daithi could tuck her away in the death plane for good. When his revival was completed, he could bring her with him and no obedience spell would have been necessary this time around.

She would have been bound to him in death.

But that's not what happened at all. Jasper's still there and...

Everything.

Is.

Dead.

"Jas is alive, Kor," my brother says, likely sharing my concerns. "I feel him."

If Zyran says he feels our brother, then Jasper Justi is still in the land of the living.

For now.

I turn from the screen and lean back in my leather chair. It doesn't give very much. None of the things "gifted" to us by our latest soul-captor ever do.

Our world has been a cold, unforgiving place since we were children. I can't remember much outside of New York, where we've been holed up for almost half of our lives.

But something deep inside of me misses Finland.

Misses the family I was supposed to have had.

A family I hope to one day get back.

"He'd better be," I say, referring to our brother's

precarious situation of life, "or I'm finally going to chop off that asshole's head."

The death stone rattles in its pedestal as if it heard me.

Zyran clicks his tongue. "Don't piss off our master. He'll be back soon, and if you take his head, I'll probably come back with two just to spite you."

"Hmm," I agree with a frown.

Daithi O'Neely is close to regenerating.

That was his plan if things ever went south. *"What good is it being an agent of death if you can't control it?"*

That had always been the ultimate goal of the patriarchs. Those who control death control the world.

Daithi's methods had primarily been through the death stone, which is an interrealm artifact.

Meaning it can be in two places at the same time. There's one in the death plane, and then one here, in my damned living room next to the decanter. Fallon probably thinks she destroyed the death stone, but it only retreated.

And it's been regenerating what the patriarchs had built since the moment Daithi died.

As his soul-captive, I'm spelled, or programmed, to care about his death. The feelings are shallow and unreliable, not dissimilar to the fake fated-mate-bond spell the patriarchs figured out.

I've had multiple soul-masters over the years, but Daithi is by far the most repulsive.

And powerful.

"We should talk to him," my brother presses. He gets up and straightens his suit. "Unless you finally want to be a little rebellious with me."

I roll my eyes and turn off the screen. "Rebellion has a time and place," I remind him.

We tried to be rebellious, once.

It nearly cost us both our lives.

He pulls a silver chain boasting a small symbol from underneath his shirt and teases it over his lips. It helps ground him when he hasn't used his powers in a while. It was our mother's, so that likely has more to do with its mystical properties than its material.

"The dukes are going to trace residual magic to New York," Zyran says. "Implicating the syndicates is against our programming. But if we volunteered to help with the investigation, we would satisfy our directives *and* we could get Jasper out."

I don't like this idea at all.

Mostly because it's everything I want. Ever since I reconnected with our brother, I wanted to tell him everything. My programming wouldn't allow it, but the longer Daithi has been away, the easier it's been.

I'm a master vampire just like both of my brothers. We're triplets, an incredibly rare assortment for our race. Procreation is something of an issue for vampires.

But our mother was a religious sort. She prayed to the goddess of death, and as a result, she was gifted with three sons.

And all three of us have unique powers, making us master vampires.

And because of our conception, we're all connected to the death plane, too—which ironically makes us susceptible to control from death-magic wielders like Daithi O'Neely.

To add insult to injury, the cost for all of this was my mother's life. As a result, I'm not much for gods or religion. Her gift was a curse, one that imprisoned her sons and took her away from them, leaving them alone with a tyrannical father.

"The dukes won't let us anywhere near Lapland," I point out, not eager to revisit memories of my father. I can remember everything except for killing him.

I haven't shared that with Fallon, either. She would not like the idea that I can't even remember the moment I took revenge—and she would want to find out why.

Regarding my more pressing issue in the present, transit is most definitely a problem. The only reason I was able to get through to Lapland before was because I traveled by portal.

We'd have to travel by plane this time, subjecting us to papers and security.

My brother grinned, showing off his wicked fangs. "They will if I show them this." He pulls a box from his pocket and opens it.

Two rings rest inside, both with garnet stones infused with our mother's blood. They're our birthrights—proof that we belong to the house of Gold and Garnet.

My eyes widen. "Where the fuck did you get those?"

Zyran shrugs. "The cloaking spell previously cast on them broke when Daithi died. The idiot hid them in his nightstand."

I'm not surprised Zyran rummaged through Daithi's things, but I *am* surprised he kept it a secret until now. "When were you going to tell me?" I ask as I pick up one of the rings.

This is how we've been controlled. Our mother is linked to our creation, and in effect, whoever holds these rings controls our souls.

Mine feels so heavy. So full of the weight of death and loss.

Zyran takes his and puts it on. "Because I knew you'd look at it like that, and I don't want to see you suffer, brother."

"I've been suffering for the past twelve years," I tell him.

He gives me a grim look, one that says he's very aware. "So, does that mean you're ready to go to Lapland?"

I sigh and make a fist, testing out the weight. "Let's go before I change my mind."

Chapter 8

Issy

Rejection should have eliminated any pull between us, but I'm acutely aware of Jasper's presence at my back.

He gave me my privacy when I took a shower, and I gave him his.

Yet all I could think about when he was under the water was his kissable jawline, his body, and his *danger*.

He'd skimmed his fangs over my pulse, but he hadn't bitten me.

Do I want him to bite me? I wonder as I clutch the bedsheets to my chin.

It scares me that I do. I want to be marked by this man.

Reclaimed.

I want him to take back his rejection and replace it with the promise of his body, his danger, and his bite.

The pain of his rejection continued to return, and by the time he's done with the shower, I'm trembling with it.

He doesn't say a word. Simply disrobes and enters the bed with me, then takes my hand.

He doesn't try to touch me, or seduce me, but just holds my hand and lets the contact ease my pain.

Or maybe it's self-preservation on his part, because touching me allows him to survive my deadly words.

"What now?" I whisper, eager to use my voice. Since he presented the opportunity, it would be a waste to remain silent.

I haven't talked to anyone since my powers manifested. Not physically, anyway, without killing them.

I was lucky that my sister hadn't been one of the victims.

Now, I wonder if fate had played her hand. I'd been in a strategic position, one that decimated my family's standing within the Outcast Coven and set a course for Fallon and me that led to this very moment.

In no other world would I have wound up in Lapland. I was a daughter of the Outcast Coven, an offshoot of the syndicates in New York.

Now, I found myself here, as the target of a mercenary who so happened to be my perfectly compatible mate.

That was either fate.

Or design.

"We sleep," he says.

Glancing up at him, I see his arm tucked behind his head and his eyes are closed. His hair is still damp from the shower—he didn't dry his like I did mine. It's silky against the moonlight coming in from the window and I want to thread it through my fingers.

He seems completely relaxed and at ease.

But his thumb is sweeping over my knuckles as if he's enjoying the contact. As if it's not just in the interest of self-preservation.

Or maybe I'm just pathetic and that's wishful thinking.

He squints one eye open and looks at me. "You're not sleeping."

"I'm not," I agree.

"Do you want to talk?"

"I do."

He hums in thought as a small grin forms across his lips. I love how he displays a hint of his fangs when he does that.

"Do you always answer questions like that?"

"Like what?"

He rolls into me so that we're nose to nose. "Like *that*."

I shrug. "I wouldn't know. You're the first person I've talked to in years." I don't voice that I can talk telepathically with my sister. That's not information he or anyone else should know.

His grin disappears, replaced by the tug of his lips into a frown I want to kiss away. "That sounds lonely."

"It is," I agree.

He moves in closer so that his breath is on my face. "You're doing it again."

"Sorry," I whisper, now a little breathless by his proximity. "I just... You have to understand. Your rejection worked on me, but mine didn't work on you. I still *want* you."

His fingers drape over mine and squeeze. "Don't worry, little witchling. I still want you, too."

A swallow works down my throat that's suddenly gone dry.

I'm wearing a thin nightdress. It's not uncommon that I sleep in the nude, but that didn't seem like a suitable option for tonight.

And he's not wearing anything except his briefs. His suit was ruined and it's not like I keep men's clothing on hand.

I could have conjured him some, of course, but I selfishly didn't volunteer that information.

"Tell me why you killed Dominique," I say. My voice has gone taut and strained, but I need to remember why this vampire is here.

To kill me.

And now he's half-naked in my bed under the guise of *keeping an eye on me*, but that doesn't change anything.

"Dominique?" he asks as if the question caught him off guard.

"The dead bear shifter in my ruined garden," I clarify. "I'm guessing he wasn't on your list if you don't know his name."

He hums in agreement. "Protocol on a stealth mission is to leave no witnesses. He was rampaging all over your property and was clearly going to be a problem."

He hesitates as if there is more to that story. "Is that why you killed him?" I ask.

"Partially," he admits, adjusting his head on the

pillow so he can better look at me. "I also don't approve of rapists still drawing breath."

A shocked laugh escapes me.

Spirits, it feels good to laugh.

"Rapist? He was my ex-date. He was angry because I stole something from him."

Jasper doesn't seem fazed by the information. "He was going to try to rape you. He was as hard as a rock. His pupils were dilated, and he wouldn't have been the first bear shifter activated by rage."

"Just because he was a bear shifter doesn't mean he was a rapist," I counter.

"No, it doesn't," he agrees. "They're not all bad, but as with every race, some are susceptible to certain traits. You stole something from him and he likely wanted his due in return."

I blink at him, stunned.

"But he was a bookkeeper," I protest.

"And a bear shifter," he counters, then he tilts his head and gives me one of his panty-melting grins. "So, did you steal a book, then?"

"Maybe."

"Hmm."

We fall into silence, but it's an easy silence. One where Jasper is looking into my eyes, seeming to read my soul, while his thumb continues to stroke my fingers.

He toys with the lines of my palm, then makes little circles on the inner side of my wrist.

It's driving me crazy.

"So, who sent you to kill me?" I ask. I have my suspicions, even if I don't want to be right.

Because it means the patriarchs haven't been fully dealt with yet.

"It was another vampire," he says.

I frown because that doesn't sound correct. The Outcast Coven doesn't typically work with vampires.

He continues those little circles on the inside of my wrist. "I didn't know it at the time, but the vampire who gave me the task was my brother."

My eyes widen. "What do you mean, you didn't know?"

His gaze drops to my lips as he talks. "You know that little memory spell you hit me with? Paired with the shock of a mate connection, it overrode something that had been done to my mind a long time ago. All these years, I thought that I had killed my brothers. My *family*." He shakes his head as if bewildered. "They've been alive all this time."

"But why would your brother, or *brothers*, want to kill me?" That question comes to the forefront, although I also want to ask how the hell he has *brothers*, plural.

It's unusual for a vampire to have a sibling, given that vampires are one of the older species in existence. Nature has a way of evening things out, so procreation has proved incredibly difficult for vampires; otherwise, the world would be terribly overpopulated with them. It's rare for them to have multiple children, much less one, but not impossible.

"I don't know," he admits. His touch skates up my arm as he talks, raking up and down on the naked skin until he leaves goose bumps behind. "But what I do know is that the name you said meant something to me. *Daithi O'Neely.*" The name is a sneer on his lips.

I stiffen against it, but I remain silent. I want to hear what Daithi is to him without my bias.

To me, Daithi O'Neely is a disgusting, worthless piece of trash. If he lives, I'll be grateful, only because I will revel in killing him all over again.

Slowly this time.

"I suspect they are working for these patriarchs of yours you mentioned. If they are, there's powerful magic at play to control vampires like my brothers because they'd never go along with this willingly." His fingers traipse across my jawline until he traces my lips. "What can you tell me about these patriarchs?"

My mouth parts as his touch coaxes my tongue out to taste him.

"Answer the question, little witchling," he says as he removes his hand but presses his forehead to mine so that we continue touching.

My entire body is shivering now, desperate to move closer.

There's still a bond between us, one that could be repaired by giving in to the pull as fate tugs on my soul.

But the conversation is proof of why I should refrain, no matter how difficult it may be.

"They're monsters," I say, attempting to focus on the thorn between us.

The reason why I shouldn't want to kiss him so badly.

"There are many monsters in this world," he says. His

lips are brushing mine now as if he feels this pull just as strongly as I do.

Perhaps the more we talk, the more our kindred death magic knits our souls back together.

We're a strange pair, one with many layers I want to explore.

"My family is part of the Outcast Coven," I say, deciding to start at the beginning. Thinking of my father is a pretty good way to squelch my sexual appetite, too. "Or they were. The women in my line are far more powerful than the men, so the patriarchs found a way to control us through a spell that forces a fated-mate bond and simultaneously allows them to leech our power."

He raises a brow. "Is that possible? To force a fate bond, I mean."

I know the question in his dark eyes is really asking if the bond between us is fabricated, too.

It's the same question I share.

"It is," I confirm. "My sister, Fallon, was put under this spell to Nikolas O'Neely, Daithi's cousin, by Daithi himself. Nikolas was later executed by King Kaspian for trying to kill the prior king."

"I remember that," he says. There's calculation in his dark eyes, showing intelligence and quick wit as he seems to put all the puzzle pieces together in his mind. "They publicized the fire, but not the event itself. What happened?"

To kill a vampire requires beheading and burning, just to be sure. I was otherwise occupied during the execution, but I know Fallon barely survived it.

"That's my sister's tale to tell," I say, stiffening my body against his touch that has gone to my lower back.

He presses himself closer to me and I allow it, both desperate for him and anxious of what our connection might mean.

"Then what *can* you tell me?" he asks, his lips tracing mine again in a not-so-subtle kiss.

"That the spell Daithi casts is real. He uses death magic. That's what the Outcast Coven is known for and it's capable of manipulating souls. *This* might not even be real, Jasper Justi."

It could all be just a very, very good impersonation of what a fated mate should feel like.

His fangs brush my mouth, giving my body a small thrill. "It doesn't feel fake," he says. "I rejected you, but I still want you."

"Isn't that proof enough?" I counter, even as I allow him to slide his thigh between my legs. I liked it when he did that before and I'm eager to experience the small pleasure again. "We can barely keep our hands off one another even though we both rejected each other."

"Hmm," he agrees, but his body is enveloping mine as he rolls on top of me.

His arousal is a brand against my stomach.

My breasts pillow against his chest. His hard muscles pin me in place, remaining taut as he holds himself still.

And his hair drapes around us, making me feel both dominated and like the center of his world.

"Maybe I don't care if it's real or not," he admits.

It sounds like a dark secret between lovers that I

shouldn't entertain, but his mouth is on mine, his tongue slipping through my lips.

And I can't stop him.

I don't *want* to.

Spirits... I don't think I care if it's real or not either.

My complete lack of willpower against this male terrifies me, especially when he works his fingers under my dress and pulls it up my thigh.

A pant leaves my lips when he reaches my breast and massages me. "Tell me to stop," he says.

There's a wild quality in his gaze now. I'm familiar with a vampire's bloodlust, but this is something different.

He wants to *devour* me in an entirely different way.

"I can't," I admit. Whatever magic is powered by fate, influenced by Daithi or not, is entirely too powerful.

He kisses me hard enough to bruise. I inhale him as if he's the only source of oxygen in the room.

Our tongues battle each other. Even though he's on top, I'm not one to be dominated entirely.

He seems to enjoy the fight as he growls and spreads my legs.

I'm wearing lacy underwear. It's a small barrier that he doesn't remove, but he grinds himself against my core, sending pleasure sparking behind my eyes.

I know I've fallen off the deep end. I've gone past the point of no return and there's no way I'm coming up for air, not when Jasper Justi is doing wicked things to me.

The temperature in the room plummets a moment later and I flash my eyes open.

Terror grips me when I realize the male on top of me isn't Japer anymore.

It's *Daithi*.

A scream rips out of my throat, but he's laughing at me.

"Insolent child," he growls, his voice no longer the vampire's, but that of the patriarch I most definitely killed. *"Your voice can't harm me, not when I'm in this body. He might be your fated mate, but that's exactly what I needed to find you."* His features flicker, moving in and out between Jasper's frame and his own less refined state. *"Fate chose* him, *but I* choose *you. You're mine, Ishara Doyle. Mine!"*

My... fated mate? I think.

It's real. It's all real.

Jasper Justi is my true fated mate.

And Daithi wants to take that from me.

His face, not Jasper's, is the one that peers down at me. Daithi is a handsome man, but I know his soul, and his soul is a disgusting, vile thing.

Issy! my sister screams in my head. *I don't know what's going on, but I'm coming. Hold on.*

It's all the warning I get to make sure my mouth is shut before my twin appears a moment later.

Nolan is at her side, his great wings blocking out half of my room as Fallon tracks her gaze to the male on top of me.

Her eyes widen when she recognizes the invading soul within. "Daithi O'Neely," she growls as she sweeps her hand.

Raw magic obeys her, blasting Daithi's soul back into submission.

He roars in retaliation, but Fallon is so much stronger than the last time he saw her.

Not just because of her mates supporting her, but because she's finally come to terms with her own magic.

She's the most powerful of us all.

Jasper's form returns a moment later, but his cheeks are sunken in and black veins swirl around his chest, concentrating on his left side.

Where his quiet heart rests.

He eases off of me and holds a pillow over his groin, giving Fallon his best smile.

"Hello, Queen of Gold and Garnet. It's wonderful to meet you."

Fallon narrows her eyes. "Nolan. Apprehend this man. *Immediately.*"

The angel's wings vanish as he approaches the vampire. "With pleasure."

Chapter 9

Jasper

I'm familiar with Nolan, one of King Kaspian's best mercenaries. He's an archangel with a penchant for death and better aim than me, so of course I'm an admirer of sorts.

Except now I seem to be the focus of his fatal attention.

"Big fan," I say, waving one hand while I hold a pillow with the other over my groin.

Because I'm sure the archangel would appreciate it if I didn't give his queen an eyeful. I'd just been about to fuck my fated mate before we were so rudely interrupted—and I'm properly equipped to do so.

But I wasn't interrupted by them, I remember with a frown.

Something else had happened.

One moment I was being drawn in by Ishara, like a drowning sailor responding to an irresistible siren's call...

And the next?

I can't remember.

Based on the look everyone is giving me, things hadn't gone well.

Nolan reaches for me and I click my tongue. "I wouldn't touch my skin if I were you."

It's not that I would intentionally use my death touch on the king's man, but I feel... supercharged.

As if Ishara Doyle sent raw electricity through my veins. My skin still tingles, but not in a bad way.

Only my chest hurts, and upon further inspection, I realize the veins around my heart have turned black.

Which really doesn't make sense. My heart doesn't beat. The blood in the veins around it is drawn *to* the source of my magic, not expelled through it. My body collects blood and power inside the containment like a vault only I can unlock.

Ishara has cracked the surface, though, allowing a more sinister presence to seep through. One that feels a lot like dark magic, the kind that someone like Daithi O'Neely would be responsible for.

"His touch kills," the queen informs Nolan, earning a raised brow from me.

"That's not widely shared information, Majesty. Care to share how you know that?" I ask.

She and the witchling, who is still in bed with tousled hair, share a look.

Hmm, telepathic sisters? My death-touch power is something Ishara would be aware of, having felt my brand of magic when I touched her.

And kissed her.

And—

"Put some clothes on," Nolan snaps. I know it's an order and not a suggestion.

"Gladly," I grumble. But when I reach for my ruined pants, Ishara snaps her fingers.

That usually means she's telling me not to do something.

She jumps out of the bed, leaving me no choice but to watch how her silky nightdress clings to her body.

She's slimmer than her sister but has no less curves. And I appreciate every. Single. One.

After a moment of rummaging in her dresser drawer, she produces a potion and another one of her nightdresses. She rips the latter in half, then pours the potion onto both pieces.

It transforms into a suit much finer than the one I was wearing.

"Well," I say with a chuckle, "you could have conjured me something to wear this whole time?"

She merely smirks and shrugs her delicate shoulders.

Wicked little witch.

I love it.

Grinning, I slip into the clothes and am about to say something to break the ice when a cold sensation slips over me.

Then my heart... beats.

Tha-thump.

Tha-thump.

Gasping on a pained breath, I clutch my chest and fall to one knee.

Queen Fallon is the first to respond. "Daithi's here," she growls.

I can't see his spirit, but I can *feel* it.

"Fuck!" I snarl as knives seem to slice through my chest. "Get him out!"

Ishara grabs her sister and drags her to me. They must be talking telepathically, because Queen Fallon's eyes widen. "You're sure?" the queen asks out loud.

Ishara nods emphatically.

Nolan grabs his mate's wrist when she reaches for me. "You said his skin is deadly."

"Trust me, Nolan," she says, and he must, because he lets her go.

Then the queen places a hand on me and my entire world explodes.

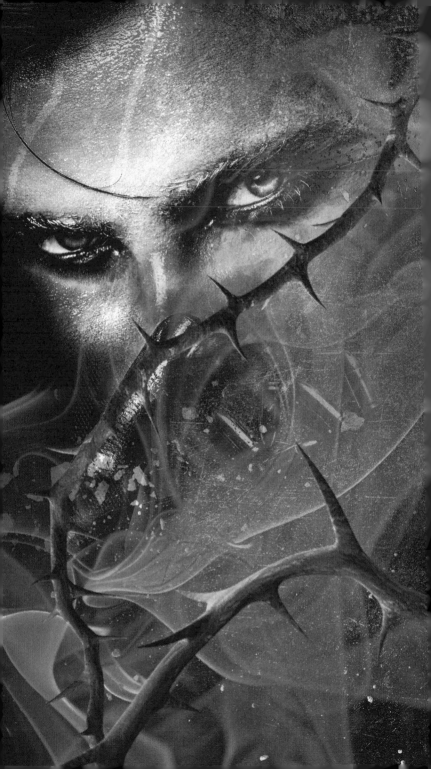

Chapter 10

Zyran

"**P**ut your glasses on, Zy," my brother tells me without looking up from his book.

Sighing, I withdraw the specialty shades from my vest pocket and perch them on my nose.

My sunglasses protect others from my power, but I tire of them. While it's not uncommon for a vampire to wear sunglasses against the sun, I'm not old enough for the sun to bother me.

Very few know that I wear sunglasses for their benefit, not mine.

The stewardess that my brother heard coming from the servant's cabin rolls in a cart of alcohol and various blood-infused beverages. She smiles at me, but I don't recognize her. Based on her woodsy scent, she's probably some sort of shifter.

"Hello, Mr. Zyran. Would you like a B-negative Valentino shot for your flight?"

I give her a slight tilt of my head in confirmation.

"You're well informed of my tastes, sweetheart."

She giggles at the endearment, although it's one I give every female I come across. Her platinum blonde hair is up in a bun and her ample cleavage is poking out from a frilly white uniform. Her fake eyelashes and fresh coat of lipstick suggest she's trying too hard.

If she were truly well informed of my tastes, she would know I prefer dirty blondes and much less makeup.

Should I want her anyway, she'd be on her back in my private cot, but lately I'm feeling a bit lethargic when it comes to sex.

It's as if the act doesn't interest me anymore. I'm far too young for ennui to set in, so I'm not sure what caused the dry spell, but at least it's given me more time to focus on our little death stone problem.

It might as well be a ball and chain on my brother and me. Although, it's a strange prison we live in, to be sure.

Daithi's methods to keep us under control are to pretend we're high-ranking members of his clan instead of the slaves that we are. My brother and I aren't impressed by finery, but we play our parts all the same.

For Jasper's sake.

It's a role we've both played for so long that I'm not sure I know how to do anything else.

I glance at Kor while his gaze flicks across the page of his book. We're both well read, but he bests me when it comes to devouring ink across the corpses of trees.

The lovely stewardess sets the shot on my table, securing it in the little slot that protects it from falling due to turbulence. She flirts with me a bit more, but when nothing comes of that, she hides her disappointment by batting her eyelashes at my brother.

Good luck with that, sweetheart.

While my dry spell has been temporary, Kor's has lasted as long as I've known him.

He's no virgin, but only one or two females ever made it past his hard exterior.

Given his particular *power*, neither of them survived it. He thought he could control it the second time around, but all it did was double his guilt.

When Kor clearly has more of a hard-on for his book on Lapland's geography—one he's read a few times—the stewardess gives up and stomps back to the servant's cabin.

I bark a laugh, earning a raised brow from my brother. "What's so funny?" he asks.

"You really didn't see her basically falling into your lap?"

Kor just looks confused. "Who?"

I laugh again as I pick up my shot and appreciate the sweet notes of B-negative blood. The whiskey mixed in adds its own spice that makes the blood a little more fiery, but perhaps it's uncouth to brag about it.

The drink is one of my own creation. I probably would have been a bartender in another life. It's my twist on the Valentino Cocktail.

"You befuddle me, Kor," I say instead. I knock back the shot and sigh a little on the inside.

Better than sex.

"If that's better than sex, then you're doing it wrong," my brother says without looking up.

I frown at him. "Didn't realize I said that out loud."

"And I didn't realize you wanted to suck your own cock. You invented that drink."

So, he *was* listening.

I chuckle. "If I want my cock sucked, I have plenty of options, brother. Perhaps you're just projecting your own desires."

Before Kor can respond to our usual banter, his head shoots up and his previously amber eyes turn white.

"Shit," I curse, throwing my shot glass and rushing to his side.

Because when Kor's eyes turn white, that means a bunch of souls just entered the death plane.

Something that can have dire consequences for my brother, a vampire hybrid with one foot forever in the afterlife. It's why we hardly ever leave the suite. The proper spiritual reinforcements are in place inside those walls, and while the airplane has been reinforced, too, it's apparently not enough.

Grabbing my necklace with one fist, I set my hand on his arm and try to stabilize him.

He's looking past me and his skin is going translucent.

Not good.

Cursing again, I rip off my glasses. "Kor! Look into my eyes."

That command would kill just about anyone else, but not my brother.

This is how I can share his burden.

I grunt when he obeys and his death-infused eyes lock onto me.

Fuck.

He holds my gaze, sending the power of death through my body as it locks around my soul like heavy chains. I admire him for how he lives with this burden every day.

While I propel death, he absorbs it.

"The spirits are pulling me in, Zy," he says through gritted teeth. "I'm not going to be able to stop it."

I don't even want to know what'll happen if Kor spirits out of a moving airplane to whatever massacre that's called him.

Because that's how his power works. When a person or creature dies, its spirit creates a vacuum in this plane as it moves to the next.

Kor has told me it feels like a black hole, and the more spirits that are moving at once, the less control he has over his ability.

Because it'll suck him and anyone he's touching right into the death site.

He can't travel to the death plane, luckily, but it does force him to create tunnels, or "pockets," in our own realm.

My vision sparks with intense white flashes, warning me that we're about to teleport out of a moving airplane to the Gods know where.

"Kor!" I shout as I grip his forearms and look into his eyes.

His magic washes through me, burns my insides, and consumes me alive.

Whether I want to or not, I'm going with him this time.

A scream rips out of my fracturing chest as my soul is sucked into time and space and we're thrust into the abyss.

Chapter 11

Issy

A few minutes earlier...

What are you doing?! I shout into my sister's mind.

I'm both terrified for her safety and worried about Jasper's soul.

Because the dead spirit of a patriarch is trying to invade his body. Fallon's presence had pushed Daithi out before, but he evidently found a work-around.

I'm tossing this bastard back to the death plane, my sister informs me as she releases another wave of power.

She's talking about Daithi O'Neely, not Jasper, the male she's releasing a relentless wave of death magic on. He just so happens to be Daithi's chosen host.

A scream rips out of Jasper's throat as he claws at his chest.

I double over when a strange thump hits the left side of my rib cage and then does it again.

Is that... Jasper's heart beating?

It feels wrong, though, as if his heart isn't meant to function in such a basic way. He's some sort of vampire hybrid, so that doesn't surprise me.

What *does* is the fact that I can feel what he's feeling at all.

Is Daithi doing this? I wonder as I rake my nails over my skin.

If this isn't the work of the patriarch, then that means it's the fated bond becoming permanent even without consummating it.

I turn to the archangel, desperate for help. If this continues, I won't be of any use to anyone.

And I certainly won't live long enough to understand why my spirit has decided to bond to Jasper's without following the rules of our world.

Fated mates have a choice, but I don't feel like fate is giving me one right now.

The archangel won't look at me. Nolan is watching the scene unfold with grim features. His muscles are coiled and he's radiating lethal energy—but this isn't his domain.

He's an agent of death, not an agent of the *already dead*.

I do notice, however, that he has a potion in his hand. It's a rare one—the same he used to bring Fallon here.

A portal spell.

My sister doesn't seem very keen on the idea of running away, though.

Fallon has her hands on Jasper's shoulders, pushing him down with the raw force of her incredible magic. Daithi's soul warps and bends in response. Wisps of him appear like ghostly fragments, seeping in and out of Jasper's form in waves.

But it's costing him. Jasper's skin breaks open as Daithi thrashes within it, as if desperately trying to root himself.

He's using the fate bond to link himself to Jasper, I realize.

Fallon is strong, but not strong enough to overpower fate. If she were, then she would have overthrown Nikolas during those three terrible years she was under his control.

Please, stop! I shout in her head as I cling to her shoulders.

She's going to kill him at this rate—assuming it doesn't backfire on her first. Jasper's death touch is in full effect and it's a miracle that Fallon hasn't gone under from it.

But she is the only witch I know who can travel to the death plane—and *return.* She's more familiar with its energy than most and that experience alone is enough to ground her in her own flesh.

For now.

This has to be done, she shoots back at me.

But you're going to kill him! I return, widening my eyes.

She sets her jaw. *That's the idea.*

I'm not sure if she's talking about Daithi, Jasper, or both.

Please, Fallon! He's my fated mate!

My connection with Jasper is real. Daithi admitted as much.

The only reason the patriarch was able to enter his body at all is because this is a true fated-mate bond. One that he intends to abuse for his own means.

That seems to get Fallon's attention. She keeps her grip on Jasper's shoulders as he thrashes, but she's looking at me. Her white-washed eyes are alive with death magic, but I can spot the sisterly concern underneath.

The vampire? she asks.

Yes! I grab onto her wrists. *And if you kill him, you'll be killing* me.

Technically, Jasper and I needed to have sex to make the bond irreversible, but it seems the rules aren't always straightforward when it comes to fate bonds.

Jasper and I are already connected, both in life and in death.

I can absorb his death touch and he can withstand my voice. Whatever exchange is necessary to make the bond permanent could have already happened.

And right now, I can feel his spirit in a tug-of-war against Fallon and Daithi. One he might not survive.

And if Jasper dies, I'll likely die with him. Fated bonds are forever.

It's a gamble Daithi is going to take because he'd rather bring me with him to the death plane than allow me to live freely without him.

"Damn it!" Fallon curses, roaring in frustration as she releases Jasper. He's left gasping for air as blood soaks the new suit I conjured for him. He's clawing at his chest, desperate to stop his heart from beating.

Because he's not supposed to be alive, not in the technical sense. Daithi is trying to force his body to be something it's not.

And in doing so, it'll give him a foothold to push Jasper's spirit out and replace the void with his own.

Body swapping with my fated mate.

I've never heard of such a practice happening before, and if I were reading about this in a spell book, I would be fascinated by the technique.

But this isn't a book. This is *real*.

I place myself between Jasper and Fallon and face her down.

This is my problem, I tell her. *If you truly want to help, then let me handle this.*

Her hair flares around her, giving her an ethereal look. She's a powerful witch, one who has power over death, just like me.

But I'm not afraid. My sister would do anything for me, even to her own detriment.

But will she do this? Will she walk away?

Her eyes burn with fury. *You* weren't *handling it,* she shoots back. *And your problems are mine, too, Issy.*

She balls her fingers into fists and stares me down. I know she's not going to leave me.

Not willingly, anyway.

I glance at Nolan, knowing he's going to have to do what I can't. I point at the bottle in his hand and hope he gets what I'm trying to say.

Remove her by force if you have to, archangel.

He can't hear my thoughts, but he can see the meaning in my eyes.

They're going to have to give me a chance to handle

this myself. In order to reclaim Jasper, I need to use my voice. And neither of them can be here for that.

"I think she wants us to leave," Nolan says to his mate.

Fallon scoffs. "You can bet your pretty feathers I'm not leaving my sister alone with this monster. Not a fucking chance."

"You should listen to your sister," Jasper says from behind me, but his voice is wrong.

It trembles with magic and an echo that comes from another realm.

The death plane.

We all turn as Daithi secures his place in Jasper's body and speaks through him. He grins at Fallon as if he's already won. *"You think I didn't have a fail-safe in place? Such a womanly thing to do, not to consider the bigger picture. Now, if you'll be a good little witch, hand over your sister and I might consider leaving you be."*

Fallon grabs my wrist and pulls me to her side. "I'm a queen now, Daithi. You don't get to tell me what to do." She shares a look with me. "We're the ones in charge. The time of the patriarchs is *over.*"

He chuckles as he takes a handkerchief from his vest pocket and begins cleaning his fingers. *"Is that what you think? Well. While you've been playing queen in this little patch of land of the living, I've been building a bigger kingdom. One that knows when to listen to its betters."*

A rumble sounds from all around us and the ground begins to tremble. My heart leaps into my throat as the whole house rattles, threatening to collapse.

What's he doing? I ask my sister, because I *feel* something coming.

My skin crawls with an eerie sensation and my chest burns as Jasper's heart continues to beat with an unnatural rhythm.

Then I notice the screams.

Thousands of them.

Do you hear that? I ask. Normally, I'm the only one who can interpret the cries of the dead, but this time they're echoing through my entire body as if they're actually here.

"Yes," Fallon replies out loud. She's cutting off the blood flow to my fingers, but I don't care.

If she can hear them, it's because Daithi is calling the spirits of the death plane... and he's bringing them *here*.

A skeleton bursts through the floor a moment later, followed by another two.

I don't have to guess who they are. I've been hearing their cries the entire time I've lived in this cottage.

It's the family of the prior owners, and apparently, they were buried underneath the house. Given that it looks like a couple and their child, it had been an unsavory ending.

Nolan reacts fast, pulling a gun seemingly from nowhere, and the resulting fire shatters the skeletons into pieces.

It doesn't do much good, though, because they just start to knit back together.

Daithi laughs. *"My children can't be killed, silly angel. They're already dead."*

Fallon tugs me back with her. "Time to go, Nolan."

Nolan sprinkles the potion, opening a portal behind us. "Don't have to tell me twice. I'll send Bane and Nox to deal with this."

Phantoms aren't going to help this situation! I shout into Fallon's mind. *I know it seems logical to bring in Bane and Nox, but trust me, only I can deal with this. And I. Am. Not.* Leaving.

Fallon's jaw clenches as I wrench my hand free.

From my experience with Daithi, once he sinks his teeth into something, he doesn't let go.

And I know if I abandon Jasper now, I'll never get him back. I'll be dooming him and myself in the process.

A particular vein in her forehead pops just like it did when we were children and I fought her on something. Except this isn't a childhood tussle. This is life and death —literally.

She reaches for me, but I back away. She sets her jaw again. "If you think I'm leaving you here with this monster, you're wrong, Issy."

The skeletons re-form and launch at us, but Nolan is ready with another set of bullets. Bone shards splatter across the floorboards that splinter apart as the ground continues to shake.

I have to reason with my sister and somehow convince her to do something she's never done before.

Leave me.

Too many souls are being forced back into their decayed bodies, I tell her as I feel everything that's going on. It's not just the prior residents of this cottage.

It's half of Lapland.

The insides of my mind feel as if they're being

shredded apart, sending lights sparking behind my eyes. The spirits cry with their endless death knells.

Because they're supposed to be at peace—a peace that's been denied.

They're suffering, Fallon, I tell her as I try to get her to see reason. *Their screams are ones of pain and they have no choice but to obey Daithi. Don't you remember what that's like? Being forced into obedience to a monster? I cannot leave.*

Her jaw flexes and I know it's a low blow, but I'm determined to make her listen to me.

"Tick-tock," Daithi says as he picks up the skull of one of the dead and strokes it. *"I've summoned the undead in the surrounding vicinity and well into the city. They're killing anyone in their way and adding to my number."* He chuckles as his words confirm what I'm feeling. *"Recently dead bodies of the more powerful families living in Lapland will be much harder to slow down, even for your trigger-happy archangel."*

Nolan's nostrils flare as he points the gun at Jasper's head. "I think it's time to end this little game. You can't control much if you don't have a body to inhabit, spirit."

I throw myself in the barrel's path and glower at him.

Nolan growls. "Fallon. Control your sister. This spirit is using illegal necromancy magic and must be dealt with."

That only pisses me off more. *Fallon, control your mate,* I retort, even though only she can hear me.

His brilliant gaze flares with heat as he continues. "Not to mention I know who this spirit is, Fallon. He's the one who bound you to that *freak*."

"I know, Nolan. But we can't kill him," she says, giving me a small sense of relief. "If he dies, so does my sister."

Nolan gives her a look that says that's not enough to stop him, but it *is* enough to make him hesitate. He slightly lowers his gun.

I don't know how long this standoff might last, and time is running out. The ground trembles with the rumble of the dead and the rising cries of the dying and recently departed.

Nolan might be the queen's mate, but he's also Kaspian's trusted warrior. He will protect the king's interests, and right now, Daithi is doing more than summoning lost spirits.

He's killing Kaspian's people.

Death rolls through me as I feel each and every one. Their screams add to the growing number, giving me a splitting headache, and I brace my temples. I know Fallon has to feel it, too.

I can stop this, but you have to leave! I shout at her.

I'm not entirely sure if that's true, but I have a theory. One that might save us.

Or doom us all.

Either way, I don't want Fallon here for the experiment that might cost us all our lives.

"You cannot stop this yourself," she snaps. "And I am *not* leaving without you!"

It's clear my sister won't leave without me.

You give me no choice, Fallon. Tightness pulls at my eyes, the telltale sign of unshed tears I'm usually pretty good at holding in.

If she refuses to leave, then I have to make sure she has no reason to stay.

Rushing to the dagger I dropped, I rear back and poise the metal over my throat.

"Issy!" she screams, but I stop her with a mental command.

Leave, I order her, digging the blade in hard enough to draw blood. *Or I swear to the spirits, I will protect you the only way I know how. I can do that with my voice... or I can scream from the death plane. The choice is yours.*

My sister is furious—and terrified. Her eyes flick back and forth between mine, as though she's desperate for another option.

I'm not going to give her one.

The ground rumbles as if to accentuate my threat. There isn't much time.

Nolan carefully wraps his fingers around Fallon's wrist. "You'll tell her when we can return?" he asks me.

I nod, ignoring the pinch of the blade against my skin.

Jasper's hand weighs on my hip as he chuckles in approval.

It proves to me that Daithi believes he can control me no matter if I'm alive or dead.

That gives me an idea, one that is unraveling in the background of my mind while my sister is slowly backing away.

"Please, Issy. *Please* don't do this," she begs.

My heart twists with her pain, but I'm doing this for her. For us.

For me.

I'll see you soon, I promise.

I just hope that the next time I see her, it'll be through my own eyes and not through the veil of the death plane.

"See you soon," she vows, then ducks her chin as Nolan leads her through the portal.

"Alone at last," Daithi says, his breath hot against my neck.

My voice won't hurt him, but that's because he's inside Jasper's body. The logical conclusion is that I need to get him out for my voice to impact him.

I only have one shot at this.

Whirling, I slice Jasper's throat open. He throws his hands over his open wound and gags.

It's not enough to kill a vampire, but it's enough to unseat the patriarch inside his body.

The spirit within him fluctuates and spills out on the waves of blood.

I don't hesitate. I draw in a deep breath... and *scream*.

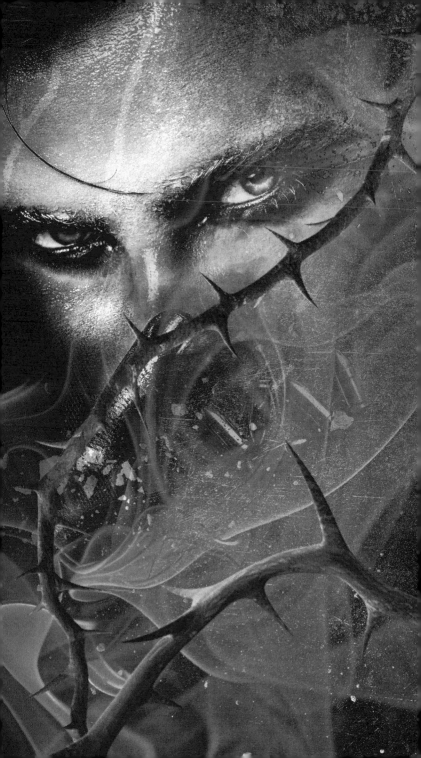

Chapter 12

Kornelius

A few minutes earlier...

I'm familiar with death, but I've never quite experienced it so up close and personal.

I'm overwhelmed with a massive migraine, leaving me dazed as I try to gain my bearings.

My world is horizontal as my cheek is pressed against the ground. Across from me, a body twitches as blood spills out of a male's open mouth. The fur sprouting all across his skin suggests he's some sort of shifter, but he wasn't fast enough against the unseen force that ripped through this place to transform completely.

Not that it would have done him any good.

Zyran steadies me by placing a hand on my shoulder. He's always been able to absorb the worst of the aftereffects of my power, but I imagine even he's struggling right now.

Regardless, his touch is enough to let me sit up.

"What the hell is killing everything?" I marvel as I crouch and watch a silvery mist sweep across the ground.

Zyran sifts dirt through his fingers. "It feels like Daithi," he says, and it does.

There's a cold sensation, and a sour taste lingers on the back of my tongue. That's always what it feels like when our soul-master is near.

But I don't see him. All I can feel is overwhelming power that doesn't make any sense.

"Daithi isn't this powerful," I counter as I straighten. I don't have a weapon, but for the first time, I feel like I need one.

My power isn't going to be of any use here. We're at the edge of the city looking in, and all I see is walking death.

Bodies crawl across the streets. Screams sound from broken windows. Blood paints the stones red.

Zyran hums in agreement, then rests a hand on my shoulder again, but this time not to steady me. He's trying to help me focus. "Where's the death stone? Maybe he can tell us what's going on himself."

Shoving a hand in my pocket, I frown, because it's not there. The mute collar developed for the witch with a deadly voice is inside, although I'm not even sure if it'll work now.

But the death stone has vanished.

"I don't know."

He stares at me.

We don't have time to argue, because someone comes at us from out of nowhere.

With a freaking machete.

Growling, I clap the blade with both hands, catching it before it skewers me in two.

The male on the other end is the half-transformed shifter I'd just been eyeing. Fur still sprouts from human skin, but the rest of him looks all wrong.

His bones are broken and twisted the wrong way. I expect that is because of his attempts to shift, but it's his eyes that aren't right.

They're completely white.

"This is some deep necromancy shit," Zyran tells me as he shoves the shifter away. Even though he's a weapon in his own right because of his death sight, he is well-trained in combat. He genuinely enjoys it and always picks up any combat mission our soul-captor allows.

Killing someone with sight can bring up questions— but death by knife wound has an easy explanation.

With a swift move, he twists the blade out of the male's hand, then disembowels him with it.

Entrails splatter across the ground as the male groans —still very much dead.

And still very much not caring.

My spelled programming says that I should confirm with my soul-captor for instructions, but that requires the death stone or a patriarch representative.

I have served the Outcast Coven for years—not willingly, but through my enslavement.

And now with the upheaval of the matriarchs taking over, I feel like I'm on a sinking ship. Not that I don't want the matriarchs to metaphorically shove their fists up the patriarchs' assholes, but because I'm not sure where that leaves me or my brothers.

We're powerful.

And we're dangerous.

In this world, that's a one-way ticket to an execution.

The ground rumbles in agreement, making me feel as if the very soil is going to melt beneath my feet.

A group of four strangers corral around a fifth. A woman in the center is screaming as the mist clings to her fingers, her hair, and hangs from her like lace.

It's not working on her, I realize, so she's not going to be allowed to live.

Either the mist kills, or blunt force will do.

Her screams go silent after a heavy thud and then she's one of them, stumbling along with half of her face missing.

The silvery mist is collecting more lives, and as Daithi's minions are killing those who seemed to repel the spell, an army is being formed.

An army... for what?

Kill her! a command enters my mind, making me double over as I grip my head.

"Fuck!" Zyran growls through gritted teeth. "Okay, that's definitely Daithi. I'd recognize that asshole's voice anywhere."

"Yes," I agree, buckling against another mental blow commanding us to kill *her*, "but where is he getting this sort of power?"

Daithi has always required the death stone to project the spell over us that subdues our will. I have no idea where the death stone is or what happened to it, but his command rakes through me like fire.

Kill her, my body screams, begging me to move.

"We should go this way," Zyran says as he drags his foot down the path. The route would take us out of the city and into the woods.

Stumbling after him, I decide to follow, but it doesn't make sense. My ring squeezes around my knuckle. It should have given me some measure of my free will back, but it didn't.

Daithi wants the witch dead. It's apparent he's having some difficulty with the matter.

Which is why we're here in the first place, but I care less about the witch Daithi wants dead and more about my brother's life.

Jasper, the brother we were forced to leave behind.

Zyran holds up a hand. "Wait, do you feel that?"

I cock my head and then sense the coming wave.

I brace myself just in time.

A shock wave of raw power rushes over the landscape, decimating everything in its path. Every single body around us falls, leaving us as the last ones standing.

"That sounded a lot like a scream," I grit out as my head spins.

"The witch," Zyran replies as he cracks his neck. "That was her, wasn't it?"

It was, but from what we know of Ishara Doyle, her voice can't carry like that.

Not without an amplifier.

"Fuck, Zyran. Fuck, I can't believe I didn't figure this out sooner."

He turns to me. "What?"

"Jasper's power is over death, just like ours. And he's with that witch right now. She could easily use him just like Daithi uses us."

His jaw flexes. "You mean..."

I nod. "Jasper... is still alive."

Chapter 13

Jasper

I wake to a gentle touch on my forehead, but it's not my mother's.

No, my mother is long dead.

Ishara Doyle, the witch I was assigned to kill, is wiping away the blood from my face, throat, and chest with a damp cloth. Her movements are slow, deliberate, and almost apologetic.

Gripping her wrist, I stop her as her intense gaze burns into mine.

I'm not sure what I should say.

I'm sorry? That seems too simple and hardly encompasses everything I'm feeling.

I tried to kill her.

Multiple times.

And now I know that I've put her in a terrible position, one where she might as well be dead already.

Because the Houses aren't going to allow her to live after this.

They won't let any of us live.

I'm not as upset about that as I should be, at least when it comes to my own life. I've gone through every day seeking a blade, seeking blood, and never quite finding it.

Today... Ishara Doyle gave it to me.

"My angel of death, how beautiful you are," I say instead.

She must not be expecting my words, because she blinks at me a few times before laughing.

The sound would cut anyone else down with its raw power, but I let it seep through me like needles through water. The effects leave behind a warm tingling sensation that has me craving more of her voice.

She licks her lips before replying with a barely audible whisper. "Nolan might take offense to me being called an angel."

"That oversized bird?" I offer, smiling when my mate laughs again. "I don't care what he thinks."

"Clearly," she says, then turns somber while I run my fingers over the inside of her wrist.

Her skin is so soft, and despite my recently slashed throat, all I want to do is pull her on top of me and explore more of her.

"If cutting you open has this effect, I'd hate to see how you react when I'm nice to you," she replies. "I've never laughed in front of someone else before. It's... nice."

I like that her voice is huskier now, my touch having its intended effect.

Because we are still fated mates.

And now, we're *alone at last*.

A frown overtakes my face when I recall speaking those words, but it wasn't *me* who said them.

It was the spirit of a patriarch named Daithi. Which is why Ishara was forced to slit my throat.

Not to kill me... but to save me.

Remembering that Daithi summoned numerous dead bodies, I glance at the bedroom window. A strange silvery film resonated around it, suggesting that a spell is keeping us protected.

For now.

"How long is that going to last?" I ask, gesturing to the glass.

She eyes an hourglass on the nightstand. Only a trickle of sand has settled on the bottom.

"A few hours at most," she says. A shadow passes over the window, but I can't hear anything on the other side.

Her shoulders tense. "There's an entire army out there."

Sitting up, I blow out a breath. "Well, I guess you'd better let your sister know that she can come pick you up." I don't include myself in that statement. Kaspian's queen would give her sister refuge—but not me. There's no way. And even if it were an option, I'd be stuck in some prison cell where I'd never see the light of day.

I couldn't be killed, or that would kill Ishara.

But I could be contained. *Secured*.

Ishara frowns and her cute brows pinch together. "I think it should be obvious I'm not leaving you. My sister would do anything to protect me, but she'd find a way to break the bond between us. After what Daithi just did to you, she's going to think you're too dangerous to keep around."

I tilt my head. "Yes, I was thinking the same thing, but she'll protect you."

She purses her lips. "And what do you intend to do? When the hourglass runs out, this place is going to be overrun."

"I'm not the one Daithi wants dead. I'll be fine."

She fists the bedsheets I'm lying on. "I had to bleed you out to dislodge his spirit from your body. I had to scream and use your magic as an amplifier to shove him back to the death plane, but it's not a permanent solution. He *will* be back and I doubt the technique is going to work a second time if he manages to possess you again."

Another shadow passes over the window, sending the room into darkness.

I prefer the darkness. It allows me to see details better —details like Ishara's silver eyes that shine bright with magic and ferocity.

She's clearly been through difficulties in her life, but she's come out stronger for it.

"You're the perfect mate for me," I say, easily changing the subject as I graze my fingers over her plump lips. I've been touching her arm this whole time, but if we're going to be here for a few hours, I want to give her a proper goodbye.

I doubt I'll ever see her again.

Because if Daithi does surpass my defenses once more, I'm taking him down with me. I *felt* what he wanted to do to Ishara Doyle, and I am self-destructive enough to make sure he never succeeds.

Even if it means I shred my body myself.

I press my mouth against hers, delighting when she parts her lips for me. My tongue tastes her fiery spirit and I enjoy it when she tastes me back.

"Your distraction tactics aren't going to work," she whispers against my mouth.

"Really? Seems to be working to me," I say as I pull her onto my lap.

It's not just a distraction tactic, though. The bond I have with Ishara Doyle gave Daithi an in, but it also helped us bring out each other's true power.

Her voice is death incarnate, but with my power, it is something so much more.

I want to give her every chance in the world to fight for herself.

I would give her everything I have to offer, because fate showed me my mate. This is perhaps everything I have been building toward.

All for her.

I know it's fate magic securing itself like hooks inside my body, making me convinced about my feelings, but that's an aspect of our world that I accept. There is enough cruelty, enough suffering.

The one good thing about our world is the true, unadulterated love fated mates hold for one another.

My mother's fated mate abused his power over her. He'd demanded a lineage and then hated her for giving him what he'd wanted.

I will not be like my father.

Cupping Ishara's ass, I pull her onto my erection. I'm still wearing pants, and she's wearing thin underwear, but her intake of breath assures me she feels an appropriate amount of pressure all the same.

"Our bond is already permanent," she informs me as she works her hips over me, grinding me and making me want to rip away every barrier between us. "Sleeping together won't change anything."

"Fucking, you mean," I correct her. I prefer to say what I intend to do to her, not insinuate it. "And I disagree, witchling. If I fuck you, I can better protect you."

She pauses over me and I dig my fingers into her hips, urging her to continue. "What do you mean?"

I spear my fingers under the sides of her panties, ripping them in the process. "When you spilled my blood, your power multiplied. Didn't you feel it?" Her chest remains unmoving and I know she's holding her breath.

She's just as affected by our bond as I am, possibly even more. My magic seeks her out like the siren she is, intoxicated by her, wanting to permeate every inch of her with my essence.

Which only proves the point I'm about to make.

"I did," she agrees as I run one hand behind her neck and tug her closer to me. I hold her in place as I kiss her again, this time angling her how I want her.

A small part of my spirit leaves my body, entering her.

Because she is my mate.

My home.

"Now," I say against her mouth, "imagine what'll happen if I'm inside of you, giving you *everything*."

"You make me stronger," she realizes aloud.

"Hmm," I agree. "Do you want to be stronger, sweetling? Do you want to see how I can make you *scream*?"

Her gaze is locked onto mine, but I see when she breaks. She can't resist fate, especially when she doesn't have a logical reason to.

My magic can protect her. She already proved that by using me to exorcise a patriarch from his host, which was no small feat.

Her fingers fumble at my pants and I grin when she lowers the zipper. "It's just an excuse to give in to what we both want," she says.

"Perhaps," I agree, then hiss when she strokes my hard cock. "But I don't see a downside to fucking you, and you said we have a few hours."

Though I want so much more than that, I'll take even a single moment inside of her.

I'm desperate for her warmth and her need.

And absolutely more of her screams.

"I don't either," she says as she peels away what's left of her underwear, exposing her beautiful wetness to me. "I want this."

I groan as I look at her beautiful pussy, wanting to taste her there. It's neat and trim with a cute little stripe down the center. Perhaps she prepared herself for her date, just in case.

Or perhaps fate gave her an unconscious premonition of me.

Her preparation only makes me want to eat her.

And I will, I vow, once I've thoroughly fucked her.

I'll clean her with my tongue and make her scream for me again.

But right now the bond between us is taut with demand, needing us to fulfill a completion that already feels like it has passed.

She positions me at her entrance and I let her take the lead.

She needs this—to feel like she's in control. How badly I want to show her how quickly I can turn the tables. I could have her on her knees for me, begging me to make her come, but I won't.

No, right now this is for her, about her, and the lust in her gaze demands my absolute compliance.

My abdomen flexes as she plays with me, soaking my cock in her slick heat as her mouth parts on a pant. She's still a breath away from my face, from my deadly fangs, and every sound she makes rips through me like a blade.

The sensation only plays on my proclivities. Fate knew what it was doing when it chose this witch for me.

This *woman*.

"You're so fucking wet," I tell her as she continues to torment me.

Based on the tension in the air, she's waiting for something, but I'm not sure what.

"I've... I've never done this," she admits, making me go still. "I mean, I don't think I'm a virgin. I don't remember..." She bites her lips as she trails off, her eyes going dark.

A growl rumbles in my throat, but the anger that surges within me is against those who hurt her.

That gives me a new reason to live. "Give me their names," I demand.

Whether they are alive or not, I'll fucking find them.

She shivers but continues to stroke herself with my cock. She moves her hips with fluid movements, rolling herself up and down my length. "I don't know all of their names. Just that they were patriarchs working with Daithi." She pauses as I grip the back of her neck, and I realize I'm being too hard. I ease my touch and lightly scratch her scalp. "I think... I was intended to be an incentive for those who pleased him."

I don't like the sound of that. But now I am doubly glad that I've given her full control of our encounter. She needs it. She needs to feel what it's like to seek her own pleasure, should she want it.

Knowing that I need to give her the full lead, I release her neck and place my hands behind my head. "My only incentive is to please *you*, Ishara."

A soft grin replaces the frown on her lips, making my heart soar. "Call me Issy."

"Issy," I say, testing out the name. It's sweet and perfect for whispering during sex. "Tell me what *you* want, Issy."

She bites her lip, the motion so adorable I want to kiss her all over, but I remain still. "I want you inside of me."

I angle my hips, pressing against her. I'm rewarded with her soft gasp. "How do you want me inside of you? Rough? Gentle? By your movements or mine? Be specific, my lovely mate."

She seems to appreciate my direction. She peels the rest of her clothes away, leaving her beautiful breasts bare

135

to me as she contemplates her answer. "I want you to stay still and let me explore."

Oh, my little witchling wants to explore what I have to offer. "As you wish," I tell her.

It seems a simple enough task, but what she does next tests my resolve. She leans back and spreads her legs, giving me the most gorgeous view I've ever seen in my life. "Sit up more," she instructs, and I obey. "Now hold your cock for me."

I do as I'm told and I keep myself in place.

Then she slowly, ever so slowly, inches forward, forcing my cock to gradually enter her. A growl rumbles in my throat because I want to thrust inside of her. I want to ravage her and show her all the power I have to offer.

But she wants to *explore*, so she stops every few moments as if she's adjusting to my size. I can't tell if she's truly a virgin or not, in the physical sense, but her anticipation tells me this is definitely her first time experiencing anything like this.

That knowledge keeps me in place until she has positioned herself all the way to the hilt. She doesn't move, but she's panting as she takes all of me like the good girl she is.

"How does it feel?" I ask her, wanting to hear her words if she's not going to give me her screams.

Her wild gaze meets mine. "Almost too much," she pants.

I grin.

"May I touch you?" I ask. "It'll help."

She bites her lip again, then nods. "Okay."

Releasing one of my hands that are fisted behind my

head, I roll my thumb over her beautiful clit. She bucks the moment I touch the sensitive bundle of nerves but then relaxes as I make small circles around it. "Relax for me, baby," I tell her.

Her hips start to move with my fingers, assuring me that I'm doing something she likes.

"I want you to come on my cock like this," I tell her. I hadn't imagined sex for the first time with my fated mate would be so slow and exploratory, but I'm about to burst. I'm enjoying drawing out her pleasure, and in effect, my own.

Her walls clench around me. "I-I don't know if I can," she says. "Orgasms don't... come easily to me."

I keep my small, consistent circles going around her clit. "That just means your body enjoys delayed gratification."

It also means that she hasn't been taught true pleasure, among other things, but I won't say my suspicions out loud. Those things aren't her fault and the assholes who did this to her are to blame. She hasn't had a chance to learn her own body or master her own desires.

Fuck. I can't have just a few hours with her.

No way that'll be enough.

A blush creeps up her chest, adding some color to her marble skin. "Or I'm just too self-conscious to let myself go," she says, admitting something I doubt she's shared with anyone else. Her beautiful gaze flicks up to meet mine while I continue to stroke her, to give her reassurance and pleasure while she shares her secrets with me. "I've had a lot of time alone. When I tried to touch myself, it only made things worse and I—" She hisses when I softly thrust my hips, moving my body in time with my circles. "Wow, that feels good," she says on a loose breath.

"Every time you question yourself, I'm going to punish you," I inform her.

"But—"

I thrust a little harder this time, making her cry out. "You are beautiful. You are perfect. And you are mine, Ishara Doyle."

Even if I have you for only a few hours, you are still mine.

It's not enough.

Not nearly enough.

"Now tell me what you want," I say, going still so she has a chance to think. I also need a distraction because my resolve is slipping.

I intended to fuck her, to give her enough of my spirit to protect her, but my pesky selfish needs seem to be getting in the way.

I'm not going to be able to let her go.

Struggling with my inner demons, I keep up my small circles just around her clit. The continuous build of friction will only help her relax and increase her pleasure at her own rate.

"I want this," she says, keeping her gaze locked on mine.

It's proof that she's not a shy little thing. She's a brave, beautiful, and powerful witch, one who is taking my cock all the way to the hilt without issue.

"Do you want to explore, or do you want me to show you how I fuck my mate?" I ask.

I need her consent if she's going to release me. While I will keep her pleasure as my priority, I can't make any promises that I won't draw blood.

She smiles as if she's won some sort of game between us. "I want to see if you can make me come. Give it your best shot, Jasper Justi. No holds barred."

A manic sense of delight rips through my core. "Hold on to me, then, little witch. Because I'm going to *destroy you*."

Chapter 14

Issy

Perhaps giving Jasper full rein was a bad idea, but I wanted to experience what a fated mate could offer.

Spirits... I had no idea.

I'm holding on to the sides of the bed for dear life as he pins me to the mattress. His strong hand is wrapped around my throat, giving me a sense of danger, while his other continues those torturous little circles of his with his fingers.

He hasn't stopped touching me for the past hour.

He hasn't stopped fucking me, either.

Countless thrusts send pleasure through me like waves in an endless ocean, leaving me buoying for any breath I can catch.

He's learned that I like it when he cuts off my air. Maybe it's a fucked-up way of dealing with being mute all my life, but every time he does it, it makes me wet.

His fingers squeeze my throat, causing my lungs to burn as I count his thrusts.

Four.

Five.

Six.

On seven, he releases me and I take in a large gulp of sweet oxygen. The next thrust is fast, hard, and deep, forcing my gasp to turn into a scream.

Then he starts all over again.

As Jasper is a vampire, I know his stamina is near infinite, but he demonstrates his level of control as he strokes me from the inside. He placed a pillow under my hips about thirty minutes ago to make the penetration even deeper, not that I needed it.

"You will feel every inch of me, baby," he promised.

And spirits, he's been making sure I do.

Over. And. Over. Again.

Even though the tension inside of me has climbed to a fever pitch, it never quite feels like I can cross over the precipice.

Maybe something's wrong with me.

"Where's your mind going, little witchling?" Jasper asks me as he pauses his intense thrusting.

I flash my gaze up at him. My entire body hums with pleasure and seems to vibrate like a guitar string left on a single note.

A sour note where I was wondering why I'm so messed up.

We haven't been sharing thoughts like I can with my sister. And thank the spirits I know how to wall my mind off from her, or else I'd be getting an earful right now.

I'm supposed to be running for my life. Not having my brains fucked out by my vampire mate—but who's she to judge?

"Nowhere," I tell him.

It's a lie.

Proving that he knows it, he pulls out of me, momentarily giving me reprieve before he flips me onto my stomach. He shoves inside of me again, making me gasp as he wraps his arm around my center and finds my clit once more.

His chest presses up against my back. The pillow keeps my hips elevated while he resumes his torment.

But it's so much more intense in this position, and he seems to know exactly what he's doing.

"Do you know what I do to liars?" he asks as he holds me in place. Each deliberate thrust sends pleasure sparking behind my eyes, but it's too much. I can't come if he's overstimulating me.

"No," I respond, eager to find out.

Because I like the idea of being punished by this vampire. He's a mercenary trained in the art of death—something that appeals to my darker nature.

"I don't give them what they want," he says, easing out of me.

Not what I expected, but when I turn to look at him, he slaps my ass hard enough to sting.

"Ouch!" I snap, but then he runs his tongue over the throbbing spot, making me go still.

"You want my cock?" he asks.

I nod, because even if I am broken and can't come, having my mate inside of me is as close to euphoria as I've ever been.

I'm not ready to stop.

A quick glance at the hourglass tells me we still have

143

time, but precious moments are slipping away.

"You lied to me, so you're going to have to earn it back," he says. "In the meantime, I'm going to indulge in what I've been wanting to do this whole time."

Before I have a chance to ask what he means, he spreads me with his fingers, then runs his tongue across my opening.

"Jasper," I hiss when he shoves his tongue inside, spearing me with it and eliciting a whole new set of sensations.

Because his fangs are pressed up against my very sensitive area, and that both thrills and terrifies me.

"Call me Jas," he says, making me flinch when his words hit my swollen heat.

"Jas," I immediately say, eager to please him.

Because his tongue and his danger might just undo me, and as much as I have been attempting to orgasm, now I'm not so sure I'm ready.

Not for the kind of climax Jasper Justi offers.

The bed shifts and I realize he's rolled onto his back. He removes the pillow, yanking it down as he catches my hip.

"Ride my face, little witchling."

His brazen words have me blushing all over again. I'm not a prude. I read more than just spell books. I have an entire collection of five-chili-pepper smut that would make even my sister raise eyebrows. Thanks to my spells, I've kept them hidden from her and the rest of my family.

Ayla is the only one who knows about my collection, because she's my source, too. She helped me begin restocking once we settled into the cottage—under a blood vow not to tell anyone about it.

It's not the lady porn that I'm shy about; it's the *kind* of books I've collected.

The ones with three paragraphs of trigger warnings in the front. Those are the ones I'm drawn to like a moth to a flame. I need to be burned alive to feel anything at all.

I definitely don't want Fallon to know that I have some pretty dark kinks. I'd like to think she'd be supportive—and she probably would be, but the self-conscious part of me worries she'll explain it away as trauma gone wrong.

The only time I can orgasm is when I'm close to death. That could mean choking myself, blood loss, or a myriad of other techniques I've come up with over the years just to *feel* something.

Jasper Justi. He's death itself.

I feel it in his touch. Each stroke of his tongue has me shivering and panting with renewed need. He dents his fingers into my thighs, demanding that I comply with his order, and I find my hips moving against him.

Rubbing myself on his face like I'm some sort of sex lunatic.

"That's a good girl," he praises, making me see stars when he sweeps his tongue all the way over my clit, then lightly nips it.

I buck when he does that and he goes still.

"Fuck, that made you wet. Do you like pain, witchling?" He chuckles as he rakes his nails over my skin, leaving stinging lines of sensation. "What am I saying? Of course you do. Fate chose you for me because you're *fucking perfect*."

It's not exactly pain that threatens to send me over the edge, but the danger Jas promises.

"Bite me," I say, eager to chase this new pleasure with him.

Pain from other sources never had this sort of effect on me. Daithi and the others hurt me and it only pissed me off.

This, though. This is different.

He growls in response, the sound one of adamant approval as he licks a line on my inner thigh.

Then sinks his incisors into my vein.

I gasp as the sharp pain spears through my body, sending a shock wave of adrenaline and warning.

Then he deeply pulls, drawing out my blood as he takes his fill.

He groans and the sound is pure sensuality. I move my hips, eager for some sort of friction to counteract the pain with pleasure, and he instantly unlatches, fills me with three fingers, then closes his mouth directly over my clit.

And sucks hard.

For the first time in my life, the climb hits me out of nowhere and my body clamps down onto his fingers. A rolling climax slams into me and I dive into a pillow to muffle my scream.

It's a reflex. I don't want to kill anyone just because I finally achieved an orgasm.

The pillow is ripped away from me a moment later

and the vampire is sucking on my clit again, drawing out intense pleasure that feels more like pain.

But it's so... so good.

He uses his fingers inside of me to push me, sending sensation through my inner walls as he forces me to ride his face, just like he commanded.

He doesn't stop until the spasms come to an end, and I realize that's part of the reason he put his fingers inside of me. To know how to make my body sing for him.

He returns to my open wound, this time licking it gingerly as he growls intelligible praises.

I'm liquid when he rolls me onto my back. He crawls between my legs and braces his elbows on either side of my head. His hard cock throbs at my entrance, but he doesn't enter me.

Instead, he just watches me as if he's evaluating my pleasure. I feel like a book he's learning to read and mine is in a unique language only he knows how to speak.

There's blood all over him, but after a moment, I realize it's not all mine.

My eyes widen as I discover that little cuts have formed all over his body. "Are you okay?"

He responds by pushing his rock-hard cock inside of me. He spreads my walls for him by his sheer size, making me whimper.

"I've never felt so fucking alive, Ishara Doyle." He growls as he thrusts into me with long, confident movements.

He's somehow bigger than before, both in length and in girth.

My eyes roll into the back of my head as I rest my head on the pillow and take in the pleasure. "You're..."

I can't finish the sentence.

I want to say that he's hurt, but he's also *larger*. It doesn't make any sense.

Vampires aren't shifters and they can't alter the size of their cocks—to my knowledge, anyway. And I pride myself on all areas of expertise, especially ones of intimate species details like cock sizes.

"Our bond definitely goes both ways," he informs me as he increases his speed. His body slaps against mine as he fucks me with a steady pace. "When you came for me, you changed me. I need you to do that again." He growls as he leans closer. "And now I know what you like, little witchling. I'm going to make you come *hard*."

Against my expectations, a new build stirs in my core.

I realize it's not just pain that turns me on—it's blood. It only took Jasper an hour with me to figure that out.

There's definitely something terribly wrong with me, I think.

But the concern is thrust out of my mind as Jasper fucks me harder. He pinches my nipple, making me yip.

"Keep your eyes on me, baby," he says as he massages my breast.

He leans in and his other hand goes to my throat, but he doesn't cut off my air this time.

He doesn't need to, because I'm panting. There's blood on his lips where he bit me and his fangs are dripping with my cum.

Why is that so hot?

He lowers his hips as he thrusts, sending friction and pressure blooming over my clit.

Then he angles my chin, exposing my throat. "I'm going to bite you, sweetling," he informs me.

"O-okay," I pant, already about to burst with anticipation.

Then he pricks me with his fangs. He doesn't sink them into me like he did with my thigh and I'm left disappointed by the brief trickle of pain.

But then he does it again farther down my throat.

And once more just above my breast.

When he returns to my mouth, I realize he was opening my veins. My own blood tastes tangy as he roughly kisses me, battling my tongue with his own.

He slams into me and keeps the pressure on my clit as he grinds down.

Hard.

"Come for me, Issy," he demands as he fills me up with his huge cock.

Against all my expectations, my body obeys him.

He's learned me so masterfully in such a short amount of time that I don't try to muffle my scream. I squeeze my eyes shut and allow the pleasure to devour me like a monster in the night.

Pure euphoria encases me like a cloud, shooting me into the stars as I fly over the precipice that always challenged me.

Jasper is right there with me, following me with a roar of release as he slams into me and fills me with warmth and *power*.

It's not just our pleasure joining, but also our magic.

149

It mixes together like a toxic poison beautifully crafted from my garden. My world shatters as Jasper empties all of his soul into my body, giving me everything just as he promised.

I should have expected such a powerful release to break the walls of my containment spell, but I can hardly hear the windows shatter or the door slamming open.

When I open my eyes, I'm stunned to find two males in the doorway staring at us.

They aren't soldiers of Daithi's undead army.

They're something else entirely. My chest tightens and my stomach flips. I've forgotten how to breathe, and it's not just because I had the most realm-shattering orgasm of my entire life.

It's because the two males in the doorway look an awful lot like Jasper.

And based on the flare of need and possession that spears through me, they're my second-chance mates.

Shit.

Chapter 15

Kornelius

Fuck.

This is the witch we're supposed to kill?

I can't take my eyes off of her. Ishara Doyle is the most beautiful creature I've ever seen in my life.

And my long-lost brother is currently dick-deep inside of her.

But his obvious claim doesn't change the intense craving that overcomes me.

Mine, a voice chants inside my head.

The undeniable bind wraps around my soul, leaving little imagination as to what Ishara Doyle is to me.

My fated mate.

I came here with the intention of killing her. That's what Daithi wants, and until I figure out a way to fight him, I'm powerless. Whatever Daithi wants, Daithi gets.

Except, harming my beautiful mate is out of the question. The kill order still throbs through my Gold and Garnet ring, but after being blasted by this witch's latest scream, I seem to be able to ignore it.

That's definitely a first.

I struggle through why I'm able to fight my soul-master's order when I never have before. Perhaps it's because I've never really tried.

Killing her aligned with my goals until now. Either this witch broke the sliver of magic Daithi had over me, or my desire no longer matched Daithi's and it was as simple as that. I was working under the assumption that the witch was *using* Jasper to amplify her power, but it seems Jasper has no qualms about being used.

I can see why.

Her silver eyes are intense and her cheeks are flushed with pleasure. My dick is already saluting and ready to complete our bond as quickly as possible. She's primed for sex.

But there's the matter of my sibling rival to deal with. I came here to save him, but he obviously doesn't need saving.

And he can shove his dick into her all he wants. It doesn't change the fact that Ishara Doyle is my mate.

"Who the fuck are you?" Jasper asks, forcing me to peel my gaze away from the breathtaking witch.

"You don't recognize me?" I quip as I press a hand to my chest. "I'm wounded, brother. It's Kornelius." I indicate Zy with my chin. "And Zyran, if you need the refresher."

Groans and shouts echo in the distance, reminding me that we don't have much time before reinforcements arrive. Ishara's screams can be felt all across the city.

But the latest one she just released was strong enough to undo Daithi's death magic spell.

Her power had come from using my brother as an amplifier. Her medium?

Sex.

Technically, she can scream again to give us more time, but I want to be the one between her legs. Not Jasper. If he can be her amplifier because he's her fated mate, then I should be able to do the same thing.

What baffles me, though, is why I wasn't ripped apart like all the corpses around us were. There could only be one reason.

Because I'm her fated mate.

Fate itself protects me from her gift.

Frowning, I glance at Zyran, realizing that he, too, is still standing.

He's wearing his glasses, but all of his attention is on the naked witch. His fists are clenched and his muscles seem taut, as if he's holding himself back.

My mouth parts when I realize what this must mean. Both his demeanor and the fact that he's still alive leaves only one possibility.

Zyran is her fated mate, too.

How is this possible?

"How convenient," Jasper says. "I suddenly remember my brothers are alive and here you are? How do I know it's really you?" He pulls out of the witch and covers her with the sheet, but his cock gleams with the evidence of her arousal.

My own cock throbs, wanting to be the one inside of her.

Zyran seems to free himself from his stunned state. He props his sword by the doorway, marches over to

Jasper, and hauls him away from the witch. "It's us, you moron. It's bad enough you didn't recognize me when I gave you the kill order, but fucking my fated mate? I should kill you right here for that."

The witch tugs the sheets over her chest, hiding her plump, beautiful breasts from view. She seems nervous as she plucks at a loose thread. "I don't know how this is possible, but I seem to be mated to all of you," she says softly.

Her words rip through me as if she shouted them. I stumble back as pain blooms through my center. Her magic wraps chains around my spirit and weighs it down as if trying to tear it free from its fleshy cage, but I steady myself, shaking off the effects.

Her words kill.

Just like Zyran's eyes.

Just like Jasper's touch.

She's an incarnation of death—making her perfectly suited to be our fated mate.

I put the pieces together quickly. Our mother prayed us into existence and because of a goddess of death, my brothers and I were born the way we were.

We've always been linked, and now it seems we share a fated mate.

A gorgeous death witch that I can't wait to taste.

"What did you just say?" Jasper snaps at her.

She flinches from his tone and I don't like that at all.

I move faster than most, and given the supernatural speed of the typical vampire, that's saying something. I practically teleport between Jasper and our witch, startling him.

To his credit, he doesn't back away.

"You heard her just fine, brother," I say, keeping my tone unnervingly steady. "It seems we're going to have to learn to share."

Zyran scoffs. "Jas was always the worst when it came to sharing. Remember my wolf blood collection? Gone. And for what? To buy a stupid blade. Didn't even need the damn thing to kill anybody, not when his skin itself is lethal."

Jasper's eyes widen as he listens to Zy ramble on, as he does.

But Zy's words just proved a point. We *are* his brothers, even if there are lost years between us. We know things about him that no one else ever would.

"I've never told anyone that story," Jasper marvels. He rubs the back of his neck. "You're... here? How is this possible?"

"It's a long story, Jas," I tell him. Even though I've imagined how this conversation would go a thousand times, it's not one we can have right now.

Another scream pierces the air and Ishara jolts. "I don't think we can stay here. My... I broke the barrier."

"Your last scream just wiped out a bunch of them," Zyran informs her. He grins, and I presume he's figured out why her last scream was so powerful. "Care to scream for us again, baby?"

"No," both Jasper and I say at the same time.

He gives me a level stare and I nod in return.

I accept that he's Ishara's fated mate. Sharing is something I can do, but my only requirement is that Ishara be respected in every way.

Protected.

Adored.

Worshipped.

Our witch swallows before responding. "I—Jasper, he's my. Um." Another blush sweeps over her pale skin as she averts her gaze. "I feel tired. I don't think I can do it again."

I'm not sure if she means an orgasm or using one of us as an amplifier.

"Then tell your sister it's time for you to leave," Jasper says. "She was able to open another portal, right? Tell her to open one for you."

I frown, not sure who her sister is or if I like the idea of my fated mate leaving my sight. Portal spells and potions are rare, coveted, and expensive.

Then, of course, there are transportation skills like my own. Convenient, but one that comes with a hefty price.

Ishara shakes her head. "No, Jas. I'm not leaving. Not after... this." She clenches the sheets to her chest, seeming to be referring to what they just shared.

Then she looks pointedly at Zyran and me.

"My sister won't let any of you into Reykjavík. And even if she does, you'll be imprisoned immediately whether she approves of it or not. Kaspian is too protective of her to let you roam free."

Zyran raises an eyebrow and it crests over the line of his glasses. "King Kaspian? Why would he be protective of your sister?"

"Because her sister is the Gold and Garnet Queen," Jasper growls.

We all fall into silence.

We're mated to the queen's sister. Great. That would have been helpful information if Daithi told us who we were targeting.

Of course, our jobs only include data on a need-to-know basis. As a soul-bound slave, I simply needed to know how to kill her. She had been portrayed as a relatively fragile target and one easy to overcome through stealth.

She is petite, but I can immediately tell by her aura of power and her intense presence that Ishara Doyle is no easy mark.

Another deathly scream rips through the air, this time much closer. The ground rumbles with the heavy weight of an army on its way.

She might not want to leave, but she can't stay here. While removing her from danger is a priority, things have changed now that I know we're all her fated mates.

"Maybe nobody has to leave," I suggest as I consider our options. I turn my attention back to the beautiful witch and ignore the raking need that continues to grow inside my core.

All I want to do is rip that sheet away from her and worship her.

Taste her.

Claim her.

But I'm a vampire of reason and logic, and right now, an army is going to tear this witch apart if I don't think fast.

"Go on," Ishara says. Her silver eyes gauge me with so much intelligence and beauty that I'm almost rendered speechless.

I'm not often shaken, but this witch has fractured me to the core. "Daithi," I say, only to be met with narrowed gazes. "He's the one sending this army. If I can talk to him, maybe I can convince him of another route of action."

Jasper yanks a pair of pants from the floor and slips them on, finally covering himself up. "You mean the asshole who just possessed my body and tried to rape Issy? No. We're not *talking* to him. If I ever see his spirit again, I'm shredding it myself."

Hearing that my captor tried to rape my mate turns my intentions murderous. The temperature in the room drops as I draw magic from the recently deceased, but more prominently the other supernaturals in my room who favor death magic. It's not intentional. It's just how my power works.

I'm a living containment of death—made to absorb its fatal attraction until I explode. My skin is already humming with spiritual energy after being sucked through time and space from our arrival. Luckily, the act of teleportation uses up my magical stores so I'm not in danger of imploding, but I can sense my well filling up again.

"Keep your cool, Kor," Zyran warns.

He knows me too well.

Grounding myself, I take a few deep breaths so I don't kill us all just because I'm pissed off. Jasper raises an eyebrow. "Well, it's nice to see you care about Issy. It doesn't mean I'm ready to trust you, though. Not until I hear the full story of what happened and why I have been walking around with the guilt of your deaths all these years."

Ishara gives Jasper a wide-eyed look. They slept together, making their fated-mate bond permanent, but he hadn't even told her his darkest secret? It seems that he's the one who shouldn't be trusted.

A rustling comes from behind us and I turn around to find Zyran rummaging through a dresser. "It's a shitty story," he grumbles as he fists a pair of lacy underwear, then pulls open a new drawer.

What in the ever-loving fuck is he doing?

Ishara protests but is interrupted by Jasper's growl. "Wait, you guys are the ones who gave me the kill order, right? Why are you involved with a dead warlock?"

Jasper might believe we're his brothers, but he invades my personal space, showing his aggression.

"We're soul-bound slaves to the patriarchs of the Outcast Coven," I inform him, not holding anything back. Raising one hand, I show him my Gold and Garnet ring. "This was how he was controlling us. So rest assured, we at least have our free will back. Your life was always his bargaining chip, anyway, and he clearly can't threaten that anymore."

Jasper's jaw clenches as if he's not sure if he believes me.

Zyran ignores the rising tension in the room and offers Ishara, or Issy, a dress and the underwear he's holding. "Here, baby girl."

She accepts the garments and stares at him when he turns around.

I do the same.

Fated mate or not, her body is her own. If she wishes to show it to me, she will.

Although, seeing her spread open and naked is an image I'm going to live off for as long as I can. I'm a gentleman.

Not a saint.

The witch is getting dressed behind us when our time runs out. Recently killed corpses rush through the doorway, leaving blood and gore in their wake.

Zyran makes quick work of them by retrieving his weapon and swiftly removing their heads, leaving a neat pile on the floor. "Whatever we're going to do, better hurry it up," he says, wiping the sword on his pants. He adjusts his glasses with his free hand, keeping them perched on his nose so they don't fall down. Just because Ishara's power doesn't work on us doesn't mean ours couldn't potentially harm her. I agree with being prudent.

"We're going to talk to the source," I decide aloud. "To do that, we need the death stone." It's a long shot that Ishara or Jasper knows where it is, but I still wish to exhaust all options before going with my emergency plan.

A magic-powered remote is in my pocket and one click would solve our problems.

It would also come with consequences I'm not yet ready to share with my fated mate. If she knows what I'm capable of, she might reject me.

But if that protects her, it's a risk I'm willing to take.

"Death stone?" Issy says. I turn to find her fully dressed and somehow even more beautiful than before.

The dress suits her well. A gossamer layer of silk hugs

her curves, leaving her pointed nipples completely visible to guide my view.

I can see why Zyran chose this dress.

"It's how we communicate with Daithi," I tell her.

She blinks at me a few times. "But Fallon destroyed it."

Right, there was one in the death plane that was eliminated. While that caused some problems with the death stone we had on our end, it was just a matter of time for it to rebuild. Both sides have to be obliterated for it to truly cease to exist.

I shake my head while Zyran dispatches another wave of corpses. A spattering of gunfire warns me that we definitely don't have much time now.

Daithi's dead are learning.

"It's too much to explain now, but no. It's not destroyed."

Ishara surprises me by running to me and clasping my shirt in her tiny fists. I can see now that she's been fighting the fated-mate allure harder than the rest of us. There are three of us in the room. I can't imagine the impact that might be having on her to complete the bonds and make them permanent. Fate doesn't hold back when it chooses soul mates.

It wants the match to work and it will push all parties to comply. To give in. To *indulge*.

She gazes into my eyes, giving me a glimpse of her spirit that glimmers behind her silver irises. She's hungry for me. I can see that much. But she's holding herself back, demonstrating impressive control. "Then you're going to help me find the death stone," she whispers with determination, "and we'll shatter it together. We'll finish what my sister started."

Her voice is soft, but her magic still hits me like a wall.

Fuck.

She's so powerful and I wonder if she even knows it.

I place one hand on her wrist, partly to steady myself and partly because I can't resist the urge to touch her. "If you were anyone else, I would say no. But you're the first witch I've met who I think could actually pull it off."

She's Fallon's sister, the only witch to have damaged part of the death stone.

It makes sense that Ishara would finish the job.

She leans in and stands on her tiptoes, bringing her lips closer to mine. "Does that mean you know where it is?"

Her words are easier to handle now that I'm touching her.

If touching her helps me learn her power, what would kissing her do?

Her lips hold me captive, enticing me to run my tongue over them before diving in for a taste. "If I knew where it was, I'd demand a kiss before I told you."

Jasper makes a sound and Zyran is busy beheading some of our new guests, or else I am sure he'd have a quip or two to add.

Ishara licks her lips before surprising me again and leaning in.

Then there's no distance between us, leaving me stunned by her incredible softness and delicious taste.

By all the death gods and goddesses, this witch is going to kill me.

She doesn't hold back like I'd expect her to. She wraps her arms around my neck and deepens the kiss. Her tongue is fierce and battles mine as if testing my resolve.

Her teeth graze my fangs and all that does is make me want to bite her.

When she's done with me, she pulls away. Her cheeks are flushed and her breaths come in short, adorable pants.

"I said *if*—" I began, but she places a finger over my lips.

"I know. I just wanted to kiss you."

Definitely my fated mate.

She leans into me. "How long can your brother keep killing things? Because I'm not sure I even want to leave now."

"We're leaving," Jasper grinds out, his voice husky with a slightly murderous tone to it.

He never was good at sharing.

Zyran yells and I twist enough to see that a wall of bodies has formed at the doorway, blocking our exit, and now more enemies are pushing their way through.

He's completely coated in blood and his glasses are dangerously teetering and half-broken. "Kor. Just do it."

"Do what?" Ishara asks against my ear. Her words send a new tremor through my body, and this time it isn't just one of pain. Her magic awakens something else in me. After sharing a kiss, I'm learning that Ishara Doyle is going to destroy my world.

And I'll enjoy every second of it.

"Yeah," Jasper growls as he digs his nails into my bicep. "Do what, *brother*?"

Sighing, I slip my free hand into my pocket and retrieve the device.

There's no getting around it now. Without the death stone, I can't even attempt to negotiate with Daithi.

And after learning he not only wished to kill my fated mate but also attempted to rape her using Jasper's body? Yeah. There won't be any talking involved when I see him again.

Which leaves us with only one option.

"Everyone hold on to me and try not to breathe."

Zyran grabs my arm before either Ishara or Jasper can protest.

I slam my thumb onto the button and a needle shoots out, piercing my skin and tapping into my magic. Five hundred souls thousands of miles away are instantly snuffed out.

It's enough to activate my power.

My world turns white as ice skates up my spine, and then we're slipping through the death plane, tunneling our way back to New York.

Back to the prison I've called home.

Forgive me, Ishara Doyle.

But after seeing you for myself, I would kill the world for you.

Chapter 16

Issy

What's happening?

My stomach drops as complete silence engulfs me for the first time in my life.

I never realized how loud the spirits were until they were completely muted.

Jasper had quieted the screams of the dead, but this is what true peace is supposed to feel like.

One problem. It's the kind of peace that's supposed to come with *death*.

But I'm not dead. I'm very much alive and my body hums with all-consuming desire.

It doesn't slip past me that all three of my fated mates are touching me right now while something incredible happens.

I'm not sure what. I just know that we're no longer in Lapland.

We're not anywhere—and yet we're *everywhere*. The sensation is disorienting, but Kornelius looks at an invisible horizon as if he knows exactly where we're going.

I'm still clinging to him while Jasper has crowded my back and presses up against me. I can feel his protectiveness as if he's trying to shield me from the void of yawning nothingness all around us.

The one named Zyran is touching me, too. His fingers have slipped through my hair and he's pressing a kiss to my temple. It feels like a natural motion and also a promise.

A promise that he's not going to be missing out while his brothers have all the fun.

Spirits. I'm mated to three brothers.

Three very hot and dangerous vampire brothers with death magic.

Their magic surrounds me like a violent wave as we travel through this unseen place. My soul feels like liquid fire inside my chest, eager to shoot free and discover everything that comes after a mundane life.

Although, my life is anything but mundane now. I'm ready to explore my future, especially if it includes three vampires who would move heaven and earth for me.

I realize that's exactly what's happening when we land. The one called "Kor" barks orders while blue flames threaten to consume me.

Out of habit, I clamp down my scream. I don't know where we've wound up or who could be nearby. Using my voice always gets me into trouble, not to mention I could kill someone who doesn't deserve it.

There could be children nearby. I'd never forgive myself if I harmed a child.

The scream is lodged in my throat as I wrap my arms around myself and bear it.

Jasper draws me into his chest while Kor shouts at him, but it does the trick.

His death touch steadies me and wipes out the flames, leaving me trembling and surprisingly cold.

I blink up at him, not sure exactly what happened, but then the sounds of the living invade my senses.

A siren blasts, its whine echoing against stone walls.

Men shout and a woman's scream rips through my core, making me look around.

We've landed in the middle of a busy foyer. There are couches framed by fancy statues and furniture while chandeliers release a bright golden glow to the enormous room.

It would be a beautiful place, if not for all the bloodied bodies strewn about.

I don't dare speak, but when someone runs up to Kor, I realize what's happened.

"We've been attacked," a male says. He has a sense of authority even though he's young. The look he gives Kornelius suggests we're not supposed to be here. "Who are they?"

Kornelius gives the youth a respectable nod. "Daithi's betrothed and fated mate," he says without missing a beat. When the other male takes a step back, Kornelius puts a hand in his pocket and pulls something out. He blurs an instant later, his superior vampiric speed making him too fast for me to stop him as he slips something around my neck and it locks into place.

"Her mute collar is on. It's safe."

I graze the icy metal with my fingers as my eyes widen.

171

An instant rush of cool energy sweeps over me, making me shiver. *Have I been betrayed?*

I don't see any children or innocents in the vicinity to keep me silent. Only misogynistic males who want to control women.

"What is this?" I ask.

Nothing happens. No one dies. No one reacts.

The male gives me a sinister grin. "He finally did it. He finally made her a fucking restraint for that damn power of hers."

I was forcibly muted before by the patriarchs, but I had never worn a collar. That magic never existed. Nothing has ever been able to tame my voice, or else it would have been a simple matter to silence me so I didn't have to hide in a basement.

A mute collar would have been a blessing once, but now? Now it feels like a chain around my neck suppressing everything I'm supposed to be.

Suppressing me.

Suppressing my *voice*.

My stomach drops and a breath catches for me to protest, but Zyran rushes to my side. "Daithi ordered us to bring her here. Gold and Garnet wants her power for themselves. They're probably the ones who attacked us, the bastards."

I only see my enraged reflection in his sunglasses, but there's an unspoken message behind his words.

Play along, baby girl, his body seems to say. *We'll explain soon.*

Jasper hasn't made a move. He continues to hold me and keep me close to him as if he's afraid someone might take me away. Based on his frown, he didn't know about the collar.

And he had been sent to kill me. That's probably something that would have been useful, so why hadn't he been given the device in the first place?

The men continue to talk over me as I'm not even there, but in my suppression, there's a strange sense of security.

This may be the only place we're safe.

Right in the middle of the enemy's territory.

Because I realize where we are on a second glance. The room screams with wealth, but my keen senses pick up other conversations.

That's a New York accent.

Languages are my forte, and so are dialects.

And I recognize the sound of home.

This time a swallow sticks in my throat instead of a scream. The urge to run is strong, but the will to survive is stronger.

The youthful male shoves Zyran aside as if he has no idea what the vampire is capable of. I watched Zyran take out an army of Daithi's monsters. This wiry warlock would be no match for him.

Still, the lustful look of interest the black-haired male gives me sends ice crawling up my spine. "Ishara Doyle." He whistles as his gaze rakes down my body.

I now regret allowing Zyran's choice of outfit. While I don't mind showing off my body to my mates, I don't want to attract attention from this male.

Because even if the patriarchs were wiped out, they could still return. Daithi was dead, but not every male

173

Outcast Coven member was killed. Where there are males, there is still a potential for their power-hungry ways to return.

It would be the matriarchs' job to keep that tendency in check. I have a feeling that they don't know about Daithi's secret afterlife operation.

Jasper growls when the male reaches for my face.

His gaze snaps up as if he hadn't even seen the vampire I am clinging to. "And who is this? Nasty fellow, aren't you?"

"My brother," Kor answers. "Daithi has charged all three of us with guarding her purity until his revival is complete."

The male gives Jasper a skeptical look, but it's enough for him to pull his hand away.

I don't dare show my appreciation to Kor and his fast thinking. He has not only brought me to the one place I might be safe from the Houses that will want me dead after Lapland's massacre, but he's also secured my safety here with those simple words.

"Hmm, is that so?" the male says. "I think you might be exaggerating. Mind if I talk to my cousin to confirm that order?"

The blood drains from my face.

Daithi's cousin?

While he wasn't one of the males forcibly mated to me, due to the fact that I couldn't feel the fake pull, he was no doubt in line. The look of vengeful lust on his face assures me he doesn't have good intentions, whatever they may be.

It's entirely possible that I killed his close family

members, leaving him a score to settle. It didn't matter if it had been an accident. When my powers first manifested, I killed many members of the O'Neely family, beginning a family feud between the O'Neelys and the Doyles.

All of this had started with me.

"Go ahead. Talk to Daithi and confirm the order, if you like," Kor says easily. His confidence is unwavering, but I'm not sure how long we can hold up this facade if his cousin can actually communicate with the patriarch.

Either he's just buying us time, or he knows something I don't.

He mentioned he needed the death stone to communicate with Daithi. If it's lost, maybe no one can talk to him. But would his blood relatives need a medium like that?

The patriarchs could visit the death plane. It wasn't in the same literal fashion as my sister, but it would be enough to communicate with any Outcast Coven spirits who were on the other side.

"Royce!" another male shouts, earning the attention of our captor. "The count is at least four hundred now. We've been checking the apartments on the upper floors and more dead keep turning up. Same method. Like a bomb went off inside their chests."

"Make that five hundred," Kor corrects. "It would take at least five hundred deaths to spirit me from another location."

My eyes widen.

Wait, didn't he press a button on a device before all of this happened?

175

Did he somehow just kill five hundred people to bring us here?

A wave of dizziness washes over me as I realize what kind of mates fate chose for me.

Dangerous.

But heartless, too.

Murderers.

Jasper had taken a life only moments before I met him. It had been for my protection, so I'd justified it, but it was still murder.

Zyran showed me his capacity for death and destruction—but I couldn't fault him for that. He was protecting us, and those enemies had already been dead, anyway.

Kor, though, makes me question everything.

He caused five hundred deaths just to bring us here. How could that ever be justified?

Royce curses. "Gold and Garnet's going to pay for this." Another shout comes from the hallway, making Royce run his fingers through his black hair. "I need to go handle the fallout of this attack." He gives Kor a pointed look. "I'll come in the morning to utilize the death stone to talk to my cousin about striking back, but also about your little witch here." He winks at me, making my stomach churn. "Do you need blood vials for that?"

Kor nods. "At least three."

"Consider it done," Royce says, leaving me confused as he hurries off with the group of youthful-looking warlocks.

Those must be male relatives of the patriarchs trying to bring their leaders back, I marvel. Terror grips my heart and I'm tempted to open up a channel to my sister and warn her, but I can't bring myself to do so.

She's been beating at my walls for hours now, but I have no idea how to explain any of this to her. I also don't want her to do anything risky, like try to save me.

This is *my* problem, one I'm going to deal with on my own. Fallon has come to my rescue too many times to count and she doesn't deserve a sister who keeps risking her life. Guilt has weighed on me too long and I can't bear one more thing on my conscience.

I already have at least a thousand souls added to my tally as it is. Five hundred in Lapland because Daithi wanted to come after me, and now another five hundred because Kor wanted to save me.

A death witch knows better than most that the medium doesn't matter—*she* is always the catalyst.

It's time for me to do my part for Fallon's sake—to protect *her* for once.

Yet, keeping her out makes my world feel more silent than ever before.

Kor approaches me as the chaos continues to surround us. His demeanor is different than it was at the cottage. Whatever fate is doing to him, he's hiding it now. And he's hiding it well.

His features are hard and cold as he gives me an order like the prisoner I am. "Let's tuck you in for the night, Ishara Doyle." He glances over his shoulder. "Zy, make sure the path is clear."

"With pleasure, brother," Zyran replies, adjusting his glasses before he takes the lead with his bloody sword still in hand.

Zyran clears a path simply with his presence as we slowly make our way to the elevators.

They called this place an apartment complex, but it feels like an understatement.

They must be right, though. A hotel would have a reception desk, but I only noticed a sitting area out front with a bar. Most of the bodies were wearing suits—likely businessmen.

This is New York, home to the Supernatural Syndicates, so there is no telling what kind of criminal activity I've found myself in.

A base of operations to bring back the patriarchs, I decide as we enter the fanciest elevator at the end of the row.

My three fated mates crowd around me when we're inside, and Zyran produces a card, then inserts it into the only available slot.

The elevator shoots up, making my stomach drop.

Jasper's chest presses against my back and Zyran guards my front.

Kornelius is silent by my side, but his hand slips out to take mine. I let him, confused and admittedly frightened now that I know I'm in the viper's nest.

His thumb runs across my knuckles as if to reassure me that he's not going to let anything happen to me.

And then we're at the top. The doors open, revealing the most beautiful penthouse suite I've ever seen in my life.

Right in the middle, though, is a pedestal that reeks of death magic—where I expect the place the death stone should be sitting.

It's empty, but the living area is filled with artifacts worth a small fortune. I recognize a few from some historical texts referring to a mythical goddess of death.

I know better than to assume myths aren't real. In my world, monsters exist.

And I'm trapped between three of them as they collectively lead me into the room.

Spirits. What have I gotten myself into now?

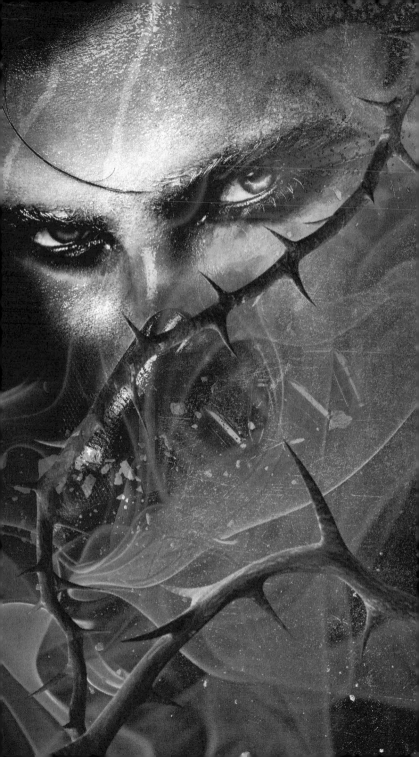

Chapter 17

Jasper

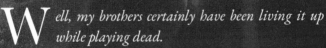

Well, *my brothers certainly have been living it up while playing dead.*

I'm very much not amused by the extravagance of the penthouse suite where my brothers have been supposedly held captive. Nor am I comforted by the decorative array of weapons on the wall.

"Home sweet home," Zyran mutters as he immediately heads to the bar. He leans his bloodied sword against the side, not seeming to care that it paints the floor and sleek maple cabinets red.

Kornelius gestures inside. "Please, make yourself comfortable. Would either of you like a drink?"

Issy's shoulders remain tense under my touch, and I'm in no mood for pleasantries, either.

"I can't be too comfortable with a damn noose around my neck," she snaps. There's definitely less of an edge to her words without her magic, though.

Kor gives her an apologetic smirk. "Sorry. It was just

for show. I can take it off." He approaches her, but she flinches. "May I?"

She blinks at him a few times, then nods.

He slips his fingers around her neck and even I can see the sexual tension between them. But he doesn't act on it and simply removes the collar as promised. I saw Issy try to remove it multiple times, so it's apparent only he can take it off—maybe Zyran, too.

Issy visibly relaxes as Kor stuffs it into his pocket. "Better? Now do you want that drink?"

"Assuming this place isn't bugged, how about 'answers' on ice?" I suggest. "With a twist of 'what the fuck is going on here?'"

Zyran smirks over his whiskey glass, already indulging in a few healthy sips. "No bugs, at least none that we know of. With some of the shit we've said in here, Daithi definitely would have beheaded me a few times."

"And castrated you," Kornelius says with a chuckle.

No bugs, then. Good enough for me.

Kornelius sobers after a moment, but his mask has slipped now that we don't have an audience. He looks like he wants to take Issy's hand again, but after seeing this place, she'd probably slap it away.

We're not getting the full truth here, considering that my brother killed five hundred people just to bring us to New York, so I'm going to maintain some reservations about Issy's safety.

As well as my own.

"Ishara," Kor says. "Would you mind if I spoke with my brother alone?"

She straightens, and even though I'm bracing myself

for the effects of her verbal magic, it still hits me like a truck. "Yes, I mind."

Zyran jolts against the bar and Kornelius flinches. Since I'm still touching her, the effect is a little easier for me to bear.

And I'm sure it helps that we're fully mated now, too.

The image of her beneath me, writhing with pleasure, shoots across my mind.

Fuck. I definitely want to do that again.

But first, I have to make sure she's safe. Being trapped in a rebel Outcast Coven fortress doesn't feel like it qualifies.

It's a pretty prison, but a prison all the same.

Kornelius doesn't challenge her. Instead, he gestures to the sitting area. "You're always welcome to be a part of our conversation. I simply thought Jasper might wish for privacy. Our discussion is going to be an intimate one."

Meaning he's going to tell me what happened all those years ago when I thought I had killed my own brothers.

Issy turns to look at me. A crease has formed across her brow as if she hadn't considered how I might feel. "I know what it feels like to have lost a sibling. Fallon might as well have been dead those years she was bound to that monster."

"Anything they have to say can be said in front of you," I tell her. I cup her chin, lifting it so she can look up at me. "You're my mate, now and forever, Ishara Doyle. I have no secrets from you." There's so much to tell her— and much of it I'm not ready for her to know.

But she deserves better than secrets.

She softens at my words, but there's determination in her gaze. "Yes, we are mates now. And because of that, I think it's best you work out your issues with your brothers before any of this goes further." She glances back at Zyran and Kornelius. "I'm not yet fully mated to them, and if I'm to remain in close quarters, I won't be able to resist the bond for very long unless I reject them. I trust you to evaluate if that's going to be necessary."

Kor and Zy blink at her. It's a logical thing for her to consider, especially after what just happened, but it's calculated and cold.

Most supernaturals have it in the back of their minds of meeting their fated mates. The way it's described is immediate, powerful, and all-consuming.

From personal experience, I can confirm that, for once, the rumors are true.

Issy hides her feelings well, but right now she's struggling. She's feeling all of the weight of fated magic times three.

She bites her bottom lip when she looks at Kor, then her cheeks flush when she catches Zy undoubtedly watching her from behind his glasses.

With a steadying breath, she slips away. She pauses when my fingers leave her skin as if she has to adjust to something painful without my touch.

"Issy?" I ask. "Are you okay?"

Kor had put a damn collar on her, and even though he removed it, I very much doubt she's okay, given everything going on.

She continues walking. "Fine," she whispers, but it's strained. "I just need some space to think about things."

Kor nods toward the hall. "There are a few guest bedrooms. Take your pick."

Issy nods before hurrying down the hall and out of sight.

Blowing out a breath, I turn to my brothers.

"Well, now that you've run off our mate, the least you can do is get me a drink and start talking."

I'm on my third beverage, this one an intricate mixture that Zyran calls one of his mystery fireball creations.

It has a nice kick, even against my vampire resistance, and I reluctantly savor it as I listen to Kornelius continue his story. Kor already explained the restriction collar for Issy and that it had been recently developed after Daithi's death. It uses a mixture of Kor's and Zy's blood, which was the key to making it work. It also makes them the only ones able to put it on and take it off of her—but Kor suspects I can take it off, too.

That's something I intend to test, because I don't like the idea of Issy being silenced and I have no power to help her, if needed.

I understand the need for us to stay under the radar and make Issy look like less of a threat than she is, but the collar isn't just for show. It does exactly as advertised, which places Issy in danger, in my opinion.

But I dutifully listen as Kor continues on about other matters that are more pressing, in his opinion. He's already told me that my brother's deaths had been staged as part of an elaborate plan by the patriarchs. He explained not only that our unique genetic makeup made us controllable by certain death witches, but also that I was purposefully left behind with the intention of being manipulated as an assassin. The patriarchs weren't sure how far the control would go, so if I was going to be a proper insider vampire, it would be better to control me through blackmail or deception.

Not to mention, my death-touch power was one the patriarchs felt to be too dangerous to contend with, as was my penchant for disobeying authority.

But what interests me more is that the patriarchs knew of our powers before they had even manifested.

"What about Zyran's power?" I ask.

Zyran leans forward in his chair. "What about it?"

Neither of them has yet shared their gifts, but I've already inferred them.

Kornelius absorbs death to the point that enough of it will suck him through the death plane to the site of a massacre. Based on the power I sense from him, he continues to draw in any form of death. Expelling it could potentially take other forms than just creating a personal portal. I imagine he might also act as a type of death bomb.

But he didn't use his powers to kill five hundred people, as far as I'm aware. He used a device to accomplish that.

So who were the five hundred people he had killed and *how* had he killed them?

I haven't yet uncovered that important tidbit, but I

told him to start from the beginning—starting with the day I thought I'd killed them.

Even though I now know I hadn't, a lingering sense of guilt still remains. My brothers had to grow up with only each other.

With their newly manifested powers.

Kor might have had an easier time managing his power, as long as there weren't any massacres, but Zy had likely run into some trouble.

Zyran holds a simpler, yet possibly more fatal, power. He'd always had striking green eyes unlike any I'd ever seen before, even though they are now hidden behind his shades.

Which suggests his power is in his gaze, and given the fact that he still wears sunglasses inside confirms my suspicions.

I take another sip of my drink before replying. "I would imagine death by sight to be more powerful than death by touch. You don't even have to get near the target to kill them."

Zy raises a brow and Kornelius produces one of his rare smiles. "Ah, but it's easier to hide," Kornelius says. He's clearly pleased that I've already figured them out.

He just gave me another bit of information I didn't have before. "You're not able to turn it off, then?" I ask, this time directly to Zyran. "I would have expected my brothers to have more control than that."

Zy scoffs. "You can turn your power off, can you? Well, I suppose you'd have to be able to, or else you'd be killing everyone left and right just by walking down the street. I thought you might be wearing gloves or something."

"I used to," I admit as I lean into the leather chair. It molds around my body and cushions my spine. "But, over time, I learned to control it. I had to."

That's one of the main reasons I became a mercenary. It was much easier to keep to myself and practice my power on targets. Sometimes it was the sort of situation where I could shake someone's hand and see if it killed them or not when I was first learning.

It took a few tries.

"Hear that, Zy?" Kor asks with a smirk. "You just need to practice."

Zy huffs. "Want to be the test subject, brother?"

"Anytime," he quips.

I listen as they banter and tease, slightly put off by their easy camaraderie.

They're my brothers, but I'm disconnected from them after so many years.

It's not fair.

"So, what about your power?" I ask Kornelius, changing the subject as I place my empty glass on an end table. "You killed all those people so that you could bring us here, right?"

Kornelius nods. "Yes. It's a fail-safe Zy and I have been working on for years."

Zy leans back, spreading out in his chair. "We figured out that his magic number is five hundred after he was yanked through to a massacre site a few times. Implanting the devices was the easy part. It was finding suitable candidates that Kor the Judgy approved of that was the hard part."

"Suitable candidates?" I ask.

"Rapists," Kor responds without missing a beat. "Zy was only allowed to implant rapists for the fail-safe."

My eyes widen as I begin to change my mind about Kor. "You managed to find five hundred rapists?"

Zy huffs a laugh. "This is No Man's Land. That wasn't a difficult feat. The bigger challenge was confirming it with the victims. They don't like to fess up to it—fear of repercussions and all that. But I started hacking into Outcast Coven monitoring footage and that helped me find a lot more targets without involving the victims at all."

"It's very important that the claims were verified," Kor says. "Our mother would have wanted us to use our power to make this world better. To take out the monsters like the vampire who sired us."

Our father was the worst of the worst, and if he had any redeeming qualities, they had no doubt died with our mother.

We were born vampires, not made, which only pissed off our father more. He had once been a human, and even though he was a master vampire, it still wasn't enough.

He hated that he had once been weak, and killed anyone who cared to remind him of it.

The fact that we had everything he always wanted and, by his point of view, had taken his mate from him, made him vengeful.

"So why didn't you implant people like Royce if it's that easy?" I ask. It's clear that there is still a danger present. These wannabe patriarchs are in charge and that is an issue that needs to be dealt with. And based on the look he'd given Issy, he likely qualified for Kor's kill list.

"It's *not* that easy," Zy says, now twirling a switchblade.

Where does he keep producing these weapons from?

"The devices aren't ours," Kor says, his mood darkening. "They're our father's and he had a say in where they were placed."

My eyebrows shoot up. "What?"

My father had disappeared years ago and I was so glad to be rid of him that I never looked into it. He could have fallen into a pit or choked on his own blood for all I cared.

Zy makes a sound of annoyance and moves to the window.

It's a spectacular view. Who knew that the syndicates and the Outcast Coven were living it up out here? Buildings and lights sprinkle throughout the luxurious townhomes and a couple of newer-looking buildings. The only evidence that we're still in No Man's Land is the horizon of abandoned structures everywhere the moon touches.

"Remember his power? He can phase through matter. It's expanded now that he can create devices that phase through matter, too. But it takes his magic to do it."

I blow out a breath while I process the fact that my father—*our* father—is still alive. "So what was his requirement for these five hundred souls you took? Because I doubt he cared if they were confirmed rapists."

"They had to be a threat to the agenda," Kor says. His

amber eyes glitter with rage. If he's been under our father's thumb all these years, I can't blame him for being pissed off. "And the agenda is reinstating the patriarchs and holding power—meaning killing anyone who isn't staying in line."

"Were any innocents caught up in this?" I ask.

Zy shakes his head. "No, I made sure everyone targeted was someone that had pissed our father off, or someone he didn't care about, and was a confirmed offender."

I hum in response. "Well, it's too bad Royce hasn't pissed him off yet. He seems like he's going to be a pain in the ass."

Zy stabs the wall and leans into the hilt as he peers outside. He's taken off his glasses and I can see his green eyes reflected in the window. He's looking at me instead of the view outside. "Those two assholes are good buddies. You need to prepare yourself, Jas, because if he's coming tomorrow, then so is our father."

"Then Ishara isn't safe here," I say as I shoot to my feet. "We have to move her. We have to—"

"And go where?" Kor says, somehow face-to-face with me even though I didn't see him get up.

Damn, he's fast.

"Anywhere but here." Letting a monster like my father in the same vicinity as my new mate is out of the question.

"Then you might as well kill her yourself," Zy says, slipping his glasses back on before turning around as he leaves the blade embedded in the wall. "No Man's Land is a dangerous place. There's a reason supernaturals ally themselves with a House. Fuck, even the syndicates are probably going to make a House of their own one of these days. Power and safety is in numbers, brother."

As far as numbers go, we have strength, but we number four.

Not a very large digit.

"I don't get it," I growl, not liking how cornered I'm feeling. "Why bring her here, then? How is this better than keeping her in Gold and Garnet territory? At least then her sister might be able to take her in."

Kor narrows his gaze. "That would likely result in the Houses going to war, and our world can't take a full-blown battle between the Houses like that. King Kaspian is a protective ruler, and if our witch is Fallon's sister, he's not going to give her up. The Houses aren't going to allow a witch that powerful to live, not now that they know about her."

"I don't want a war, either," I snap back. "But you're not the ones in charge here. What'll happen to her when Royce comes tomorrow and finds out we don't have the death stone? What happens when our *father* sees her?"

If he finds out we're mated to the witch, then he'll fully exploit that.

He'll probably take her for himself just to prove a fucking point.

Kor rests a hand on my shoulder until I realize I'm growling.

His touch does something strange to me. When we were children, we had a strong connection. More like a magical connection, one that allowed me to feel the intentions from my brothers.

Kor's intentions are pure. Everything he's said is true and his feelings for our witch are roiling inside of him like a storm.

He's very good at hiding it, but he can't hide it from me.

Not when we're bound by blood and magic.

He doesn't continue until I've settled. "I know this is a lot to take in, Jas, but you're going to have to remember how to trust me again. Zy and I have been working out this plan for years. When Daithi made his move, we were going to make ours. Nothing's changed in that regard."

"Everything's changed," I growl. "Did your plan include protecting Ishara Doyle?"

"No, but it can be adapted to do so. The Houses might pose a threat to Ishara, but they will target any creature with too much magic that upsets the balance."

"Creatures like Daithi," Zy points out. "I don't think coming back from the dead is going to be looked at very kindly. We just have to show them what he's capable of and they'll pivot." He shrugs. "Two birds, one stone, and all that."

Kor nods. "Trust us to keep to the plan. It's already in motion. Gold and Garnet will catch wind of this attack and blame another House, maybe even the syndicates. It'll cause the distraction we need to buy us time."

"Time for what?" I snap.

"For the next stage of the plan," Zy says. "All of this hinges on placing the blame on Daithi. He's fucking that up by putting it all on Ishara, but that's okay. We have a witch who can help us prove her innocence."

"I've already called her," Kor says. "Amala will be here

in two weeks. She says she's going to wait for the heat to die down, and I don't blame her for that. She's exiled by the Outcast Coven and is taking a risk by even coming here. We just have to keep up appearances until we can prove Ishara isn't a threat."

"How is some witch going to help anything?" I say. "Ishara *is* a threat. Her scream *did* kill people."

"Amala has already said she can help with that," Kor responds.

I raise a brow. "This sounds like you already knew about Ishara."

"We didn't," Zy says. "But Amala must have known. She's the one who reached out to us, originally."

"And you trust this witch?"

"We do," Kor says. "She wants the matriarchs to win. After the latest upheaval with Fallon, they're on the winning team, but they're disorganized. Amala has taken an interest in anyone fighting the patriarchs, and when she discovered we weren't here of our free will, she offered her support where she could."

"She'll want to expose Daithi," Zy says as he rubs the growing stubble on his chin. "As long as that remains our directive, she'll help us."

It's a sound plan, but it still doesn't assure me of Issy's safety.

"Fine. We can play along with your plan, but Ishara cannot be here tomorrow."

"Agreed," Kor says. "That's why Zy's going to take her to his townhome."

Zy's eyebrow shoots over the rim of his glasses. "I am?"

194

"You are," Kor says.

A frown tugs at my lips. "With me," I add. These might be my brothers, but they're fucking mad if they think I'm going to leave my witchling alone with either of them.

"That's fine," Kor says. "Our deception hinges on Daithi's order being believable. As the three of us have been slated for possession by patriarchs, it's reasonable that we would be charged with being her guardians."

My nails dig into my palms as I make a fist. "I think that's enough information for today."

My brothers are alive.

We're all mated to the same death witch.

We're in the middle of a brewing war.

Oh, and apparently we're body bags for the patriarchs when they decide they're bored of the afterlife.

Fuck that.

"I'm going to check on our mate. You two have fun with... whatever is going on here."

Zy and Kor chuckle and seem to share an inside joke as I storm off and look for Issy.

I had intended to taste her again, but now my fate-bound heart compels me to tell her everything I just learned.

She should have been there for that conversation.

When I find her room by following her floral scent, I open the door and see why she'd left the room.

She's clutching the edge of a dresser and gasping for breath. It's evident she had a shower again, because her hair is damp and a silky robe clings to her wet skin. A water droplet runs down the center of her cleavage as her body trembles.

Her gaze meets mine across the dresser's mirror. "Jas," she breathes, the version of my name dripping with sex. "Please. I tried to relax and shut them out, but nothing is working."

"Shut who out?" I ask, but I already have an idea.

"The dead," she whispers. "There are so many of them and they're so *angry*. I can hear them. They're—" Her words cut off on a gasp as she squeezes her eyes shut.

I don't ask for her to elaborate. I can put two and two together.

This is why she flinched earlier. My touch grounds her.

It would kill anyone else, but not Ishara Doyle.

Not my fated mate.

It is exactly what she needs, so I don't say anything as I close the distance between us and wrap her in my arms.

She immediately settles into me, but her body is still trembling.

I've got you, my mate. And I'm never letting you go.

Chapter 18

Issy

Jasper immediately gives me a sense of peace as his touch muffles the screams.

And then silences them entirely.

I hug his arms around my chest as I gulp in air. It's as if I've been underwater and he's just brought me to the surface.

Hearing the screams of the dead is nothing new. I deal with it on a daily basis, but I've never been in the middle of a massacre.

Aside from the one I caused when I killed my father and his supporters, but that still didn't number in the hundreds. And I can't remember the actual event anyway.

After Daithi started killing people in Lapland, it was worse than I remembered it ever being. But the cries I had heard while in the cottage only hurt when Jasper didn't have his hands on me. Even then, they had been muffled.

Perhaps having all three of them in the same room with me provides some sort of buffer.

But that buffer couldn't stand up to five hundred

dead in the immediate vicinity, and it wasn't just the number, it was the kind of souls that had died.

Visceral, *evil* souls.

It frightened me that Kornelius would take so many lives, but now I wonder if he'd targeted criminals to activate his ability. Bad people wouldn't be very hard to find in syndicate territory just a stone's throw from the Outcast Coven.

"Better?" Jasper asks.

I'm shaky, but at least I don't feel like throwing up. "Better," I agree.

He grins at me, showing off his lengthy fangs. "Good."

Based on the hungry look he's giving me, I expect Jasper to make a move, but he continues to hold me while pressing a light kiss against my throat.

He grounds me.

He's simply here with me, in whatever capacity I need him.

Even if my body wants him, I'm exhausted. I also can't deny the effects that fated magic is having on me. Fate chose these three vampires for a reason.

The screams of the dead nearly overwhelmed me when I'd let go of Jasper a few hours ago. I didn't realize how much the triad had been protecting me.

I'd been in this room trying to shut the screams out ever since, but the more I tried, the more fate reminded me that the three brothers were my cure.

I need *them.*

When Jasper skims his teeth over my neck, I picture Kornelius on the other side using his fangs.

When Jasper licks my ear, I imagine Zyran licking me somewhere... else.

Spirits, save me from this craving.

I've studied fated-mate magic more than most. The reason it works so well is because it's, well, fated.

Our ideal matches are out there and fate knows who they are. When we find them, it gives us a little boost to speed things along.

Without it, one might walk past their soul mate and have no idea. Fate magic makes sure we know, then gives us a chance to embrace our perfect match, or walk away. We're still given a choice, but at least we won't miss the opportunity.

In my case, fate chose three brothers. It's unusual, but most things in my life generally are.

My sister had been under a spell that forced a fated bond where there shouldn't have been one, giving me a reason to study the magic more intensely. If it could be replicated where a bond shouldn't exist, there was no telling what kind of other dangerous possibilities were out there.

On top of it, there had been an obedience spell locked in place that not only took away her free will, but completely blocked me from her mind. It had been horrible, devastating, and—

I freeze when I realize I'm doing the exact same thing to my sister. I may not be trapped in a fake bond, but I'm blocking her out when she has no idea if I'm alive or dead.

My desire to protect her is clouding my judgment. For now, I'm not in immediate danger.

Although, Jasper's dangerous gaze reflecting in the mirror suggests otherwise.

He must sense my change in demeanor because he instantly backs away while keeping a hand on my shoulder. "Talk to me, my witchling."

I force a swallow down my throat as I tighten my robe around my body. "Maybe I should tell my sister what's going on."

He sighs. "I'm not sure if that's such a good idea. My brothers had a lot of concerning things to say, and if tensions progress, we're going to be in the middle of a war with Gold and Garnet. Perhaps all the Houses, once they realize you're here. Many of the dead are syndicate members."

That didn't sound good.

"Kaspian hates the syndicates," I say, knowing that he's right. After all of this, a war might be inevitable. Kornelius told Daithi's cousin that the Houses are to blame. The Houses will know what happened in Lapland and pin all one thousand deaths on me.

They won't let me live if they think I'm capable of death on that scale. Even if, technically, I am, I would never use my power like that.

"We're going to have to brace ourselves," Jasper says.

I reach up and grab his hand. "All the more reason to talk to Fallon."

I don't give myself another moment to doubt as I open up a channel to her.

Issy? Oh, Gods! You're alive! Are you hurt? Where are you? I was so worried!

I swallow, guilt swelling up inside of me. Tears sting

at the edges of my eyes when I hear the panic and relief in her voice. Of course Fallon would think the only reason I had walled myself off from her was because I was either spelled, or dead.

Hey, I begin. *I'm safe. I just... I needed to figure things out on my own for a bit there.*

A moment of silence makes my stomach churn.

You mean, you weren't talking to me on purpose?

I expected the anger I hear in her voice, but not the crack of pain. That breaks me a little inside. *I'm sorry,* I say, knowing an apology isn't enough. *I knew that if I reached out to you, you would portal in and save the day like you always do.*

And what the fuck is wrong with that? she snaps. Whatever worry she had has now been replaced with fury. *I'm your sister, Issy. I'd do anything for you.*

I know! I snap back. *That's the problem. That's why I couldn't talk to you, Fallon. I couldn't risk your life, not again. Okay? You can't just rescue me every time I'm in danger. That's not fair to you.*

I don't give a fuck about fair. Gods, Issy. If something happened to you, I would lose my shit.

I know, I reply softly. I've seen what happens to Fallon when she can't save me. It's not something I want to put either of us through again, but this situation is different.

Now, I'm not alone.

You don't have to save me, not this time, I tell her earnestly. *I'm safe, like I said.*

Okay, she says, the tension in her voice easing. *But I still need to know where you are, Issy. I need to know what's happening.*

I swallow as I debate how to answer that. *I'm home.*

I don't know what else to call it. I'm originally from New York, and even if I'm not in my father's house, I recognize Staten Island from the window. It spans out, revealing all of the Outcast Coven's territory through an array of town houses and well-kept buildings. The outskirts are easy enough to see, too.

No Man's Land.

Home? she asks. *You mean you're still at the cottage? That place is a warzone! It's all over the news. Kaspian is on another call with Khaos handling the fallout. Everyone is blaming you, Issy. I told them you didn't do it, but I don't have proof. If you're at the cottage, Gods, please leave.*

I'm not at the cottage, I say. *I'm in New York.*

Stunned silence lingers and I grip Jasper's hand. He's watching me through the mirror, and even though I know he can't hear the conversation, he can read the expression on my face.

I can't hide my feelings when I'm talking to my sister. She's everything to me.

W-why are you there? How? I don't understand.

I take a deep breath before responding. *I found my fated mates, Fallon. They're three vampires. Well, some sort of necromancy-vampire hybrids, anyway. One of them has a teleportation ability, but there's something I need you to know.*

Mates? she shrieks, but she's excited this time. *Oh, Gods, Issy! I'm so happy for you! And* mates, *as in plural?*

Of course she'd be distracted by the news that fate chose multiple peens for me. Exciting, yes, but I was not in the headspace to imagine all the possibilities that would mean.

Fallon, listen. I'm trying to tell you something important. Gold and Garnet is going to be blamed for five hundred deaths, and most of them are probably syndicate members. That's how Kornelius's power works. If there's a massacre, he's sucked into the area by the flux of death.

What? Are you serious? Another moment of silence passes and I'm not sure if she's talking to one of her mates or thinking. *They're going to blame you for that, too, Issy.*

That's why I can't be with you in Iceland. This is exactly what Daithi wants. He wants to put a bounty on my head so big that all the Houses come after me, and whoever tries to protect me will start a war. Don't you understand? I can't be anywhere near you right now.

Issy, she says, emotion drenching the word. *Please, at least tell me if you're protected there. These vampire hybrids, they sound powerful. But can you expect them to stand up against all the Houses? If the syndicates attack because they think Gold and Garnet killed their people, there's going to be a war and you're going to be at the center of it.*

She's right.

"What's she saying?" Jasper asks. He's whispering as if he's trying not to interrupt, but Fallon can't hear him.

"She says that all of the Houses are going to come after me. She's right, Jasper. Nowhere is safe." I squeeze his hand. "Anyone with me is in danger."

He doesn't look as concerned as he should be. "Well, it's a good thing Amala is going to tell us how to prove your innocence in two weeks."

My eyes widen. "How do you know that name?" Amala is the witch who helped me learn all about fated-mate bonds. She knows how to break the ones that are spelled—although, it turned out not to be necessary for Fallon because her fake mate was executed. She's an exile of the Outcast Coven, so I have no idea how they even got her to agree to come here. I've only been able to learn from her indirectly through Ayla, who was allowed to visit me when I was imprisoned. Meeting her in person was never an option, even after I moved to Lapland, because she often kept to herself.

Probably because she is very powerful. She poses as a healer—which is comical for a death witch. But it gives her the perfect front to hide behind and be considered inconsequential by most.

He shrugs. "I think she's a fan of yours. She must have been monitoring the situation, because she reached out to my brothers and said she's going to come help once the heat dies down. We just have to play along and keep a war from breaking out until then. Oh, and we have to keep an eye on Royce, that asshole wannabe patriarch, and did I mention my father, Zane, is in the game, too?" He clicks his tongue. "Just what we need—a sadistic vampire added to the mix."

That's a lot to process, so I just blink at him.

Two weeks, I tell my sister, deciding to focus on the most pressing issue. *Find a way to stall the Houses for two weeks. By then, I'll have figured out how to prove my innocence.*

I'm not sure if I can trust Amala to pull that off, but it's my only option.

And I'm also not confident we can evade Royce and Zane and whoever else wants a piece of me by then, but that's my problem, not Fallon's.

My sister sighs on the other end of my mental connection. *Okay, Issy. I will do my best. As Queen of Gold and Garnet, and your twin who loves you, I promise I will do everything I can to buy you time. But when the two weeks are up, I'm going to find you and hug you, no matter what the world looks like.*

That sounds pretty good to me. *Deal.*

Chapter 19

Zyran

I adjust my glasses as I take a left turn onto the back roads that lead to my personal town house.

The shorter routes are packed with security and matriarchs. I'm grateful to get off the main roads to avoid questioning. We've already been pulled over twice.

Luckily, the spell Kor and I came up with—unfortunately, with the help of the patriarchs—did its job of keeping us away from prying eyes, meaning I didn't have to put Issy's collar on, either. She did not seem to care for that and I didn't blame her.

Something big is going on, though, and it's not just syndicate deaths. Something else has happened and I make a note to ask Kor about it when we return.

For now, it's a day of R&R for my new mate—maybe a little seduction if I can get the stick out of Jasper's ass so he doesn't get in the way.

Rather, I hope he encourages Ishara to accept me after what we shared with him last night. It's not every day one meets their fated mate. I've been looking forward to mine, and I have every reason to protect her.

She's Daithi's target, and I don't want that asshole laying his ghostly hands on her.

She's also perfect. But I think my brother is already intimately aware of that.

I've thought long and hard about meeting my fated mate. It doesn't happen for everyone, and being that Kor and I were trapped with the patriarchs and rarely let out to play, I wasn't sure if it ever would.

"Doesn't it bother you? You can't be a man whore anymore," Kor said last night when we were alone.

"Not one bit," I replied. *"Think of it this way, brother. Every girl I've been with has been practice for my mate, and now I know many, many delicious things to try on her, when she's ready for me, anyway. When I'm done, I'm going to be her favorite."*

Kor laughed at that, and he doesn't often laugh.

I think he was in a good mood, though, mostly because we now have two weeks with our mate with nothing else to do other than spend time with her and stay out of trouble. He has the short end of the stick, dealing with our dad and Royce, but he's patient. He doesn't seem to mind if I warm her up while he placates our captors.

He's good at that.

And I can be charming when I want to be.

My town house is beautiful, too, and jam-packed with aphrodisiacs. That doesn't hurt.

My place isn't as impressive as the penthouse apartment, but it's *mine*. It's the one thing I have in this world that doesn't belong to anyone else.

I don't even have a fated mate who's solely my own, but I'm not upset about that. The witch at my side makes my blood hum with new life—and for a vampire that doesn't have a heartbeat, that's saying something.

"So, how does this work?" Ishara asks as she peers out the window. She's tense, but curiosity seems to be getting the best of her.

Jasper, though, is glaring at me through the rearview mirror and hasn't taken his eyes off me.

I'm not sure what he has to be so pissy about. He's the one who spent the night in Ishara's bedroom.

Alone.

"How does what work?" I ask as the BMW iX—one of my personal favorite vehicles—seamlessly deals with a sharp turn. It's one of the many toys granted to me by being in line for patriarch possession. They think placating Kor and me with luxuries will keep us amenable to an early death.

In truth, it's probably just preparing our roles for when they take over. Every luxury a patriarch could want has been granted to us because we're eventually supposed to be vessels for them to be reborn.

It's been described as body-sharing to us, to lessen the blow, but after I saw what happened to Jasper, there was no sharing involved.

No, if the patriarchs get their way, my brothers and I will be kicked out of our own bodies so some dead guys can live.

Ishara waves a hand to indicate the neighborhood.

"This is clearly an Outcast Coven sector. Vampires wouldn't be allowed here."

Jasper's still staring at me while I pretend to be invested in the back-roads route that I have memorized. "My brothers and I have enough death magic in us to pass as Outcast Coven members and Kor knows a spell to enforce it by shrouding our vampire nature. Or rather, it just makes witches less interested in noticing it." Jasper would have received a dose of it, too, just by entering our penthouse apartment. The spell is activated by our genomes, and his genetics are nearly identical to ours.

"But I knew you were a vampire right away," she says, blinking at me.

"As my fated mate, I'd expect no less," I respond while flashing her a smile.

She instantly blushes and flinches back to her view.

She wants to deny our connection because Kor and I scared her off after killing five hundred people. Understandable, but she killed five hundred people first, if we're keeping score.

Not that it was her fault. I know that Daithi set this all in motion and he's going to pay for that.

Dearly.

If I didn't already hate him for his role in what happened to my brothers and me, messing with my girl is a good way to get on my shit list.

We arrive at the town house and I park the car, then get out to open Ishara's door.

Of course, Jasper's already there with his hand on the handle. He gives me a dangerous smile that suggests he might bite my hand off if I get too close. "I got it."

Nodding, I wait for Jasper to let Ishara out. I don't comment when they hold hands.

She's been very touchy with Jasper, but I catch how she looks at me.

Her bond with my brother is secure, but fate must be pushing her to complete the one she has with me. It burns in my chest, urging me to push my brother out of the way if he's not going to participate equally.

Because Ishara Doyle belongs to both of us. Just because he found her first doesn't change the fact that I'm just as much her mate as he is.

And I'm the pretty one, if I'm being honest.

To prove a point—or stir the pot—I loop my hand around Ishara's waist as I guide her to the town house.

"What do you think?" I ask, ignoring the fact that she's still awkwardly holding on to Jasper's hand.

It's not exactly modest from the outside. A gardener tends to vibrant vines that wrap around the exterior, and roses of all colors flood the front flowerbeds.

There's a water fountain and a statue of a naked woman with long hair. It reminds me of the death goddess and I like to think that if I talk to her, my mother can hear me.

Ishara seems mostly interested in the flowers, though. "Do you grow all these?"

I slip my fingers lower on her hip. "No, I have a guy for that. But if you like this, you're going to love the roof. That's one I tend to personally." Her eyes light up for the first time when she looks at me.

"I'd love to see that."

Jasper is practically growling, likely pissed off that I've not only discovered one of her tastes but also share it.

So, Ishara Doyle likes gardens. Good to know.

Maybe it's because I'm inundated with death, but gardening is one of my hobbies, too. Being surrounded by life is a refreshing change after the things I have to deal with day-to-day.

Taking out my keys, I unlock the door and gesture for them to go inside.

"Please, after you."

Ishara passes the threshold before I remember I spelled the entrance.

She doubles over and squeezes Jasper's hand. "Oh," she breathes right before the scent of her arousal hits me like a truck.

Jasper's nostrils flare as he glowers at me. "What the fuck did you just do?"

Chapter 20

Issy

J asper curses before rushing to my side. I'm about to
protest when I realize he's securing my arm before
my knees give out.

When they do, he's there to catch me.

Jasper makes a sound from behind me that lets me
know he's not amused by any of this.

Because they're vampires, I know they can pick up
what's going on with me.

My arousal was already bad before, but now it's
spiked for some reason and my lady parts are on fire and
screaming at me.

"Over here, baby," Zyran says, lifting my chin with
his finger. "I didn't mean to do that to you. It must have
been active since my last—since last time."

I look up at him but only see my panicked expression
in his glasses.

Does he never take those things off?

I have an absurd urge to rip them away so I can see

what his eyes look like. They must be beautiful, if only to match the rest of him.

My gaze drops to resist the temptation, but I quickly realize that was a bad idea.

He's wearing an off-white silk shirt that's unbuttoned all the way down to the center. He must have loosened it recently, because I feel like I would have remembered the glimpse of pure male underneath.

The sleeves are rolled up to his elbows, revealing thick veins and muscular arms. And his sharp jawline has a hint of stubble, suggesting he hasn't shaved recently.

Was he thinking about me?

Was he *talking* about me?

Logically, I know that I must have been a topic of conversation between the brothers, but a part of me wonders if they relived the moment fate bound us together.

I'd been in a compromising position with Jasper blowing my mind, my body bare to the three of them when Kor and Zy had walked in.

They'd seen everything.

And I'd enjoyed it without even knowing who they were other than my fated mates.

I shouldn't trust fate to be infallible, but in the moment, I hadn't cared. All I'd wanted was to ask them to join us, and if there hadn't been an army of undead on the way, I likely would have.

Spirits. I need to stop thinking about it.

My breath is coming in short pants now as Zy begins a chant. He sweeps his thumb roughly over my lips as if he's trying to remove lipstick, but I'm not wearing any.

"Hurry it up," Jasper growls.

Hurry what up?

The overdosed haze of lust only lessens when Zyran's finished and I realize that he dispelled some sort of trance I'd been put under.

I'm not sure if I even want to know why he has a lust spell on his entryway, but given that I am his fated mate and we have yet to finalize our union, it doesn't much matter. The pull toward him isn't going to go away, no matter how much dispel magic he performs.

"Better, baby?" he asks.

I can still see my flushed cheeks in his glasses and the way my cleavage moves with my heavy gulps of air.

His hands are still on me, keeping the screams away just like Jasper does. The one near my face has slipped through my hairline and he's lightly scratching my scalp.

The other has found my lower back and he's pressed me closer to him, although I don't think it was intentional. It just feels natural to be close to one another.

And even if he wasn't hit with an arousal spell, fate is already doing a number on him. His erection presses against my belly, encouraging me to weaken my defenses.

"Not really," I manage to say. My mouth feels dry and my entire body throbs.

"I'm sorry," he apologizes again. "The spell is only activated by someone who wants to sleep with me already. It's to make things more exciting, but also tells me if I've misread the situation."

I blink up at him, not sure if I should be offended, jealous, or impressed.

He doesn't want to ever take advantage of a female and this is his safeguard against any misunderstandings.

But this also means that he now knows I definitely want to sleep with him. While that shouldn't be a surprise, given that he's my fated mate, it still leaves no question about it.

"This was a bad idea," Jasper says as he squeezes his massive arm around my middle, wedging it between Zy and me. His breath is hot on my ear when he talks, sending a shiver down my spine. "Fate is going to push this even if she's not ready."

Even if I'm not ready?

I'm not sure what to make of Jasper's words, but they certainly sound like he's already approved of his brothers.

As if his body disagrees with his statement, he squeezes the life out of my lungs as if in protest of the idea of sharing me.

Although, I do enjoy being the center of this delicious vampire sandwich, either way.

I sense a connection between him and Zy. Even if they've spent their adult lives apart, they share the same mother, the same birthday, and the same blood.

I know better than most how close a bond that can forge.

Zyran trails his fingers over my jaw, then slips a loose strand of hair behind my ear. I practically melt into an Issy-shaped puddle of need. "She's more than ready, brother, but she makes the call of who, how, and when. Fate is merely another form of magic, and this witch is strong enough to decide her own path."

I blink at him a few times, stunned.

Zyran and I only met last night, but he seems to have captured a picture of me in a short amount of time. He believes I'm more powerful than fate itself, even if I'm not.

But it's his belief that gives me strength.

I swallow and lean back into Jasper, reminding myself that *he* is my mate and Zyran is still on parole. Jasper proved himself to me by rejecting me to show me our choice was real, but what did Kor and Zyran do?

Other than kill hundreds of people.

And lie to the Outcast Coven, presumably to protect me, but also so they can keep me to themselves.

It could all be a farce to take advantage of me and use me for my power, just like every other male in my life seems to want to do.

But they are Jasper's brothers. Triplets born of a mother's prayer.

Fate chose them for me because they're my perfect match.

I deserve them all, don't I?

An inkling of selfishness enters my mind, reminding me that I've been jealous of Fallon and her gorgeous mates.

Yes, of course I'm happy for her. It's all I ever wanted for my beloved sister.

But to say I'm not jealous is a lie.

I want to be happy, too. I want to live a life of abundance when so much has been taken from me.

Don't I deserve to be surrounded by protection and love, just as my sister is?

Zyran still has one hand on my hip, but he's moved

away as I lean into Jasper's chest while contemplating everything.

"See?" Zy says. "You're not throwing yourself at me. You're in control, aren't you?"

Perhaps.

Barely.

Instead of responding aloud—which is truly a luxury —I nod. I have no practice at hiding the emotions in my voice because I've never had to.

Zy blows out a breath. "Okay, I need a drink. Shall we?" He gestures further inside the town house.

It's a beautiful home. There's abstract art, tasteful decor with ruby and silver tones, and plenty of places to relax.

Or do other things, my mind supplies as I eye a chaise lounge near a countertop that could, technically, act as a handhold.

A different sort of jealousy flutters inside my chest. After being hit with a lust spell and now seeing the layout of his personal home, I'm getting the picture that Zyran is a bit of a playboy.

How's that going to work if he wants to be my fated mate?

I am well aware that fate chose three mates for me. It would only be fair if I shared them as well.

Except, the very thought of it leaves a sour taste in the back of my throat.

Maybe this isn't going to work after all.

Because just as my mates seem intent on me choosing them, I want them to have a choice, too.

If Zyran isn't the type of vampire to be pinned down, then I'm not going to tell him what to do.

But would I be able to live like that? To wonder where he is at night when I'm with one of his brothers?

That wouldn't be fair to anyone, not Jasper or Kor, and certainly not me.

I should reject him right now. I stare at his back, watching how the silky shirt ripples around him, as I try to form the words.

They don't come—because I don't *want* to reject him.

Spirits. What am I going to do?

I struggle with my jealousy as Zy leads us through a cozy living room and then into a kitchen. "I don't have a bar like at the penthouse," he explains as he sets his keys on the counter. "Not even a butler's pantry, but I make do."

Jasper has his hand secured around my hip as he easily holds me against his side. If it weren't for his support, I would likely fall over. My knees still feel like jelly.

Plus, it helps my sanity not to hear the screams of the dead that are still raging like an echo chamber in this region.

"What are you talking about? This is basically a bar instead of a kitchen," Jasper says.

He's not wrong. Various liquor bottles are lined up in glass cabinets where dishware should be. There are rows of shakers and stirrers, as well as shot glasses.

Zy points at the lonely stove. "I cook, sometimes, when I have a—um, guest, who eats food."

I can't see his expression behind his sunglasses, but he

adjusts them as if it's a nervous tic and goes about making three drinks.

It doesn't take a genius to know what he means.

Just like I suspected, he brings girls here, and likely often.

When he hands me a pink drink with a cherry, I decide to rip the bandage off. "So, you fuck around a lot?"

Jasper had already been taking a sip of his drink and he snorts into the glass. He takes out a handkerchief to dab away the mess. "Damn, Issy, you don't mince words."

I could say it's because I don't have practice with words, but the truth is I don't want this to linger. If he's going to fuck around, then this needs to be dealt with one way or another.

Zy waves his brother's comment away. "She has every right to know what I'm like. Yes, I have fucked around a lot, but that's over now that I've found you."

I raise an eyebrow, definitely feeling skeptical of that. "Just because fate introduces you to your ideal mate doesn't mean you're going to change who you are." I glance at Jasper as I take the cherry out of my drink. "Plus, if we went through with this, you'd have to share me with your brother."

"Brothers," Zy instantly corrects, pulling my attention back to him. There's a little smirk on his mouth and it forms a dimple.

Spirits. I want to stick my tongue in it and then lick him.

"Kor is your fated mate, too," Zy continues as he

swirls the ice in his glass. He has a tube of something red that he pours into it.

Blood.

My body is instantly hot as I watch him empty the contents. "That doesn't sound very fair," I say, continuing to talk so I don't do something else, like try to bite him. "You mean to share me with two other men, but you think you're going to stay loyal to me in return?"

He nods as if that's a simple idea. He takes a sip of his bloody concoction before responding. "Of course. Believe it or not, I've thought a lot about what my mate might be like." He smiles again as he seems to look toward the ceiling in thought. "Delicate. Beautiful, of course. Sexy as fuck and wields a feisty spirit to match her powerful magic. A mate who can keep me in line and be my equal instead of being dominated." He runs his tongue over his lower lip. "One who likes me buried deep inside of her when I *bite*."

I realize I've made a little sound when Jasper steadies me.

He's been possessive, but now he has a crease in his brow that's new. "What's wrong?" I ask him, desperate for a distraction from Zyran, who seems intent on tormenting me.

Jasper takes my cherry and holds it by the stem, then rolls it across my lips while he talks. "My brothers are right that I'm not one to share, but there's something I've forgotten when it comes to my siblings. Do you want to know what it is?"

I hum against the cool cherry, focusing on the heat of the alcohol drizzling onto my tongue.

He gives me a wistful smile, one that's almost painful. "I can feel their intentions. I didn't notice it until last night, but there's a connection I share with them. It's a magical one, almost as if I can read their minds."

I lick the cherry before taking it back from him. I know I'm being a tease, but I can't seem to help it. I'm a complete introvert around most people, but these guys bring out that smutty heroine character that always kicks ass and gets all the hot guys.

That can be me, right?

Although, my ability seems limited on the "kicking ass" part. I only have a few fighting lessons from Bane to lean on, but I could totally have the hot guys.

What Jasper just told me gives me hope. If he has a connection to his brothers like I do to Fallon, it might give me some much-needed insight.

"That sounds similar to how Fallon and I can talk telepathically," I say aloud. It's not exactly the same, but it has the same principle of being emotionally connected to each other. I tilt my head as I toy with the cherry's stem, sending the red orb swirling around. "So what are Zy's intentions when it comes to me?"

Jasper looks at his brother. "He's telling the truth. He's going to give up his lifestyle not because he has to, but because he always planned to when he found his fated mate." He licks his lips as he looks at me. "When he found *you*."

A swallow sticks in my throat.

Spirits. How am I supposed to reject Zyran now?

Jasper surprises me by letting me go. He blows out another breath as if he's made up his mind about something. "I came here because I didn't trust you alone with him. But now I think I made a bigger mistake by leaving Kor by himself to deal with Royce and our father."

My eyes widen. "He's alone with them? Is that such a good idea?"

"Probably not," he says, giving me a tender kiss on the cheek. "You'll be safe with Zy. As much as I hate to admit it, he's right about one thing."

"What's that?" I ask, looking into his eyes.

He leans in and whispers in my ear, "I've never been good at sharing. So I'd better leave before I spread you open and taste you right in front of him just to show him what's mine."

He nips my earlobe, making me jolt with the nip of pain. He chuckles, then pulls away. He doesn't look back as he returns down the hall, grabbing Zy's keys on the way. "Take care of her, Zy. I'll be back tonight."

"Hey, not my BMW, you assh—" Zy begins, but the sound of a door slam cuts him off.

With that, Jasper's gone and I'm alone with a very hungry-looking vampire. It's hard to tell, but he's gone extremely still and he seems to be staring at me as his nostrils flare.

I run my fingers over the small hurt Jasper left behind and find my fingertips tipped with blood.

Then the screams come back. I school my features so Zy doesn't notice.

I'm not sure why I'm hiding it. Maybe I'm ashamed that I can't control my power.

Maybe I don't want him to think I'm a freak.

Zyran smiles, revealing dangerous fangs. "He's such a

brat. Stealing my car and marking you? Cute, Jas. Real cute."

I reach for a napkin on the counter, but Zy blurs to my side and grabs my wrist. He clicks his tongue at me before bringing my fingers to his lips. "Never waste this beautiful blood, sweetheart."

He pulls a vial from his pocket and collects any loose blood. It's only a few droplets, but he seems to treasure it as he pockets the find, then finally allows me to use the napkin. He plucks the cherry still dangling from my other hand and offers it to me. "Let's continue the tour, shall we? Would you like to see the roof?"

I obediently nibble the cherry from his fingers, now feeling relaxed again that he's touching me, then nod in agreement.

He seems pleased with himself when the cherry is finished, leaving only the stem. He places it on his tongue, closes his mouth, and then a moment later reveals that he's tied the stem into a knot.

"You hold on to that while we look around," he says, handing it to me. I stare at it as he takes my drink away and then slips his fingers through mine. "I know you're worried about how many women I have been with before you, but now that I've found you, I'm all yours, if you want me. Everything I've learned is for you, and every sensual skill I've mastered will be a thousandfold better on your body." He squeezes my fingers and tugs me along. "Now, on with the tour, baby girl. I have a surprise for you."

Spirits. I don't think I can handle any surprises, I think as Zy leads me to a winding staircase.

I very much change my mind about that when I see the roof.

Because there are roses *everywhere*. They're of every color imaginable and I can't spot a single defect in the winding array of gorgeous petals.

Spirits. I think I just fell in love.

Chapter 21

Kornelius

My father looks like the prick he is as I peer at him over my steepled fingers.

Slicked-back blond hair. Dead blue eyes. And fangs still tinted red with blood from his latest victim.

He usually kills someone before he comes to visit, knowing that it gets under my skin, but this time he's actually brought a girl to sit on his lap.

She's half-conscious as she teeters on his thigh. Blood drizzles down her neck and chest, soaking into her silver-sequined dress.

The scent makes me dizzy, but not hungry. I haven't fed in days, but my control has always been strong when it comes to my vampiric nature.

Perhaps it's because I'm only half vampire and half something else.

It's the "something else" that always pisses off my sperm donor. The cloaking spell that the patriarchs came up with for us works on our shared death magic. I can walk freely on Staten Island.

He cannot.

Royce is peering out the window, frowning because he is disappointed Ishara isn't here. "A safe location?" he repeats. His tone has gone whiny and is grating against my ear.

"Yes," I reply, leaning back into my chair. I keep myself completely at ease as if there aren't two murderers in my den. "As I said, Daithi gave us an order to protect her virtue while preparations are being made for his resurrection."

"An order we conveniently can't confirm," my father says as he nuzzles the poor female's neck.

Based on her scent, she's some sort of shifter who must have been picked up in No Man's Land. My father mainly frequents the Vampire Syndicate in the Bronx, but he does enjoy hunting, too.

I don't know how the vampires in the syndicates operate and I don't care. What little blood needs I have are met by the bags in our freezer. I don't know where the supply comes from and I don't ask, but I do make a point to ration as much as possible.

Only the Gods know where the patriarchs are getting their blood supply for their little pets from.

I tire of their tactics just as I tire of being a *pet*.

Royce taps the glass. "Yes. I'm not sure if I buy your story about the death stone disappearing due to so many deaths."

"It's simple," I say, easily formulating the lie that will be enough to buy us some time. Especially if I pull at the threads of Royce's weakness, which is his arrogance. "You do know what happens to the death stone when a thousand spirits pass, don't you?"

He frowns. Of course he doesn't know, because it's not something we've ever had to encounter. But I act like this must be common information, which already puts him on edge.

He hates to be ignorant, of which he's guilty quite often.

"Of course," he snaps. "It just makes sense that it would weigh the stone down. But if you expect me to believe that—"

"So it has sunk like a stone to the bottom of the death plane; is that what you're saying?" my father asks.

There's a twinkle in his eye that suggests he's playing along, but I'm not sure why he wants to help me.

It most likely has something to do with the little witch we've taken custody of. Royce wants a taste, and my father no doubt wants a *bite*.

Neither of them is going to get the opportunity before I rip their heads from their bodies.

The murderous urge is only quelled by the knowledge that if I did so, I'd have nowhere to keep Ishara safe for the next two weeks. Previously, it was the suppression of my will magically bound by my soul-captor that kept my violent needs at bay. It's ironic that now it's my protective nature that stills my hand.

"That's a good metaphor," I say, forcing my mouth to praise my father, even if it's all a ruse. "With that many spirits, the death stone has sunk, and we simply have to wait for it to surface again." I turn to Royce and give him a fake smile. "I'll be sure to let you know the moment it's returned."

He snarls, which is a cute sound coming from a warlock. Vampires are more intimidating, at least.

"You asshole," he snarls. "You just want to keep the witch pussy for yourself. You think I don't know your brother is hiding her somewhere on Staten Island? I'll find her myself and when I do, I'll—"

His words are cut off when the elevator dings. I raise my eyebrow when Jasper enters the room.

His presence here is unexpected, but not unwelcome. It means he's grown to trust Zyran a lot faster than I would have expected, but then again, he can read our intentions when he touches us.

I learned as much when I saw it happen last night. It must be some consequence of being triplets, or being brought into existence by a goddess. Either way, I'm grateful for the connection. I need Jasper to be on board and on our team so we can focus on protecting Ishara.

He stares at our father, his mood instantly darkening when he sees the poor girl on his lap. "Father," he says.

Zane practically beams. "Jasper, is that you?" He slaps the girl's thigh, making her squeak. "Fuck, let's celebrate! Here. This bitch is on the house."

I've never seen a hand severed so quickly.

Chapter 22

Jasper

My father's hand rolls across the floor, thumping over the wood as my chest heaves with anger. I grabbed a sword off the wall and acted on instinct.

Fucking asshole.

Well, not entirely on instinct. My instinct had been to behead the bastard, but for some reason, I didn't.

Even though my unbeating heart throbbed for violence.

Even though the telltale signs of bloodlust had been so easily activated. If I don't reel it in, I'm in danger of losing control for a few hours. It doesn't escape me that I just tasted Ishara Doyle, my fated mate and an extremely powerful witch.

As a vampire, I could be prone to bloodlust simply by tasting her, and I've had more than my share recently.

Bloodlust is a dangerous thing for a vampire, even a hybrid such as myself. It sends the creature into a frenzy, one where fucking, feeding, and maiming are all one can

I steady myself against it when I recognize the signs. Ishara would likely be my target, and she doesn't deserve that kind of treatment.

So I take a steady breath, flaring my nostrils as I take in the metallic tang scenting the air. My handiwork satisfies a small part of me, but I still deeply crave to saw my blade across his throat.

Why did I aim for his hand and not his head?

Maybe he deserves a more prolonged death than that. Or maybe some remaining logic centers buried in the back of my brain understand I'm out of my element here and my father, as much as I hate him, is vital to the plan my brothers have put in place.

He can phase objects through matter, which is the only way Kor can kill the number of people needed to activate his magic. I'm not sure if he's going to need to pull that particular stunt again.

Not to mention I don't fully understand the politics involved. I hate politics, always have, but right now I wish I knew what was going on.

Because without understanding my father's role, I can't do something stupid.

Like kill him. That might endanger Issy. And I need to put aside my own bloodlust to protect her in any circumstance—even if it's from myself.

But I wonder who's going to protect the poor shifter still on my father's lap. She's frozen in time with blood splattered all over her. His fleshy stump is on her lap. The wound slowly closes as my father's vampire nature heals him.

He's older than me and my brothers. Much older,

which tends to make a vampire stronger, so if I'm being realistic with myself, he might have even *allowed* me to sever his hand.

If I had tried to behead him, I might be the one bleeding all over the floor.

The shifter female draws in a deep breath and screams.

The sound breaks the small eternity of stunned silence in the room and my father shoves her off his lap. She must already be weak, because she unceremoniously thumps to the ground. He shreds the bottom half of his shirt and wraps it around his wound.

"Son," he says fondly as if I hadn't just removed his hand, "it's been too long."

Royce chuckles from his place by the window. He's leaning against it with his arms crossed as he basks in the blood and violence. Kor is watching us over his steepled fingers, but I sense the tension in his body as if he's ready to act.

Royce starts to laugh in earnest. He would have made a good vampire. He's just like the rest of them amused by gore and cruelty.

He slowly claps as he pushes away from the window. "If that's how your family greets you, Zane, I don't want to meet your mate."

I have a feeling that Royce knows my father's mate is dead. The way Zane goes still pleases me more than my action of dismembering him.

The hand will grow back, but his pride? That's something that'll take longer to regenerate.

As if my father has been reminded I'm the reason he

239

no longer has a mate, his smirk dies before floundering into a scowl. He's turned his back on Royce and now approaches me until we're nose to nose.

He looks even younger than I do, with blond hair, blue eyes, and a lean frame. He's taller than me by a few inches and he's maintained the intimidating sense of power I always feared growing up.

I feel like a teenager again when he lightly slaps me on my cheek with his remaining hand. "Jasper, my boy. Now that that's out of your system, let's celebrate our reunion, hmm?" He gestures to the whimpering female behind him. "I know you're spoiled by the life of a mercenary in Lapland, but here, fresh shifter blood is a rarity. It would be disrespectful to waste my gift."

I have no intention of sampling his *gift*.

A creak sounds as Kor stands from his chair. He calmly walks over to the weak female and places a hand on her head. She shrinks into herself at his touch, but she seems to fear him less than the other two men in the room.

Wise girl. "Jasper isn't familiar with our ways, Zane," Kor says. "May I suggest she stays here and I'll warm Jasper up to the idea?"

I raise a brow, but I have learned Kor's tic by now that shows when he's lying.

His tic is that he has none at all. He's completely calm and believable.

My father barks a laugh. "Fine. Brotherly bonding, is it? Can't say I understand. I never had a brother." He snaps his fingers. "She's yours."

Kor nods. "I'll restrain her in Jasper's bedroom." He

glances at my father. "Be good while I'm gone. I'll be right back."

With that, Kor drags the crying female away. My father chuckles as if her terror greatly amuses him.

He'll restrain her, and probably scare the poor girl to death, but he won't touch her. I imagine he knows how to help her escape, but he has a part to play while we still have an audience.

I remain silent when I'm left alone with Royce and Zane, two males I very much want to behead.

My fingers tighten around the hilt of my blade as the girl's screams heighten, and then are muffled.

"Relax, boy," my father says as he taps my cheek again, then finally backs off. He goes to Zy's bar and pours himself a drink. "You can fuck out your anger on my gift when we're done here. For now, Kornelius is right. We have business to attend to."

I came here to support Kor against our father and Royce. It felt wrong to leave him alone, especially when I made the decision to trust Zyran to protect Issy.

A warmth flutters inside of me wondering what she might be doing right now. Would she give in to the fate bond with my brother?

I'm not sure how I feel about that.

With my father leering down at me, all I want is to wrap Ishara in protection, no matter what form that takes. Zyran is a powerful vampire, and one that would protect her with his life.

I *felt* that from him. He had told the truth when he'd talked about waiting for his fated mate. Sure, he'd been a playboy like Issy said, but that didn't mean much to him. It was all practice in his head.

And now he wants to share all he learned with his new mate. He wants to introduce her to all the pleasure he can offer, and for that, I'm happy. I don't know the full extent of Issy's past, but from what little I heard, it had been a dark one.

She deserves everything.

And everything is what my brothers and I will give her.

Kor returns, wiping blood away from his chin, painting a very different picture than my sentiments.

I'm not sure if it's the girl's blood or if it's another ruse. Uncertainty sours my stomach, but I try to hold on to the faith that my brother hasn't crossed any lines.

Zane grins. "I do hope you saved some for Jasper."

Royce seems to have had enough of our banter and claps his hands again. "Forget the fucking girl. Back to *business*. When will the death stone resurface?"

I glance at Kor to answer. Politics are his jam, not mine.

"My best guess would be a few weeks," he says with a shrug. He ventures to the bar and pours himself a drink. He wipes his thumb over the blood on his chin, then rims his glass with it. "Give or take."

Royce frowns. "Then you have two weeks."

Kor raises a brow as he slowly takes a sip before answering. "I can't guarantee that. Like I said, I estimate a few weeks."

"Give or take," our father purrs. "You can do something to help it out, I'm sure, to guarantee you meet that timeline."

"And if it doesn't return by then?" I ask, sensing a threat.

Royce licks his fingers, then chants a few words under his breath. The air frosts and ice clings to the hairs on my skin. "Then I will send you to the death plane myself to retrieve it."

A chill slips up my spine, and it's not just from the temperature in the room.

This male can't be older than twenty-five, but he has the power of a patriarch. I believe him when he says he will send us to the death plane.

Even with our hybrid magic, that's not a trip we would survive—leaving Issy to fend for herself.

Not an option.

"Two weeks," Kor agrees, likely coming to the same conclusion.

I stare at him. It's a risk to not give ourselves any leeway. The plan is to wait for the rogue Outcast Coven witch named Amala to help us expose Daithi, but simply exposing him isn't enough to protect our mate.

We still need to get her out. We still need to do more than prove her innocence—we need to prove she's not a threat.

Which will be hard to do, given that she *is* a threat. Her voice kills and it's something she has no control over. I've seen it myself.

Royce flicks his fingers and the temperature warms again. "Very good. And in the meantime, you'd better hide that witch of yours well. If I find her, I'm going to take my sample as a patriarch in line for her power." Kor opens his mouth, likely to protest, but Royce raises a hand. "I will deal with my cousin if he disapproves." He grins. "You're lucky I like games of cat and mouse. It'll be so much more satisfying when I find her and see the look of terror on her pretty face."

A growl rumbles in my chest, which only seems to amuse Royce. He barks a laugh as he walks out of the room. "Stay sharp, vessels."

The elevator dings as my father takes another swig of his drink. He stays silent for ten seconds, and I realize he's waiting for Royce to be out of earshot. "I thought that asshole was never going to leave."

Kor gestures for me to take a seat, so I do.

Apparently, this circus isn't over yet.

I'm still holding my blade and I decline a drink when Kor offers me one. He looks annoyed when he sets it on the table, but I don't have to pretend like I'm on board with this.

That wouldn't be believable anyway. My father knows how I feel about him.

Case in point, the bloody hand on the floor.

"We're going to need more devices," Kor says as he makes himself look comfortable leaning against the wall.

I know he's anything but. When he touched me earlier, I sensed his unease. He might look confident, but he's playing a dangerous game with our father.

Zane seems to consider the request. "You're pinning the deaths on the House of Gold and Garnet. I want to know why you're intent on starting a war, first. The plan was always to create infighting with the syndicates."

"I have a better plan," Kor says. "You want a war between the other syndicates and the Outcast Coven, but that's thinking too small. For the number of deaths you want, it needs to be on a larger scale."

What in the death plane are these idiots going on about?

Zane scoffs. "I'm also interested in a world remaining when the death goddess has surfaced. We've talked about this."

My eyes widen. "You want to summon the death goddess?"

Zane grins. "Of course. I intend to fuck her, then show her what death looks like. She must be tired of watching everyone else die. It's time she took a turn."

What a noble goal.

Kor blows out a breath. "If you really want the death goddess to surface, it's going to take a lot more than a thousand deaths. All we managed to do was bury the death stone."

Zane hums. "You don't have to lie to me, son. I can see that you've broken Daithi's control on you and the death stone is hidden, not gone. You're playing a game of your own, which is why I put a little fail-safe in place to keep the patriarchs in charge. They're key to my plans, because once I take the death goddess's power, I'll *own* them." He runs his tongue over his lower lip. "So you'd best be on my good side, son. I'm going to be very powerful by the time this is all over."

Kor frowns and I have a feeling my father's done something to worsen our situation.

"What kind of fail-safe?" he asks instead of

responding to our father's threat.

Zane smirks. "I had some extra devices placed in key figures that'll wreak havoc on the Outcast Coven and buy the patriarchs some time to figure their shit out. I still need them in charge for my plan to work. The patriarchs will handle their women—and I will handle *them*."

I don't like the sound of that.

"Meaning?" Kor presses.

"Four matriarchs are dead."

Kor doesn't move. In fact, he remains perfectly still and unresponsive.

Which means he's *pissed*.

"The matriarchs took control of the Outcast Coven when Ishara Doyle killed the patriarchs," Kor says with a level tone. "You think disrupting them and sending their fragile leadership into chaos is going to help you achieve your goal? You've only made matters more difficult."

Zane doesn't seem to agree. He takes a lengthy sip from his drink, then swirls the ice as he rests his bandaged stump on the arm of the chair. It's not bleeding anymore, but there's enough residue to stain the upholstery. "No, I've simply made sure you can't fuck things up for me, my son. You're going to be a vessel and I'm going to make sure that you keep to your role. I need the patriarchs to help me contain the goddess, like they do the matriarchs, and when I drink her blood, I'm going to become the most powerful death-magic vampire hybrid the world has ever seen."

His eyes sparkle with the pathetic goal.

It doesn't surprise me that he wants to force the

goddess to turn him into what his sons are—to prove to his fragile ego that he is still the best. It's so... unoriginal.

"You're worse than the patriarchs," Kor snarls, finally allowing his mask to slip.

Zane beams as if that's a compliment. "I would hope so. They settle for their females, try to control them and siphon their power, but the death goddess they don't even recognize is the true prize. They think I'm a fanatic believing in a lost deity. Imagine their faces when I bring her to our realm and feast on her blood." His blue eyes sparkle with cruelty. "Imagine how she'll *taste*." He licks his lips. "Maybe I'll join Royce's game to find this little witch of yours. She's the closest thing to a death goddess any of us will taste until this is done." He grins. "I, too, have no problem indulging in a hunt to pass the time. If you manage to keep her from both Royce and me, then you'll prove a worthy vessel." He shrugs. "And if not, well, at least I'll have a taste of one of the most powerful death witches to exist. Not a shabby runner-up prize."

I take a page from Kor's book and remain stoically still as my father finally takes his leave.

If I move, I'll fall into bloodlust and have his head—or die trying.

And I'm not sure what'll happen next. Would I hurt the shifter in my room?

Or would I find Issy and do something worse?

The answer is a bloody smear in my mind as silence envelops us and Kor finally blows out a breath.

"Change of plans. The matriarchs are going to be in chaos right now and looking for someone to blame. I doubt they'll buy that it was the other Houses. They're going to be looking for allies to the patriarchs and they're going to sniff out this place. Let my father deal with that."

"I don't give two shits about matriarchs, patriarchs, or the Houses," I growl. I flex my fist around the hilt of my blade and scrape the point across the floor, leaving a groove. "Zane and Royce threatened Ishara."

They both need to *die*.

Kor nods. "Yes, and we're going to have to split up and make sure they don't get anywhere near her." He waits until I meet his gaze before he continues. "Do you want Royce or our father?"

My fangs ache as I make an easy choice with those options. "Zane's mine."

Chapter 23

Issy

An hour earlier...

"Do you like it?" Zyran asks while I stare at the most beautiful collection of roses I've ever seen.

Like it?

I'm in shock.

Numbly, I nod as I venture farther onto the roof. The screams don't seem so bad up here, as if the beauty of this place insulates against death.

There's too much life for death to overtake it.

The intense aroma immerses me in floral perfection as I trail my fingers over silky petals. They're all shades. Pinks, blood-reds, and even blues.

"I've only read about these," I say as an excited tone enters my voice. I scamper to the blue roses and cup one of them as the texts I read flutter across my mind's eye. "There was botany science introduced before and further developed after the Great Sacrifice, but I've still never seen a blue rose in person. This would have required genetic manipulation by adding the blue pigment delphinidin."

Zyran chuckles. "You sure know how to seduce a man, Issy."

I blush, more so because he used my nickname instead of calling me "baby." Although, I enjoy it when he does that, too.

I stare at the rare, spectacular roses and marvel at holding one in my hands. "This must have taken years to cultivate."

"*Ten* years," Zyran clarifies. His touch runs along my wrist, then he sweeps his thumb over the petal I'm admiring. "It took some trial and error on my part. Then Kor converted one of the empty suites into a library so we could learn death magic and develop that side of ourselves. It's something of an unspoken competition between us who is better read than the other. I found the potion books more interesting. Only the perfect roses are suitable for potions, apparently, so I learned a lot that way."

I smile. "A library? I'd like to see that."

And the fact that Zyran and Kornelius enjoy reading as a pastime—spell books, no less—seals the deal for me that fate knew what she was doing.

When I turn to Zyran, I would have kissed him.

But his glasses are still in the way. I could kiss him even while he wears them, but I prefer to first meet his gaze.

I reach up to take them off, but pain shoots up my wrist when he roughly grips my arm. "Never take off my glasses," he warns, his tone going dangerously low.

I frown. "Why?"

His grip on me doesn't loosen, but I don't try to move away.

I want to see his eyes. There's nothing he can tell me that would scare me off.

Does he have a wound he's embarrassed about? A horrible scar? Or something else?

"My power," he says. "Anyone who meets my gaze dies."

My eyes widen.

Something else indeed.

"And anyone who hears my voice dies as well," I tell him. "Yet here you are, listening to me. I'm not even wearing that collar Kor put on me."

He doesn't realize how rare and incredible all of this is. Each effort to form the foreign words with my tongue exhausts me. I'm fluent in many languages, but I never had to speak the words aloud.

It was too dangerous. I trained myself to be a mute and talking so much is starting to make my throat hurt. I need more practice.

With Zy, I'm up for the challenge.

"We don't know if you'd be safe from me," he says, his touch trailing up my arm until his hand is caressing my face.

A whole new set of nerves comes alive at the sensation. My heart skips a beat and surely Zyran must hear it.

"Fate would not be so cruel," I decide aloud. "Let me see your eyes, Zyran. This isn't negotiable."

He grins, the gesture showing his fangs.

The thrill of the danger he offers only excites me more.

Spirits. What's wrong with me?

He might not comment on the changes in my heart rate, but he seems to be cataloging my reactions. His touch glides lower across my collarbone, then along my throat.

Just like with Jasper, my heart practically stops when he gently dents his fingers into my skin.

"You fascinate me, little witch. You're my equal, or my better, perhaps. Your power is incredible. I can feel it with every vibration of your voice—yet, your preference is for me to take your control away."

Is that my kink? I know that Zy's experienced, but he seems to enjoy figuring me out.

It almost doesn't seem fair, given that I haven't had a chance to discover my tastes on my own.

"I've been controlled all my life," I practically snarl, insulted by the idea that I am so damaged that my trauma would turn into a desire. "That's not what I want."

He hums as he leans in closer, not kissing me, but I can feel his closeness all the same. "It's not that you wish to be controlled... no. There's something else." He moves in and glides his nose across the column of my throat, then deftly licks my throbbing vein. "You want it hard. You want sensation. You want to feel *alive*."

My eyes widen when I realize he's spoken the truth.

My truth.

It's why I respond to blood—specifically my blood. It's why pain excites me and why everything he says is true.

It all reminds me I'm alive.

"Yes," I decide aloud. "That's exactly what I want."

He faces me again and I desperately want to rip off his glasses so I can see the lust in his eyes. Surely I'm not imagining the tension ready to snap between us.

Mine, my heart tells me.

I will take what is mine.

When he moves to stop me again, I strengthen my voice.

"No."

The word has enough power in it to make him stagger. He's momentarily stunned as I slip off his glasses.

He's squeezed his eyes shut, but I can already see that he's beautiful.

"Open them," I command. The air shimmers with magic and it's the first time I've ever manipulated the power in my voice. Perhaps knowing that a collar could silence me makes me appreciate it even more.

Efforts to block out my power were always ineffective, but I never tried to make it stronger.

"Issy, please," he begins, but I press the matter.

"I will be fine, Zy. You cannot hurt me. You're my mate."

My patience runs thin, but I wait until he finally opens his eyes.

My entire world slams inward as I soak in his power.

Spirits...

My soul is bathed in vibrant greens, the kinds that come from a garden of life I have yet to sample.

"Zy," I breathe with amazement. His power is undeniable, but I imagine it must be what my voice is like for him.

His gaze envelops me with relentless magic. It's a wild, unrestrained power that he can't control not because he lacks skill, but because his magic is pure.

He's an open channel to the death plane, just like me, and his eyes are the windows to a sea of souls.

When he kisses me, I'm cut off from his world of magic and am instead thrust into an ocean of desire.

More.

My need to claim him, to make our bond permanent, thrums through my veins. I claw at him and rake my nails down his chest, popping buttons in my wake.

There's a beautiful silver chain that ripples over his collarbone and I leave that alone. I don't have time to analyze the unique symbol dangling from it. My attention is definitely elsewhere.

He rips his belt from his hips and wraps it around my wrists, binding my arms behind my back. With one quick motion, he secures the makeshift cuffs.

"Mine," he says aloud, repeating the mantra that's consuming my mind.

The blood flow to my fingers cuts off, leaving them tingling as he resumes exploring my skin with his tongue. He gently nips on the same ear where Jasper had drawn blood. A stinging sensation lets me know he's reopened the wound.

A groan escapes him as he takes a moment to collect himself.

"Fuck, sweetheart. You taste…"

I gaze up at him through my eyelashes. "Good?" I guess. Jasper seemed to enjoy the taste of my blood, too.

He gives me a flushed look, one of ravaging hunger that makes a chill run up my spine. "You taste like raw magic, like I just electrified my senses on undiluted power. You're *incredible*."

I smile, pleased that my new mate enjoys my taste. An instinct arises in me to give him more of what he likes and I don't think about it when I sink my teeth into my lip.

Hard.

The sting radiates over my skin and my flavor is metallic to my senses, but Zy's growl says I did something dangerous.

I lean in to offer him more, but he bruises my arms and holds me in place. "This isn't safe, sweetheart. You could awaken bloodlust in any vampire that tastes you." His gaze flicks up to meet mine. "Jasper was feeding on you when... Did he hurt you?"

I think about that. No? Yes?

I don't really care. I enjoyed what Jasper and I did and I want more of it.

"You won't hurt me," I assure him. "Just like your gaze can't hurt me, you will never lose control with me."

He releases a shuddered breath. "You don't know me, Issy. You don't know what I've done. What I'm capable of and—"

"I know that fate chose you for me," I cut him off. My hands are still bound behind my back, but I'm glad they are or I would be forcing the matter. I'd grab him and bring his face to mine so he could stop second-guessing himself and let this happen.

"Is fate enough of an assurance?" he asks as a pained look crosses his features. "My parents were fated and my father did horrible things to my mother."

"You are not your father," I decide aloud. He's right that I don't know him, but I don't have to.

Because I have the same story.

My father was cruel. He only wanted to use the women in my family and take their power.

His death had been satisfying, but it wasn't nearly enough. Not for all that he put me through.

But now maybe I understand why I haven't been able to pull up the memory of my revenge.

Because it is something I must experience with my mates, to share with them and help them understand that we do not have to follow in our parents' footsteps.

We make our own paths.

And if we don't like the person who created us, we shred them to pieces.

"Kiss me," I demand. "And don't stop when I show you something. I'm going to cast a spell."

He seems to be teetering on the edge of desire, but now I've piqued his curiosity. "A spell?" He grins. "Is it like my arousal spell?"

Hardly, but it'll bring us closer than lust ever could.

"You might not even want me after I show you this, but it's a part of my past that I think I'm supposed to relive with you. Do you trust me?"

Now he's definitely intrigued. Mischief has entered his fluidly green eyes as magic courses between us. He doesn't know it, but having him just look at me gives me so much more power to work with.

Enough to break down the walls I've put up around a memory I wasn't ready for.

"Do your worst, Ishara Doyle. I trust you through this life and the next."

When Zyran runs his tongue over my wounded lip, I begin the spell.

And then we're both drawn into the darkness, our bodies surrounded by the beauty of life while our souls seek death.

Chapter 24

Issy

A memory from the not-so-distant past...

Beep. Beep. Beep.

My body is frozen as I suffocate on tubes lodged down my throat, forcing me to breathe. A machine continues to send a pulse throughout the room, irritating me.

I'm not sure how long I've been like this, but my soul is wandering an endless hall and is nowhere near the annoying machine. I pick up a book and thumb through it.

All the pages are empty.

This is a mental prison created for me by the patriarchs while my body is *preserved*.

My stomach rolls as I locate the faraway sensations of tubes in my body and air pumping through my lungs, keeping me alive.

A powerful spell silenced me, and now an archaic

machine breathes for me because I'm too weak after all of the abuse and oppressive magic.

My arm stings where a saline drip is keeping fluids regulated in my flesh, and there's another tube running to my stomach to feed me.

I'm not supposed to notice any of this. I start to slip back into the comforting illusion until I sense a sudden disturbance.

My sister is at my side. I can feel her, but I can't see her.

Fallon! Please!

This state is too horrible to live in—too cruel to exist.

She pushes power into me, but power isn't what I need. I have plenty of that.

It's the invisible chains she needs to do something about.

Then Fallon is gone. Devastation sinks to my gut until I realize she hasn't left me.

She's just somewhere else.

She pushes power into me again, but not into my body.

Into my *soul*.

Warmth floods through me and my body struggles to take a breath, but the machine is still in control.

I seek refuge in the mirage the patriarchs made for me, quickly losing scope of reality.

Safe. Home. Calm.

The mantra of the illusion comforts me and I almost fall back into it until I hear Fallon's voice.

You're still unconscious, she says.

I am? I reply, confused because I don't feel unconscious. *I'm in my room.*

No, you're in a freezer. I'm looking right at you.

Oh...

I try to frown when I realize she's right, but my body doesn't obey me. *I knew something was wrong when my books kept showing me blank pages.*

I am teaching her the spell to free me when a new presence invades our space.

Daithi.

Terror winds through me when he casts a spell on Fallon, forcing her body to mimic death.

It's the same he performed on me—perhaps a little too well, given the machine required to keep me alive.

Rage fuels my soul as I remember everything he's done.

Forced a fated-mate bond on me.

Given my body and soul to other patriarchs like I'm currency to be traded.

Chaos explodes when another female enters the room. I instantly recognize her presence.

Ayla has not just been my roommate, but also my only friend besides Fallon. She's a cousin, although not by blood, but she's family all the same.

And she's here.

She's done something to Daithi, but it's only temporary.

He lashes out and Fallon is cast from the room and sent sailing across the building.

I don't know how high up we are, but Daithi

wouldn't have cast her out unless it would seriously hurt her.

Pain rips through me as Ayla breaks the spell holding me captive, then slowly tugs on the tubes.

I'm gagging and mortified and rip them out while she screams.

"Issy! You're going to hurt yourself!"

I don't care. I need to be free. I need to *breathe*.

I need to make sure Fallon is okay!

When I finally open my eyes, I take in the dim freezer and flickering lights.

The view through the window shows an angel diving where my sister just fell.

Nolan!

Residual power from what my sister just gave me pours through my spirit. I'm trying to counteract the impact spell to save her—but she's not stopping, only slowing down.

I can only hope I've bought her enough time.

Fallon! I scream, hoping she'll reply. *Fallon!*

Issy? She whispers back, sounding dazed, but not in terror like she should be.

Which means she's okay.

Oh, thank the stars, I breathe. *I tried to give him time to catch you. But I was worried... I was worried it wasn't fast enough.*

Fallon remains silent as if processing everything.

Daithi is clawing against a golden noose around his neck, but it's already starting to disintegrate.

I flash a look at Ayla and quickly work my fingers.

They're stiff, but enough blood has flooded back into them to form sign language.

He's mine, I tell her.

She nods and portals out while I continue my conversation with Fallon.

He used *me to hurt you,* I tell her. *He* froze *me under an obedience spell.* Infiltrated *our mental connection to let the patriarchs talk to you through me.* Mated *me against my will.*

He. Will. Die.

Wait, Issy— Fallon says.

No. No waiting. He. Will. Die!

*But we don't know how the forced bond—*she continues, but I slam our connection closed.

And then Daithi is mine. He writhes against his restraints.

I don't waste any time. I grab him by the throat and lean in, grazing my lips against his ear as I utter the single word to unravel his soul.

"Die."

When I stumble outside, chaos has ensued. The women of the Outcast Coven are free and they are *furious.*

The streets are painted with blood as spells launch against one another, but the women have always been more powerful.

That's why the men wished to control us, to use our magic because it's superior to their own.

I have one more target to find, but I stop when I spot three shadows in the distance.

Three vampires.

They're watching me and their forms don't quite line up how they should. Dark wisps writhe around them and one of them has brutally green eyes that seem to pierce through the dark.

The other two have distinguishing features as well. One has strange face paint that reminds me of a gothic skeleton, but it's not makeup.

It's his magic.

It's sucking in all the chaos around him, drawing it in like a void at the center of a galaxy.

His body draws in death—his soul a link to the afterlife.

And the other gleams with dark silk as if his skin is made of velvet.

He communes with death, too, and is completely comfortable with it.

I'm not sure who the three men are, but there's a connection that tells me I will one day.

So I let them watch, because there's one more task to complete.

My father.

I can't see him in the mass of chaos, but I work a spell to locate him. It's easy enough. All I have to do is tell my magic to find my own blood.

It spears in two directions, one of them weak and far away.

That one is my sister. The other leads to my parents.

I fear for my mother, but I head toward the street where my house is.

It's at least a fifteen-minute walk and my legs are tired by the time I reach it. The bloodshed is far behind me, but all of the death has given me a boost.

I'll be able to overcome my father's defenses—but I'll only get one shot at this.

Rolling back my shoulders, I enter my childhood home. The winding staircase is something I never get to scale, but I do today.

I take my time going up each step, letting my bare feet slap against the expensive metal.

Then I'm in a hallway that feels unfamiliar, but simply because I'm only allowed in the basement.

No more.

Never again will I be so suppressed and hidden.

My mother's scream makes me hurry and I burst through a cracked door to find I'm too late.

The blood drains from my face as I take in my mother on the ground with a thick black line drawn across her throat.

A beheading spell.

Her eyes are wild and furious—not weak and submissive like I'm used to.

Fallon had done something to free the women of my coven. Even our mother.

But she wasn't enough to stand up against our father. Her husband towers over her and seems to gloat as he juts out his chin. "Useless woman," he snarls, then spits on the ground.

I open my mouth to scream, but the muting barrier is active in this room.

Even though I'm ready for it, it'll take my magic time to saw through it.

The air shimmers as my father turns on me and chuckles. "Oh, Ishara. You've come just in time to see the fallout of our family. You're lucky that I need you alive—but you're not supposed to be here." He clicks his tongue and whispers another few words of a spell, sending the black line deeper into my mother's neck.

She gurgles on her own blood.

A scream is lodged in my throat, but I can't move. My entire body is frozen just like it has been under Daithi.

Bastard! I scream in my mind, but the words don't come out.

"You're supposed to spread your legs for your new mate," he says, circling me with a cruel grin on his face. "That's all bitches are good for. That and giving us their power, because none of you know how to use it properly. Don't you see? Only the patriarchs can bring the Outcast Coven to power. So witness what happens when you *disobey*."

He makes a fist and my mother's body lurches. Tears are rushing down my cheeks and my entire body trembles. I'm screaming inside my head, and my magic is like a bubble about to burst, but it's not enough.

My mother locks her gaze with mine and there's an unspoken need.

She can't talk to me like Fallon can, but I don't need to read her mind to know her intention.

I'm sorry, she seems to say. *I'm sorry for everything. Do not... let him win.*

Her lashes flutter over her eyes and her lips move on a spell.

It's the kind of spell a witch can only cast once.

When her spirit pops free from her body, all of the magic generated by her death explodes through the room, breaking the barrier holding my voice and body at bay.

I scream. I release all of my fury, my rage, and my sadness.

It rips into my father, shredding into him unlike I've ever seen my magic do before. His skin splits as if I've cut him with a thousand knives.

He falls to his knees and trembles as blood wells across his skin, soaking into his suit.

I shuffle forward into the room and run my fingers over his cheek. Blood smears with the gesture as I crouch down so I can see his face.

I want to see his terror when he dies.

"Goodbye, Father."

Chapter 25

Zyran

S unlight struggles to warm my cool skin as I finally stir from the spell-induced dream.

A dream where my fated mate killed her own father.

And Daithi, too. That was hella satisfying to experience.

She allowed me to watch her darkest memory, one that felt so buried I am sure even she hadn't relived it since the event itself.

But something feels wrong as I struggle to open my eyes. The sun is annoying to a vampire, but not unbearable, at least not at my age. Yet my fingers ache as if they don't have any blood in them.

I don't have a heartbeat, so my blood travels differently in my body. Magic is what keeps everything flowing, but a stabbing sensation makes me wince when I flex my fingers again.

When I move, I disturb the beautiful witch lying in the sea of roses with me. A few of the thorny stems have caught in her hair, making it appear as if she is wearing a floral crown.

She groans and her brow furrows, then I see her arms are still trapped behind her back.

And her fingers are completely blue—still bound by the belt I had selfishly wrapped around her wrists. I had been rooting out her desires—which apparently ran dark.

But I hadn't factored in that playing with a witch came with risks, such as being put under by a spell.

"Fuck," I curse as I immediately free her.

She whimpers as blood rushes back into her hands and she curls into a ball.

"I'm sorry," I whisper as I press my forehead against her spine. "I'm so fucking sorry, Issy. I... I fell asleep and..." No excuse feels good enough for nearly making her lose her hands.

She takes a moment to collect herself and she remains still against me for a long time. She finally relaxes as she blows out a breath.

"I'm fine," she whispers.

Her words still hold incredible power and I flinch against the whiplash of magic when she speaks.

Her power is easier to manage when she's looking into my eyes. I noticed that before when she took off my glasses and her words transformed into something sensual and delightful rather than painful.

Although, right now, maybe I deserve the pain.

But I need to know she's truly okay, which means judging her for myself.

Helping her to turn toward me, I look into her eyes

again, no longer afraid I'm going to hurt her with my power.

But still, it doesn't mean she's safe with me. Case in point, her blue fingers.

"You're not fine," I whisper. "I hurt you."

"You would never hurt me," she counters, even if it's not entirely true. Neither of us can deny that I most certainly had.

I hold her freezing hands that seem cold even to my touch. "This is the danger of being with me, Issy. I can't promise you'll be safe. Not even from me."

She sighs against me, but she's not pulling away like she should be. "It was an accident. It won't happen again."

"No, it won't," I agree. "We're going to make a safe word."

She blinks up at me. "A safe word?"

"Yes, and not just a word to let me know if I've crossed a line. A word that we're going to spell together so that whatever is happening will stop. It should work on my brothers too if we bind it to blood. Do you understand?"

She seems to consider that, then smiles. "If that'll make you feel better, then okay. I think I can help make a spell like that." She glances around us. "It's a spell that'll need the perfect rose. I'm not sure where we might find something so rare."

I know she's teasing, but it's a game now, one I want to play. "Indeed. Quite the conundrum. It'll take an unblemished red rose, a deep red, not a light one. And it needs to have long, wicked thorns. A protection spell will make good use of that."

"Hmm," she agrees, sitting up. She rubs sensation back into her fingers. They're still the wrong color, but the fact that she can move and flex them is a good sign. It means the flesh didn't lose oxygen long enough to die. "How about a race, then?"

I grin. "Oh? A race for the perfect rose?" I lean in. "And what does the winner get?"

She bites her lip, stoking fresh need through my body. We have yet to make our bond permanent, and my cock is painfully aware of that, but my mate wishes to play.

So play we shall.

"The winner gets to decide the safe word," she says without hesitation. There's a sparkle in her eye and I'm not sure if I want to win or let her win.

Either way, it'll be fun because if I win, I know the safe word I intend to use.

A word she'll never, ever say during sex.

Because when I finally have her, I'll never want the fun to end and I'm just selfish like that.

"Deal," I say. "I'll give you a head start, sweetling."

She raises a brow but doesn't protest special treatment.

Instead, she runs.

I watch with amusement as she weaves gracefully through vines, deftly perusing her selections.

I'm tempted to give her more than a few seconds' head start, but this is a rare opportunity.

We'll only be making a safe word once. It will not change. There's a training period to make sure she knows how and when to use it, and also for my mind to react enough to be pulled out of lust.

Ishara Doyle has the potential to take me under and drive me to dark places I've never visited before—a safe word is very much a necessity for my new mate.

I know the garden better than Issy does, but she's had no trouble finding the healthiest section closer to the sun where I've recently fertilized.

My nose guides me where to go, but Issy works on instinct.

We both find the perfect rose at the same time, and even with my vampiric speed, she beats me to it.

Maybe I let her, or maybe she was just faster than me.

I smile when she holds it up in victory.

"Ah, you've won," I say, surprised that I'm not more disappointed. "What safe word have you chosen, then?"

She twirls the rose as her silver eyes glitter with magic. For a death witch, she has so much life to give. "Whenever I'm in danger, there's only one word that comes to mind. It's a name, actually."

I'm not surprised she's chosen her sister's name. "Fallon?" I guess.

She grins. "Yes, it seems fitting. And it's not a name I'm going to want to say during sex, trust me."

I chuckle. It's a good compromise. "Very well. 'Fallon' it is."

She makes a face. "Is it really necessary to attach a spell to the word?"

I nod. "Very." If she pushes me into bloodlust, I'm going to need more than willpower to stop.

"All right, then. I need your blood," she says, holding

out her palm. "Just a drop will do."

Making a show of pricking my thumb with the tip of my fang, I squeeze it and offer her the growing drop. My wound will close within seconds, so I allow her to squeeze my finger to drop the blood onto the rose.

She reaches up then and trails her finger over my jawline, sending tingles over my skin, especially when she presses her finger against my fang.

Her blood lingers on my senses when she adds her droplet of blood to the rose, then begins to chant a spell.

It only takes a few moments.

"Fallon," she whispers, naming the safe word and finishing the job. The rose puffs into energy, sending ruby-red motes into both of us.

A ripple curls through my body, securing the word to a sense of restraint.

I sigh, glad that's done.

"So," she says, slipping into me as she wraps her arms around my middle. "What word would you have picked? I'm curious."

She stands on her tiptoes, eager to kiss me, but she's waiting for my response.

"Oh, that's easy," I say, yearning to devour her, to begin the rest of our lives as bonded mates. "The word I would have chosen is a name, too. But one of my siblings, not yours. Probably Jasper, just because he's an ass."

Her eyes widen. "Really? Why would you choose his name? They're my mates, too." A blush sweeps over her porcelain skin. "If we're really going through with this, I expect I'll say their names at some point."

"That's precisely why," I say as I nuzzle into her. She

smells like magic and sex, awakening a raw need inside of me that has a dangerous edge. "I have no problem with sharing, but I do have a competitive side. When you climax, I want *my* name coming from your lips." I lick her pulse, eager for more of her delectable blood. But only if she offers it. Now that we have a spelled safe word, I feel less hesitant to indulge when it comes to my new mate. I'll drive her mad until she's begging for me to be inside of her—both my fangs and my cock. "But I do believe we were in the middle of something that I'd very much like to finish."

Her breath shudders against my lips, drawing me in. "We were?"

"We have to test that your spell is effective. It's only prudent," I say, continuing to play our game as I graze my tongue over her lower lip. She flinches when I nip her.

"Perfectly prudent," she agrees, her words going husky and low. Her power still rips through me with every sound she utters, but I'm growing used to it.

I *like* it.

And I mean that I want to test her safe word. I want to know her limits now that it's safe to do so.

She makes a sound of pleasure, not pain, when I dig my fingers into her hip and yank her against me.

She complies when I growl, wilting against me like a perfect rose.

She bares her neck and it's too fucking much. Too tempting.

I sink my teeth into her, relishing her cry.

No safe word yet? All right then, little mate.

It's time to play.

Chapter 26

Issy

Zyran is going to be the death of me, I decide as he
works his jaw against my throat, then pulls my
blood into his mouth.

He's feeding on me. It should be terrifying, or at least
painful.

But it's neither of those things.

It's... *euphoric*.

Warmth tingles through my body as he continues and
I realize there's something different about Zyran's bite.
He's a hybrid vampire, and his other half includes death
magic.

I've looked into his eyes. He's powerful, maybe even
more powerful than Jasper.

Jasper has learned how to disable his death touch, but
not Zyran.

Zyran's death sight is something he deals with every
moment of every day. He *can't* turn it off.

Perhaps that's not a lack of skill or willpower, but
rather a testament to how much magic he really has.

When his hand slips over my collarbone to secure me against him, I clench my thighs and make a sound.

He pauses, as if he's listening for the safe word we just established, but I certainly don't want to call on my sister right now.

She might disapprove of the darkness I sense in my mates. But they're necromancy-vampire hybrids—what does she expect?

However, the truth is that my sister would disapprove of the darkness my mates bring out of *me*. They feed my deepest desires, ones I've hidden out of shame.

Because it feels like there's something wrong with me.

"There's nothing wrong with you, baby girl," Zyran says against my ear.

I realize he's stopped feeding on me, and either he's developed the ability to read my thoughts, or I said those words aloud.

My legs shake when he kisses me, my blood a powerful flavor on his tongue. "You're *perfect*," he insists against my mouth.

I love that he praises me, that he doesn't judge me or make me feel ashamed. When my hands go to his waistband, he stops me.

"No, not here." He grins as he gives me another leisurely kiss. "I won't have anyone seeing you naked on this rooftop. You are *mine*."

The possession in his tone makes my blood rush to my sex, and I gladly allow him to guide me back into his town house and to his bedroom.

He doesn't give me time to process the oversized bed that would more than fit him and his brothers—*spirits, am I already considering sleeping with all three of them simultaneously?*

Zy perches me on the end, then peels away his shirt.

My mouth salivates at all the hard *man* before me. Then he leans over me, and I think he's going to take me.

But he doesn't. He's reaching for something in the dresser and pulls out a small blade.

Surprised by the glint of silver, I stare at it as he drags it across his arm.

"I'm good at sharing," he reminds me when I blink up at him with confusion. "You're going to drink my blood, just like I drink yours."

"I'm not a vampire," I protest, but my gaze has gone back to the red painting his muscular forearm.

Why does that make me... hungry?

"You don't need to be," he says. "If I've learned anything from witches, it's that my death magic exists in my blood and you can absorb it by drinking it."

Jealousy curls into an ugly knot in my stomach. "Other... witches?"

"Yes," he says without shame, even though I feel like he should at least be remorseful to admit to prior lovers.

Not that it's a secret, but he doesn't have to flaunt it. Especially when I was as good as a virgin before I met his brother.

Then again, maybe I should be the one feeling guilty. I slept with his brother first, after all.

"I never allowed a witch to feed on me, not willingly, anyway," he elaborates. "It's happened, though. A witch tasted my blood and I learned how my magic is inside of it. If you want my apology, you have it, my mate," he says, his voice changing to a softer tone. He drags the blade over the wound again, reopening it. "I will give you all my blood if it'll pacify the rage I see in your gaze. But trust me when I say now that I have found you, everything I have is yours. My body is yours. My *blood* is yours." He offers me his arm that's now dripping with such rare immortal blood I could probably buy a mansion with just a few drops. "All of it, my little witch. Every last drop."

My mind swims with desire as I give in and run my tongue along his cut.

He shivers, then groans when I use my teeth.

A strange need arises in me, one that wants to *bite*.

"Fuck," he groans again when I lock my jaw onto his wrist and mimic the pulling sensation he'd done on me.

Blood fills my mouth, causing my senses to fizzle into madness.

Black spots sprinkle over my vision, making me dizzy, and all sense of self melts into aching need. I'm yanking on his pants, snarling, going mad.

I want to bite, fuck, *devour*.

"Issy, *Issy,* slow down," he says, but I don't listen. I need him inside me *right now*.

"Mine," I snarl as I use his blade to cut away his pants. It leaves marks on him, but that only encourages my growing madness.

A distant part of me warns of what's happening. It shouldn't be possible, but Zyran's blood has sent me into a frenzy.

The kind vampires get.

Even with that little voice reminding me—I don't *care*.

I straddle him as I yank my underwear aside, not having time to wriggle out of them. I line him up with my entrance and then sink down, releasing a breath when he's sheathed in me.

He groans and seems trapped by indecision. I've clearly been affected by his blood, but the fate bond must be riding him too hard for him to comment on it.

He opens his mouth as if to say something, but I wriggle some more on him, making him dig his fingers into my skin.

He hasn't gone in all the way. He doesn't fit, but I'm determined.

He makes a pained sound when I start to roll and move, working my body to accept him.

Pleasure spikes with the intensity of his size. I don't have experience with this and my body is still sore from Jasper, but I can't feel any of that as I chase my goal.

Mine, my mind chants.

He promised me his body. He promised me his blood.

But this desire? It'll demand his fucking soul.

Chapter 27

Kornelius

I haven't gotten much sleep in the past few days, especially after the vivid daydream Issy had shoved into my head.

It had taken me a moment to figure out that she was showing us all her past. It haunted me, but brought me closer to her all the same.

Fatigue has dragged me down, despite my best efforts to remain vigilant.

But I'm wide awake now.

Royce isn't the reason I've jolted straight up in my seat. My vantage point shows me exactly what Royce is up to, all from the comfort of my inconspicuous vehicle —not the overpriced hunk of metal Zyran drives around.

The wannabe patriarch fucked one of his pets during the night—or multiple ones, I wasn't sure, and he had a late start to the day. Now he's making rounds, talking to his contacts, likely trying to find Ishara Doyle.

I know exactly where she is. I also know exactly what she's feeling, and something's wrong.

Lust shoots through my body, but it isn't the lasting ache that first appeared when I laid eyes on my fated mate. It's the kind of violent lust that comes with a vampire's need.

I'm not sure what Zyran and the witch are up to, but they've shared more than just magic. Perhaps they've shared blood, too, which could prove dangerous.

We don't know what our combined hybrid powers will do to the death witch, much less one bound to us not only by fate but also by a spell from the death plane.

Daithi still intends to take Ishara as his mate, and he's already chosen Jasper as his vessel. All the more reason I'm okay with Jasper trailing after our father instead of spending more time with the witch.

Zyran has dark tastes, but I trust him.

Now, though, it seems Ishara is the one I need to worry about.

The telltale signs of death magic are tugging at a weight in the center of my chest. My powers gather it up, suctioning it until I explode.

In the case of a surge, such as a massacre, I'm drawn to the death site.

I don't understand why I feel the same sensations. Tingling zings over my chest and I rub my fingers into my sternum, trying to dispel it.

If I'm spirited out of my vehicle, I'll lose track of Royce.

My vision splinters with silver as death magic pulls at my center. My soul is thankfully linked to my flesh, so it won't yank me out, mostly because I've learned how to intertwine the two.

Yet, now I feel like I might be torn apart if I resist the magnetizing pull.

Closing my eyes, I allow it to happen.

My world transforms, swirling in power and magic as I'm sucked through time and space.

The distance I need to travel is short, and I find myself surrounded by familiar walls.

I've been in Zyran's bedroom before. His town house isn't a place I often frequent, but I've come to retrieve him more than once when needed.

Just like those times, I find him in his bed with a female. I never did understand why he had made sure the mattress was a triple king—not even something that could be regularly found. He only slept with one woman at a time, and given his vampiric tendencies, the sheets were a bitch to change. Or at least he'd complained about it more than once.

Now, I see that blood has soaked the bed and splashed onto the pillows and comforter, but it's not from the witch.

She's feeding on *him*.

"Ishara?" I ask, both stricken with shock and a fresh wave of desire that has me immediately rock hard.

She snarls as she looks up at me. Through her haze of lust, I notice her once silver eyes are now red.

Not good.

"Zyran. Get away from her," I order.

Whatever blood- or magic-sharing is going on needs to stop until we understand what's happening.

"Fuck," he grounds out when Ishara rolls her hips, sending him deeper inside of her. She claws her nails down

287

his chest, leaving faint red lines. "I'm not going anywhere," he pants. "But she's clenching even harder around me now that you're here. I think... she wants you to fuck her, too."

I've never shared a female with Zy, but I can't deny the invitation in Ishara's red eyes. She seems accustomed to conveying what she wants with her expression.

And her full, parted lips and swollen breasts indicate only one thing on her mind. The sight threatens to obliterate all of my logical senses.

She wants me to join her.

She wants *blood*.

Something's not right.

I don't know how it's possible, but Ishara seems to have entered into a state of bloodlust. Something I know my brothers are prone to, but somehow, she's channeling what Zy should be experiencing.

Ishara leans back, riding my brother as her dress inches up her thighs, giving me a gorgeous view.

I want to be the one inside of her. I *need* to be the one stretching her open.

There's a small, logical part of my brain shouting somewhere in the back of my mind, warning me that something is terribly wrong.

My power only transports me to the site of a massacre. It requires the transfer of five hundred souls for me to portal somewhere.

Maybe that works differently with my fated mate. She's clearly manipulating death magic in a new way, and she needs me.

She *called* me.

But to yank me through time and space when it normally takes untold death? That should frighten me.

Instead of keeping my distance, I'm doing the opposite. My knee makes the edge of the mattress dip as I undo the buttons on my shirt. I suddenly find my clothes far too restrictive to tolerate.

Ishara continues to roll her hips on my brother, drawing out her pleasure in a way that has my instincts snarling.

The truth of it is, I've been lying to myself.

I'm just as prone to bloodlust as my brothers, perhaps more so because I deny myself pleasure.

The pleasure of blood, and the pleasure of a supple female in my bed.

Today, though, Ishara Doyle is breaking all my walls. She's shattering them with her power, her gaze, and her call.

Mine, her gaze tells me, and I am done.

My own possessive need rakes through me as I kiss her for the first time.

Fuck.

She tastes even better than I could have imagined. Blood lingers on her tongue and I ignore my brother's vampiric tones in favor of her floral, decadent taste that hints underneath.

They've been blood-sharing for sure, which gives me a prelude to the meal.

"Bite me," she says against my mouth.

My desire for her has a secure lock on my soul, not allowing me to reject the delicious offer.

She tilts her head to the side, showing her neck that still has Zyran's handiwork.

I want to add *my* claim. I want to leave *my* mark.

Choosing a spot closer to the vein, I delicately break the skin. She moans in response as if the act is pleasurable.

Maybe it is. Maybe nothing is how it usually would be when it comes to my mate.

You're perfect, I think when her blood hits my system.

It's as if she was made for us. Her power is in her blood and I understand what has happened now.

Fate has tied us all together, but so has other forms of magic. My brothers and I were formed by an ancient power, one we don't fully understand but we know lies in the death plane.

Ishara is a witch with a direct link to it. While all Outcast Coven witches have that power in some capacity, it's nothing like this.

"Kornelius," she whispers, and even though my name was said softly, *reverently,* the power behind her voice hits me straight in my core.

My cock throbs and I'm desperate for her, but she's not done with Zy yet.

"Knew I should have made the safe word," he hisses, then growls when Ishara rolls her hips again.

I'm not sure what he's talking about, but I'm glad they've already established such precautions.

I suspect it'll be needed.

"Harder," she demands, and I realize she's talking to me.

Talking to both of us.

Zyran pulls us down so that he can bite Ishara's neck on the other side. She groans when he latches on.

Then we're drinking from her together.

I shouldn't indulge, but I can't help it. A red haze overtakes my vision as I lock my jaw and *feed*.

She cries out and the sound goes straight to my cock. I can only imagine what she's doing to Zy, because he thrusts into her and growls.

I know she's coming and she's taking Zy with her. It makes me angry because I want her climax. I want her clenching around me.

Violent possession makes me bite harder and something shreds underneath my teeth.

Then there's blood everywhere, screams, and a sense of wrongness that only worsens when Ishara stiffens against us.

Zyran snarls, giving in to the bloodlust just like I am. He's not shredding into her, though. He's exchanging violence for sex, continuing to drive into her with rough, deep thrusts even though he already reached his climax.

Both of us show no signs of stopping, but magic snaps through the air when our witch cries out a name.

"F-Fallon!"

Magic hits me, but I don't stop.

"Fallon!" she cries again, this time the word weaker.

Zyran growls as he fucks her, grabbing her hips as he amps up for another round. A violent one I'm eager to join.

Then Issy screams, her magic hitting us hard before she goes limp.

I gasp when my heart beats for the first time in my life, sending agony through my limbs.

It's only one and then it's over, but it's enough to break the hold bloodlust has on me.

Zyran and I immediately freeze as our mate sags between us, slipping into unconsciousness while her blood freely seeps down onto the bed.

Zy blinks and wipes the blood away from his chin and assesses the damage to our mate.

His side isn't so bad, but mine goes straight down to the bone...

My stomach churns with her blood, and nausea strangles me like a noose.

Fuck. What have I done?

Chapter 28

Issy

Pain consumes me as I struggle to open my eyes.

I can't seem to do it. Everything *hurts*.

"We need to call that witch, Amala," Kor's voice says.

"How? She's in hiding, remember? We need to call her sister," Zy responds.

They're talking about me.

My spirit seems weightless as the room comes into view, but I'm not using my eyes to see it.

I'm dying, I realize.

It should frighten me, but it doesn't. Death is more peaceful than I would have imagined.

Restful.

"Her heart is slowing," Zy says, his voice dropping with concern. "Issy!" he says, gently placing a hand over my heart. "Can you hear me? Please. *Please* don't leave us. We're so sorry."

Sorry?

For killing me...

My spirit lowers to the ground, setting my feet on the

floorboards as I stare at Kornelius and Zyran leaning over my body.

I look so fucking pale and weak.

"You don't deserve for me to stay," I snarl. My words come out garbled and strange, as if spoken with ethereal magic instead of the vibrations of a biological body.

They both jolt and whirl on me.

My body is there, but my spirit isn't inside of it right now. I feel the tether to my heart that rests underneath Zy's heavy hand.

Kornelius seems resigned. "We don't," he says.

The hurt in his gaze makes me flinch, but I won't fall for his puppy eyes.

Flashes of what happened roll through my head.

They were biting me.

They were killing me.

And when I said the safe word... they didn't *stop*.

"Why?" I ask. My eyes burn as if tears want to form, but my spirit can't produce them.

Zy hangs his head and stares at my body, which is going ghastly pale.

Kornelius is the one to answer. "We're vampires, Issy. There is no reasoning to explain what we did. There is no apology that could make up for it." His jaw flexes. "Although, if you choose to stay, I'll do everything I can to make it up to you, or spend the rest of my life trying."

"Me, too," Zy says without looking up. The agony in his voice makes me want to give in.

But then I look back down at my body. Blood has soaked through the fresh bandage.

They did this to me.

Ishara? a voice asks in my head. *Are you coming?*

I don't recognize the voice, but apparently Kornelius and Zyran can hear it, because both of them snap up their gazes to look at me.

Who are you? I ask.

I'm... it's not important who I am. The real question is, you're dead, but you don't want to be, do you? I can help with that.

I sense that the voice on the other end is coming from the death plane. A rush of ice slips up my spine as she talks and a growing sensation of pressure spreads through the left side of my chest.

In response, Zy flinches away as if my skin has burned him.

A bloody, circular mark appears on my chest just over my heart.

"What the fuck?" Zy says under his breath. He glances at me. "Don't listen to whatever is calling you, Issy. Stay here. I *beg* of you."

The voice on the other end must be a spirit, perhaps an ancient one. She's offering me a chance to restore my life.

If I stay here, I get to watch my body die with the mates who killed me.

No, thanks.

"Goodbye, Zyran. Goodbye, Kornelius," I say with finality.

Both of them stare at me as I watch their hearts break.

My only regret is leaving Jasper. He's done nothing but protect me. For his sake, I plan on returning.

But his brothers deserve this pain. They deserve to

watch me go and wonder if it's the last time they'll see me.

But when I really think about why this happened, I question whether there's more to it.

If there's a reason I should forgive them.

Because if there is, I will certainly return.

If there's not... they can wallow in their guilt for eternity.

Chapter 29

Jasper

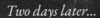

Two days later...

"I s someone going to tell me how the fuck this happened?" I growl.

If the two males before me weren't my brothers, they would be dead.

Or at least barely kept alive so I could flay them over and over again until they begged for an end.

While I had been trailing Zane for the past two days thinking Issy was safe, she had actually almost died.

And no one had fucking told me.

It bothers me that I hadn't sensed it, either. We're a bonded pair. I should have felt her brush with death, but I hadn't.

Some theories come to mind, but I'm in no mood to entertain them.

She almost died!

My vision threatens to go red again, but I sober myself by looking at my mate, who is still alive, in the center of Zy's massive bed. She still needs me to be here for her.

She looks so small and fragile. Her blonde hair wilts around her like the fallen petals of a rose left out in the sun too long. Her skin is abnormally pale and a winding bandage hides the majority of her neck and collarbone from me.

I've seen vampire feedings gone wrong. I don't have to see underneath the gauze to know she's lucky to have survived.

Kor's sulking by the window while Zy takes a swig directly from a whiskey bottle.

There are several empty ones around him. It might be difficult for a vampire to get drunk, but Zy seems determined to try.

"I thought it was the fate bond doing it," Kor says quietly, still looking out the window. "But I was wrong."

"Doing what?" I snarl. "Making you two lose your fucking minds?" I take a step forward as I clench my fists. "Tell me who did this."

I know it wasn't Zane. I had been following him without fail. He'd been underground for the most part, sending out lackeys to attempt to find Issy, but he himself hadn't gone anywhere interesting.

It couldn't have been Royce unless he had suddenly turned into a vampire and I didn't know it. This was clearly a vampire-related injury.

Zy doesn't answer me. Instead, he takes a long swig of his bottle.

Kor remains calm as he peers out the window, seemingly fascinated with the view.

That tells me all I need to know.

My eyes widen as rage threatens to force my unbeating heart to stutter. "One of *you* did this?"

It's bad enough that I thought they'd *allowed* this to happen.

But that one of them nearly killed our mate?

Murderous intent rolls through me when Kor finally turns around. "It was me."

He was ready for my response. I flashed across the room, fangs bared, and went for his neck.

He caught me with his arm and my jaw locked around it until bone snapped underneath my bite.

He didn't even flinch.

"You have every right to destroy me, brother. Trust me. I want to do the same to myself, but that won't help Ishara." He glances at her. He *dares* to look at her. "She woke briefly after it happened. She almost died, but an ancient spirit called her to the death plane and it's preserving her body. It must want her power for itself— and it's not a patriarch."

Unlatching my jaw from his arm, I snarl as blood drizzles from my mouth. "Already trying to make excuses for losing control, *brother*?" I use the term loosely. As far as I'm concerned, my brothers died a long time ago.

After this? They can stay dead.

"I told you he'd need proof," Zyran says. "Shall I show him?"

Kor glances at me and must see my resolve to rip his throat out, because he agrees. "Very well. Go ahead."

Zyran gets up and approaches Ishara. I'm on him in an instant.

"Neither of you gets to touch her again. *Ever*," I grate out. And I fucking mean it.

Zyran backs off, which is probably a wise move if he likes his head attached to his body.

"It's on her chest just over her heart," he explains. He nods to the unconscious witch when I don't move. "See for yourself."

I frown, but curiosity wins out over my anger and I approach Issy's still form.

Her chest rises and falls in a slight pattern. One too frail for my liking, but the sheet is pulled up to her shoulder. I tug it down, only to find more bandages in place.

"Did you go for the heart?" I growl, fresh rage building inside of me.

"No, Issy's magic stopped me the moment I went too far," Kornelius insists. "We covered it up. I'd remove the bandage, but you seem like you might rip my arm off if I get near her."

Damn straight.

Ignoring my brother, I gently peel away the layers of the bandage until angry, bruised flesh is exposed to the air. A growl rumbles in my throat.

Because I want to kill whoever harmed my mate.

I want to rip out his entrails and ring it around his neck, choking him until the last thing he sees is the heart I've ripped from his chest before death takes over.

Too bad the person on the other end of that would be Kornelius in this case.

And Zyran next, because he looks just as fucking guilty.

But once I see past the bruises, I notice a very circular

mark, one that doesn't line up with vampire bites or scratches.

No, there's a pattern. One that forms a witch's symbol.

"What is this?" I snap. I'm not experienced enough with witchcraft to know exactly what sort of symbol I'm looking at—but I know a curse when I see one.

"The ancient spirit," Zyran supplies. He places his bottle down as he stands.

He wisely doesn't approach, but he does lean over to look at the mark.

"It's angrier," he says with a frown.

That doesn't sound good.

The mark isn't quite bleeding, but the skin is raised and discolored. Ishara's marble skin is now deathly pale, and I realize it's not just because of blood loss.

It's because of whatever this curse is doing to her.

I run my fingers over it, instinct wanting to help my mate.

My power is through touch, but even my magic doesn't seem to penetrate whatever barrier has been put in place.

"What do we do?" I ask. "Can we use the death stone to talk to this spirit? Why the fuck would it do this to her?"

"We let her fight this battle," Kornelius says with a sense of resignation. "The death stone is still lost. I did not lie about that, and as for why an ancient spirit has given her a death curse... I can't answer. Not without more information."

"Then *get* more information," I demand.

Zyran rakes his fingers through his hair. He's wearing his sunglasses, but even I can tell he hasn't slept at all based on the slump of his shoulders. "Kornelius knows a lot more about the death plane than most witches. If he says we have to let Ishara handle this one on her own, then all we can do is wait."

So, that's what they've been doing.

Waiting with their thumbs up their asses.

I realize now why Kornelius is so calm. It's not just the guilt of his actions, but it's also how he handles stress. It's got to be eating him alive to know that something is after our mate and the only thing we can do is rely on her to save herself while we *wait*.

"What the fuck use are we if we just sit around and do nothing?" I snarl.

I don't care how *informed* Kornelius might be.

This isn't how fated mates are supposed to work together. They bring out each other's strengths. They *help* one another.

Fate didn't introduce me to Ishara Doyle just so I could watch her die.

Ignoring my brothers, I rake my fang through my palm, then place my hand directly on the curse brand on my mate's chest.

Nothing happens at first, but after a moment, my hand begins to *burn*.

This began with blood. We'll end it with blood.

I glower at my brothers, who are just staring at me. "Well, are you going to gawk like idiots, or are you going to help?"

Chapter 30

Issy

A few minutes earlier...

W*hat a strange library.*

I feel like I've been wandering the same section of this massive library for ages. It's the largest collection of knowledge I've ever seen in all original texts and languages—and that's saying something.

Although, I can't remember how I got here. Or when I arrived... or *where* this is at all.

Oh, look! A Sarcee dialect original spell book!

My excitement over a rare find takes over as I gently grasp the ancient tome and scamper back to my ever-growing pile on the desk.

A desk in the middle of an enormous room.

An empty space that should be thriving with witches, students, and scholars.

Except, it's just me.

Or it was until a few moments ago. There's a woman

between the dark arts section and the herbal remedies who's staring at me.

She's tall—but not intimidating. Her soft silver hair that cascades down to her waist gives her an elegant look only accentuated by the smile she offers me.

I nod in response when she approaches. Her light blue eyes glitter with intrigue as her gaze dips to my mountain of books.

"I see you've been enjoying my library," she says as she trails her fingers over one of the stacks. "Can you really read so many languages? You have at least eight different ones that I can see." Her brow rises when she sees the book I just retrieved. "Make that nine. Is that the Tsuut'ina spell book? I've yet to find a spirit to translate it for me."

A "spirit"? What an odd choice of words.

I point to my mouth and shake my head, indicating to her that I'm mute.

Well, I *can* speak. She just wouldn't live long enough to hear anything I have to say.

She chuckles. "Oh, the death speech? Don't worry about that. It can't hurt me here."

Frowning, I remember that I still don't know where *here* is, exactly.

A sharp pain radiates across my chest, ripping a sound from my throat as I double over onto the table. The spell book I had been holding tumbles to the ground, breaking its spine in the process.

"No, stop!" the woman shouts, and at first I think she's upset that I damaged a rare book.

But she's looking at my chest right where it burns. Not at the collection of pages on the floor.

Peeling my hand away, it comes back wet with blood. But it's not *my* blood. I don't have a cut to explain it, so I dumbly stare at the substance while the room begins to tremble.

The woman growls. "Those damn mates of yours. They're going to kill the both of us at this rate. Don't they know that the women are talking?"

I glance up at her, blinking, and *see* her for the first time. Magic bleeds from her as if she doesn't know how to contain it. She leans onto the desk and the wood transforms under her touch. What had once been dark oak now glimmers with silver, then gold.

My eyes widen.

I've only read about manifestation spirits. They are more myth than reality—even in our world of supernaturals. "You're a mani-spirit," I breathe, stunned.

She rolls her gorgeous eyes. "I hate that term. It sounds like I'm about to get a mani-pedi. I prefer to go by my name. Which is Jewel, by the way."

I smile, instantly liking her.

Even though I shouldn't like her. I should run in terror because this spirit is probably why I'm trapped in a spelled library.

In the death plane.

The atmosphere makes sense, as does the sensation that I'm not quite grounded in reality. The patriarchs tried to perform this exact same holding tactic on me when I had been placed in a magically induced coma.

Only, the books I'd read hadn't had anything written

on them. Jewel conjured an entire library for me to explore. Although, it sounds like she had conjured it long before I came along.

Because she's been here for a while?

Another stab of pain makes me hiss and I realize that my mates are pulling me back to my body.

Jasper. Zyran.

Kornelius.

My mouth goes dry when I remember what Kornelius had almost done to me.

"I came here to get away from them," I recall, but I was enraged by what had happened.

I didn't stop to really think why it had happened.

"Do you have something to do with this?"

Jewel shrugs. "Maybe, possibly? I don't know. My magic isn't something I can control too well, but I will say you're someone I've been waiting for, and for a very long time, mind you." She clicks her tongue. "Your men are just going to have to wait," Jewel says as she holds my hand in hers. I immediately feel more grounded and the tug on my chest eases. "First off, I'm sorry for cursing you. I thought you were working with that asshole, Daithi, and I was just going to steal your power. But after watching you for a couple of days, all you've been doing is reading books and working on spells to break his hold on you. You're not *bad*. You actually know what you're doing, too."

She smiles, the gesture infectious and disarming.

Are all manifestation spirits this charming?

"Maybe you'll be able to help me," she adds with a

wrinkle of her cute nose. "And I won't have to kill you. For real, anyway."

Comforting.

I'm not sure what help I could offer a spirit in the death plane. I also don't recall working on spells, but then I realize there is an open journal with my handwriting in it.

A quick skim reveals spells in multiple languages that I don't remember writing. But they're all related to fate magic.

Parts of it are things I learned from Ayla, who had worked with the rogue witch, Amala.

Other bits are new.

I pick up the journal and read over it. *This could work,* I think.

The female loops her arm through mine and sighs at the words on the page. "You really are brilliant. I've been wandering around for a while now, collecting scattered knowledge left over by other witches in this plane. But I can't interpret it like you can, even though I used to be a witch before the manifestation power took over."

I blink at her. "How long is a *while*?" I know that technically a manifestation spirit can create pretty much anything given an applicable medium to work with. Their power comes from a great sense of need or an inciting event of incredible willpower that fuels the rare magic.

A manifestation spirit can do almost anything, create whatever they can imagine.

But an entire library?

It must have taken her ages.

She shrugs, her warmth strangely comforting against my spirit form. I'm not quite corporeal here, but the curse she put on me is keeping me in place and allowing me to interact with her creation. "Weeks? Months? I'm not sure, to be honest. I feel like it's been much longer than that, but I was recently freed from some sort of siphon state. I walked out of a grave and there was a broken headstone." She shivers as if it's an unpleasant memory. "I tried to leave, but I still seem to be stuck here."

"But you're not dead," I observe. She's a spirit, yes, but that's her natural state.

Her skin is warm.

Her flesh is real.

Everything about her is alive—she's just trapped here, like she claims.

And it's her observation of a "siphon state" that tells me all I need to know.

My fists clench when I realize that she is yet another victim of the patriarchs. They've been in power for ages and there's no telling how many women they've bound and used for their own selfish purposes.

"The patriarchs trapped you and were using your magic," I observe. If she was still alive when she had been pulled into the death plane, it could have been the incident that transformed her into the mythological species.

She shrugs again. "Yeah, that's what the other spirits told me. It seems to be a common problem around here. At least, until all the headstones broke. Now the patriarchs are coming up with new tricks."

"They're not the only ones," I lament. "Apparently, my mates' father, Zane, is trying to control power, too.

314

I'm not sure how he's involved, but he poses a danger just as much as the patriarchs do."

I saw the fear hidden in Jasper's eyes when he mentioned his father. I wasn't going to forget that threat.

The walls tremble and my gaze shoots up. Shadows filter over the reflective windows and my heart kicks in my chest.

"The patriarchs are here," I realize aloud.

Of course they are.

Daithi is here. I can sense his magic and his disgusting lust. He wants me.

He wants my power, just like everyone else.

And if he gets into this library, I won't be able to stop him.

Jewel curses and runs to the shelves. She pushes the books into a pile on the floor and places her hands on them.

They begin to melt, then change into raw energy.

"I thought they were after me, but they're really after you," she tells me, her eyes glowing with manifestation power. It's *incredible* and unlike anything I've ever seen. "Let your mates bring you back. I'll buy you time."

"But what about you?" I ask.

She shakes her head. "I'm trapped here until the bloodline who bound me is destroyed. Not just dead, but their magic gone forever. I... I don't know why I can't just dismantle his spirit. My powers don't always work as they should, especially on men."

Don't I know it.

"I can relate," I grumble. Although, I've made progress on that front.

Maybe my lessons are something Jewel can learn to move past whatever block she has. Manifestation spirits are powerful, but the magic can be finicky because it's based on belief.

If she doesn't believe in herself, she might fail. And the one thing that can't be manifested is courage.

Courage has to be learned.

Something I'm very well acquainted with as well.

Jewel sends some of the energy into me and the pain in my chest lifts. My mates have already dismantled part of the curse through the power in their blood, but Jewel finishes the job.

Then she readies the rest of the glowing energy to fortify the library walls. "Go," she tells me.

My vision wavers and my spirit shimmers.

"I'll find a way to end him," I promise her. It was already my goal, but now I have a new drive to make sure he's gone. Not just for me, but for all the women he threatens.

It won't end with me.

The power glittering in Jewel's eyes hides the hint of sadness. She doesn't believe me. "I hope you do," she says.

She makes a flourish with her fingers, then a new symbol appears on my wrist. "It'll protect you and link us together," she says by way of explanation.

And then my world goes black.

Chapter 31

Issy

I wake to the sensation of being watched.

And mind-blowing pain radiating down the left side of my neck and shoulder.

Ow...

My eyelids are so heavy that lifting them proves a challenge. I manage it after a few attempts, only to find Jasper's beautiful face taking up my view.

It's a very welcome sight after being trapped in the death plane.

"You're alive, little witchling," he says as if that alone is worthy of praise.

And it is, really. The way I feel suggests I have been dancing with death.

Or hanging out with it in a library.

I look down and realize that Jasper's hand is lightly pressing on my chest, which is why I'm not hearing the screams.

But there is blood everywhere.

"What's... going on?" I ask, my voice coming out

tired and scratchy.

"We almost lost you," Zyran says from somewhere behind Jasper. "Again."

Peering around Jas's massive shoulder, I find the brown-haired vampire adjusting his glasses. He resumes cleaning a cut on his hand with a handkerchief.

We've already established that his death sight doesn't harm me, but I'm not sure how it works with his brothers. I'd imagine they'd be immune to each other, or at least be able to channel each other's death magic.

Which leads me to the conclusion that Zy is hiding behind his glasses. The urge to rip them off takes over again as I remember what we'd been doing before...

Before Kornelius.

"You mean you and Kor almost *killed* her," Jasper snarls over his shoulder, confirming the gruesome memory.

I know my third mate is in the room. Even if I can't see him, I can sense him.

Meaning that a bond has already formed between us just like it had with Jasper before we finalized fate's choice.

I'm learning that the fate bonds transcend the standard links normally severed by death.

When my mates are necromancy-vampire hybrids and I'm forever linked to the death plane, that changes things. It changes the *rules.*

"I want to see Kor," I demand. My voice is coming back stronger now, although the ache along my neck and shoulder still blooms with blinding pain.

Jewel had something to do with what happened,

meaning Kornelius and Zyran might actually be innocent in all this.

My rage is justified, but perhaps misplaced.

"No," Jasper says, the word nonnegotiable. "Kornelius was just leaving. Weren't you?" he asks over his other shoulder, where I presume Kornelius is standing.

"You're not listening to me," I say, keeping my voice low and steady. "I said—" My words are cut off by incredible pain as I lean forward to sit up, rendering me speechless. Deciding to relax back onto the pillow, I hiss at the overpowering sensation as dark spots filter over my vision.

The sound of wood cracks and Jasper moves over me as if to help, but it allows me to see Kornelius, who is just a few feet away.

He's gripping the wooden frame so hard it's splintering underneath his fingers. His gaze is locked somewhere outside as he remains unnaturally still in a way only a death vampire like him can do.

"Do you remember what he did to you?" Jasper snarls in my ear. His hand continues to press on my chest and the places where his skin touches mine feed me his magic.

It eases the pain and I allow it to seep through me like the invading force it is.

Overpowering. Masculine. *Angry.*

He's not angry at me, but his rage is palpable. I'm honestly not sure why Kornelius is still in one piece with the amount of hatred stemming from Jasper's unbeating heart.

Jasper begins to tremble, his need to protect me making him cage me in with his arms as if he wishes to be my shield. "He fed on you, Issy. He ripped into you like a piece of fucking meat. The only reason he's still alive is because killing him might hurt you more, and I will do every fucking thing in my power to protect you—even if it means sparing his worthless life."

Kor's gaze flicks from the window, allowing me to see amber orbs of his reckless emotion.

He seems the type to always be calm and collected, which is why what he did was so out of character.

Or maybe it was inevitable. He can pretend to be in control—but no vampire exists without living with the risk of bloodlust.

I've never had to experience bloodlust, but after sharing it with my mates, I realize how similar we are. We are creatures of death. We live in darkness, no matter how much we seek out the light.

Adding a manifestation spirit's curse into the mix is a recipe for disaster.

"I'm glad you spared his life," I tell Jasper honestly, matching his gaze with my own. "Because he's my mate and I would not have forgiven you had you taken him away from me."

I might not have even survived it. As I'm coming to learn, our bonds transcend this plane. Whereas most deal with insanity when they lose their fated mate, I think my bonds would take it much further than simply breaking me.

If one of my mates moved into the afterlife, I would likely follow him or be torn apart while trying to. I don't expect my vampires would go to the death plane. That is a place for witches.

They would go someplace else, somewhere darker.

And we'd never again see the light we so desperately seek.

Jasper's dark eyes widen. "Do you not remember?" he asks again.

"I remember," I immediately counter. "And I will talk to Kornelius and Zy about that, but for now, there's something more pressing to address. I met a spirit in the death plane and she changes everything."

"Is that so?" Zyran asks with a curious tone.

"It changes nothing," Jasper snarls, making my skin prickle with irritation. "It changes nothing. He hurt you, Issy. You're not safe here. Don't you hear what I'm telling you? We need to *leave*."

Fury rises in me. "Leave?" I snap, unable to move underneath his body, which is more of a cage now than a shield. His hips pin mine, and despite my anger, arousal lingers beneath the surface of my rage.

Because he's my mate; he's the first of the three. No matter what happens, I will always want him.

But it doesn't mean I can't be pissed off when he's not listening to me.

"And go where?" I continue, grazing my nose against his. I realize that more skin contact is easing the blinding pain across my side, giving me the strength to oppose him. "The Houses want me dead. The syndicates will, too, if they learn I'm here. Don't even get me started on the enemies lurking in the Outcast Coven."

"Like Royce," he snarls. "We don't even know where he is because Kornelius was supposed to be tracking him. I've been following Zane—our father, who also wants to rip into you—and I only came back when I was sure he was down for a few days. This is the time to move, Issy. This is—"

"No," I say. The word is a whisper, but my magic is behind it, making Jasper and the other vampires in the room flinch. "Overriding me when I'm trying to talk is a good way to get on my bad side, Jas. Now, are you going to listen, or are you going to be an asshole?"

He frowns at me but finally backs off.

The cold that seeps in to fill the void between our bodies makes me shiver, but I ignore it.

They need to know my plan.

Still, I slip my fingers through his, needing his touch. It's not only because I need him, but also because it is giving me strength.

"I'm going to contact my sister and convince Amala to come to us early. She's going to heal me, and then we're going to face our problems instead of hiding from them."

"Problems like Royce and Zane?" Zy asks.

I can't nod, so I purse my lips. "Yes, and when they're gone, Daithi will be next."

"How will we manage that?" Jasper asks, now from his position at the end of the bed, still close enough to keep hold of my hand. I haven't told him that his touch helps me, but he seems to already sense it.

He's still between me and Kornelius, but at least he's not towering over me. "If it were as easy as killing them, I would have delivered their heads to you on a platter, witchling. We need Zane for his phasing ability. That's how Kornelius was able to kill five hundred people at once—by phasing bombs into them without them even being aware of it."

"That's changed," Zy says. "Issy was able to activate Kor's teleporting ability without death. We don't need him anymore for our plan to go after Daithi to work."

Jasper raises a brow, but a new look has entered his gaze.

Violence. He's eager to kill, and I am happy to offer him the death his violence demands.

He just has to agree to my plan.

"And Royce?" he hedges, talking to Zy now. "I assume he's been kept alive for a reason."

Zy looks at Kornelius, but he hasn't said a word this entire time and doesn't look like he's going to start now. "Royce isn't alone," Zy finally says. "He has many warlocks working behind him, trying to resurrect the patriarchs. Cutting off the head of a hydra doesn't kill it. That just pisses it off."

Jasper's gaze moves to mine. "If we're killing Daithi, then that's the heart of the hydra, isn't it? Royce can still die."

"Yes," Zy finally agrees. "If we can eliminate Daithi and the threat of the patriarchs coming back, it'll eliminate any chance of rebounding on us if Royce is gone."

A devious grin spreads over Jasper's face. "Then tell me how this plan of yours works, little witchling. I'm all ears."

I grin, too, because I quite like my idea. It'll give me a chance to finally face my nightmares instead of running from them.

I'm done running.

"We're going to set a trap—one where I'm the bait."

Chapter 32

Kornelius

I watch with a sense of envy as Jasper carefully adjusts Issy on his lap. He uses his shoulder to prop her head up as she winces with every movement, but it seems that his death touch is ironically helping her heal, at least a little bit. It'll have to do until Amala can come and finish the job.

They're both naked minus a bra and panties for her and boxers for Jasper. The deathly pallor has left her skin, returning her to a goddess made of marble.

Every curve begs for kisses and entices me to draw closer, but Jasper is the only one allowed to touch her right now.

That's not exactly what I'm envious of, though. It's the fact that he was able to not only wake her up after she had left us, but also relieve some of her pain.

All I can offer is my regret, which isn't worth much.

She's still horribly injured and two days haven't been enough to promote the kind of healing she needs. My presence has done nothing other than allow my guilt to fester.

Not after what I did to her.

My stomach churns again, something it's been doing constantly for the last forty-eight hours, making me uneasy.

I almost killed her.

This is all my fault.

"It's a sound plan," Zy says, joining in on the conversation that's been going on while Jasper helps Issy heal.

"It's a plan that we're not pursuing," Jasper immediately replies.

Issy has enough strength now to roll her eyes. "I'm sorry. Have I missed the part in the past hour where you had a better one?"

His jaw flexes as he continues to roll his thumb over her knuckles. It's not until she flips her wrist to tickle his fingers that I realize there's a new mark on her arm.

And I've only seen it one place before.

Zyran notices it, too. He immediately straightens and adjusts his glasses. "Where did that come from?" he asks.

Issy looks down at her wrist while Jasper helps her lift it to examine the mark more closely. "Oh, right. The spirit I was talking about gave it to me to connect us."

Jasper frowns. "I don't like that. We can't trust some random spirit you met in the death plane. Especially one powerful enough to stand up against the patriarchs. We could just be trading one enemy for an even worse one."

"We can trust this spirit," I say. It's the first time I've spoken since Issy woke up, but it's also the first time I felt like I had something of value to say.

An apology wouldn't mean anything, and neither would my regret.

But this... this is something that changes things.

Jasper raises a brow. "And why do you suddenly trust this spirit? So far, all we've learned in the past hour is that a witch was trapped by the patriarchs, just like they have been for Gods know how long, and something changed her into a manifestation spirit. Which are unpredictable and dangerous, by the sounds of it."

He wasn't wrong about any of that, but this spirit could most definitely be trusted.

"Show him," I say while still looking at Jasper. He reminds me of a predator, and if I look away, he will pounce and I'll be dead in a matter of seconds. Perhaps he's held off this long because he doesn't want to hurt our mate by risking what'll happen to her if I die, but instincts don't think things through like that.

Zy pulls the silver chain from beneath his shirt. It's the one he always wears and the symbol icon dangling from it is small, but it has a noticeable design.

One that matches the mark on Issy's wrist.

"This was our mother's," Zy explains. "One of her friends told me that she treated it like prayer beads. Although there was no goddess represented by this icon, she didn't care. She prayed to it anyway."

"A prayer that came true," I clarify. "That's how the three of us were born."

It wasn't a goddess.

It was a manifestation spirit that created us from our mother's plea.

There is no way it's a coincidence that this spirit

found a way to bring Issy to the death plane and marked her.

My mind spirals with all of the possibilities. Everything is connected.

Our mother. Our birth and our magic. Our fated mate.

And our destiny to destroy her enemies once and for all.

Issy wrinkles her nose. "Manifestation spirits aren't gods. They don't respond to prayers."

Jasper presses his lips against her hair as he seems to think. "Doesn't manifestation magic work through belief and willpower? Maybe our mother wanted us so desperately that she manifested the will on her own."

Issy purses her lips. "I suppose that's possible. It takes an incredible amount of magic and willpower for a supernatural to turn into a manifestation spirit. I'd never met one before, or even heard of one documented in history, but I have read ancient transcripts in dead languages about them. If your mother was on the cusp of becoming a manifestation spirit, she could have had enough of that magic to reach out to Jewel."

I presume that's the name of the spirit she met in the death plane. "Fate has been behind the scenes, driving events, but this puts everything in our court. Fate set the stage. Now it's time to execute the play."

Zy scoffs. "There are only two endings in the script. One where we kill all of our enemies."

"Or another where we fail, and we all die," Jasper adds darkly.

Issy blows out a breath. "I know which one has my vote." She winces when she tries to move.

Jasper shushes her and wraps his arms around her middle, securing him closer to her. "We'll talk more about this plan of yours, little witchling, but you can't save the world if you can't even move."

Her breath comes in sharp pants now and my guilt returns tenfold at seeing her in pain.

"Maybe... maybe if all of you touch me, I can heal faster. The death magic you have helps, but it's just taking the edge off."

Jasper glowers at Zy, then gives me a murderous look. "They're never touching you again, Issy. Not if I have a say in the matter."

"You don't," I counter, and not just because I want to touch Issy.

Fuck. I want to apologize with my tongue. I'll gladly go on my knees for hours, *days*, to show her how sorry I am.

But this is about getting her out of pain, and if my touch can do that, then I will push the matter.

"Kor's right," Zy says softly. "Issy is the only one who decides who can and can't touch her."

Jasper remains still, but he clearly doesn't like any of this. "Tell me what you want, sweetheart, and I'll give it to you."

Issy looks at Zy, then at me.

There's longing in her gaze, and fuck, I don't deserve it.

"I want you to leave me alone with them."

We all stiffen because that sounds like a terrible idea.

"My touch is helping you," Jasper wisely counters. "And I'm *protecting* you, sweetheart."

She slowly shakes her head from side to side. "No, Jas. You're possessing me, and if we're going to win against Daithi, we need to be able to work together. We need to be able to trust one another." She looks at me when she adds, "And they need to be able to trust themselves. If none of you have faith, let me have faith for you. Let me show you that we can move past this."

An unfamiliar sensation pinches my unbeating heart.

I'm not sure what it is at first, but my mate's words move me. None of us deserve a mate like this.

We've murdered. We've sinned. We've failed her.

Yet, she's enticing me again, believing in me even though I've obliterated any trust between us.

I hope she has an infinite amount of faith, because I certainly have none in myself.

"Jasper," she says as she lifts herself from Jasper's chest. I'm not sure where she's getting the strength. Her bandages are soaked through again, suggesting her wounds have reopened. "If there's any love for me in your soul, if you ever want this to be a partnership instead of a relationship designed by fate, then do as I say. Respect me enough to trust me."

Jasper looks like he's pinned between two choices. One of them is to snatch Issy away and never let us see her again.

The other is a dark shadow, one that will destroy him, because it requires leaving her in our care.

"If I'm going to do this, then I need something from all of you," Jasper says, his voice taut.

"Name it," I reply without hesitation. I'm eager to make amends in whatever form that might take.

"Make a soul promise. If you harm Issy again, I *will* kill you."

It's not a threat. It's simply his line. He won't be capable of restraint if this happens a second time.

I don't blame him. If I did hurt her again, I would beg him for death myself.

It's an easy choice to make. I prick my thumb with my fang until a droplet of blood swells. "Deal."

Zy does the same, and so does Jasper.

We all shake hands, mixing our blood together to bind the spell.

Then Jasper leaves the room, and I'm relieved to know that if I fail a second time, I won't have to worry whether I deserve to live.

Because my brother will make sure I don't take another breath.

Chapter 33

Issy

I'm once again alone with Zy and Kornelius, but neither of them approaches me after Jasper leaves the room. The screams slowly filter into my mind, but I allow the sorrow of the dead to mix with mine. Sometimes it feels less lonely to hear someone cry with me when I'm sad.

I can sense that Jasper remains just outside the door, but he's keeping his word. He's trusting me to prove a point.

The way Kornelius looks at me breaks my heart. I can't tell him that I empathize and that I forgive him for what he did.

I understand it.

He won't believe me. And if I've learned anything from my brief interaction with Jewel, it's how powerful belief can be.

For better or for worse, belief makes dreams—or nightmares—come true.

Despite all that, bloodlust is a nearly uncontrollable

state. The only reason Zy didn't rip me open was because he was already inside of me, taking out his need through sex. Not to mention the curse Jewel had put on me had probably set off my mates in the first place rather than any severe lack of control on their part.

Tasting Zy's blood had begun a process she'd put in place long ago, whether or not she realized it. I've read enough about how magic works to understand it could have been an unconscious move on her part.

My working theory was that Jewel wanted to be free of the death plane, so she had willed a path where that possibility could happen. By planting her will inside the blood of the triplets her magic had helped create, she had planted the seed to call me to her side to set her free.

And it had worked. The moment I'd tasted Zy's essence, bloodlust had hit me just as it would have a vampire.

And I'd enjoyed it until they'd gone too far.

Even uttering the safe word we had established hadn't done much good. It was my *magic* that stopped them.

I had kept it as a safe word, though. When I'd screamed my sister's name, I hadn't opened the mental channel to her. She was probably going crazy with worry, but I would talk to her soon.

Once my mates realize that they *can* control themselves, if given the tools.

"Come to me," I order them. Now that Jasper is gone, pain returns to my senses and I need death magic to battle it.

I'm also figuring that one out based on some of the journals Ayla has let me read. Amala is a death witch just like me. She's learned how to manipulate the spirit and the magic within it to heal the flesh.

It seems that I can do the same, but I need more practice.

More power.

Zy is the first to respond. He approaches the bed but doesn't climb onto it. My weakened state reflects in his glasses, making nausea wind through my stomach.

"Are you sure about this?" he asks.

"Very," I respond without hesitation. I know things they don't, but words won't convey the truth to them. I don't want to be weak anymore, and even if they don't see it, I know how to be strong.

But I can't simply tell them how this works. Only a few scholars can read words on a page and learn the world's secrets. Most have to experience truth for themselves to fully understand it.

"We almost killed you," Kornelius says. The emotion in his voice betrays how affected he is by all this. "I'll never forgive myself for what I did. You shouldn't either."

Zy nods in agreement. "I... I disrespected the safe word we established. Don't you know the punishment for that? Death."

I'm not sure who decided that rule. Perhaps it was a punishment that fit the crime, but this wasn't a black-and-white situation.

Sighing, I wince with the effort it takes to stay conscious. "Listen, if you two don't touch me right now, I'm going to pass out. So *help me.*"

That seems to force their hands. Zy's jaw flexes before

he climbs over the mattress and places his palm on my thigh. I relax as the screams fade into silence.

Kornelius does the same and gently holds my fingers.

It's not how I want them to touch me. The desire riding me to experience my fated mates to the fullest is still strong.

Perhaps it'll never go away.

I hope it doesn't.

Relief rushes through me as the first wave of magic comes, but it's faint compared to Jasper's power. "I need you to use your strengths, not just your touch," I clarify. "Jasper's gift is his death touch, so touch alone transfers his magic." I turn to Zy. "Yours lies in your beautiful eyes. Take off your glasses and give me what I need, Zy."

His throat bobs with a swallow before he obeys, taking off his glasses. Kornelius isn't affected, which confirms my theory that the brothers can absorb each other's magic like they do mine.

The hit of Zy's gaze goes straight to my core.

Just like last time, magic swirls with incredible power in those bright green orbs. They're glorious and beautiful and every bit as enticing as the rest of him.

Taking in a deep breath, I allow the magic he offers to swell through me. It fills my spirit to the brim, giving me energy to work with.

Transferring it into my flesh is a difficult matter, but now that I know what I'm trying to accomplish, I manage to stop the bleeding along the gash on my throat. A tingling sensation sweeps over fresh skin as a delicate layer forms.

"Take off the bandage, Kornelius," I tell him without

looking at him. I need to keep my gaze on Zy, but Kor's power is going to come into play soon.

He silently obeys and tenderly pulls at the soaked gauze, peeling it away until cool air meets my skin.

A strained sound leaves his throat. "Issy..."

I know it must look bad, but he needs to see this through.

The other end of failure is a lesson learned. And I have one to teach him here.

"Lick the wound clean," I tell Kornelius.

Both of my mates go extremely still.

"I don't think—"

"Do it," I snap when Kornelius tries to protest, then I turn my tone softer. "Trust me."

Zy's eyes have widened and his gaze immerses me in his magic and concern, but he doesn't look away. Instead, he gives me what I need when Kornelius gently runs his tongue along the firmer part of my skin near the wound.

That tingling sensation grows when his arousal releases his magic into the air.

He's like a battery, one that transforms energy and holds on to it until it's released.

Jasper amplifies it.

Zyran is power itself.

Zyran and Kornelius *together* are a deadly duo, creating the perfect mixture of magic I can manipulate as Zy looks into my eyes while Kornelius continues his slow, gentle work.

His breath puffs against my neck as he inevitably feels the pull of my blood. I'm not cursed anymore. We shouldn't go into a spiral of bloodlust again, but I suspect that Kornelius is a vampire who has denied himself in all things. He's far too calm and reserved, as if he's hiding something. Hiding *himself*.

That's a recipe for disaster, as I hope he's finally learned.

"I don't think I can do this," he whispers, his words tickling my skin.

"You can," I say. "You're sorry for what you did, aren't you?"

He presses his forehead against me. "Fuck. You have no idea, but an apology means nothing in comparison to... this." He's staring at my wound. It's going to leave a nasty scar and that hurts me more than the pain, because I know my mates will always be reminded of what happened when they see it.

"Then show me you're sorry," I say, eager to take my fill.

I might not be cursed, but fate still has a debt to be paid.

And I have not yet bonded with Kornelius—while what bond I have established with Zy is frayed.

Both issues that need to be dealt with immediately.

I've always dreamed of what it would be like to find my fated mate.

I found not only one, but three, and I'm not going to let anyone or anything take that from me. Not even their own regret.

It's a risk, but I break Zyran's gaze to give my full attention to Kornelius.

We kissed once before, but our first kiss was marred

by a curse. When I wrap my arms around his neck and press my mouth to his, the walls around his soul break.

And his magic spews forth, making me feel like I'm floating.

Mine, I think, lazily drunk on his power.

Something in him finally seems to snap and he listens to the demands my body is giving him.

He draws me into his lap and I'm painfully aware of the restrictive bra and panties I'm still wearing. It was more for their comfort than mine that I opted to wear underclothes while absorbing Jasper's death touch.

Now, I wish I weren't wearing anything at all. There shouldn't be clothing separating me from my mates, not when it feels this amazing.

I demonstrate my desire by unbuttoning his shirt. He helps me, giving me what I want.

What I need.

Zyran's touch glides over my shoulder as he resumes where Kornelius left off. His tongue follows my wound, not touching it, but cleaning any lost blood around it.

I enjoy his heat from my back while I continue to help Kornelius disrobe. He backs up, leaving me in Zyran's care while he finishes removing his clothes.

Then my gaze rakes over him as he stands there, giving me my fill.

Spirits.

Kornelius is incredibly beautiful, and it's something I couldn't fully appreciate before in the haze of bloodlust.

Now, though, I take my time to memorize the shape of his muscular arms. His brown hair falls over his amber eyes as he watches me. My gaze dips to the "V" along his abdomen and his impressive cock proudly on display.

My mouth salivates at the glistening of precum at the tip. Tasting my blood has him rock hard, or maybe it's knowing that I'm admiring him.

"Do you like how my brother looks?" Zyran asks, his breath tickling my ear. His voice ramps my desire up another notch. "I want to see him inside of you."

Kornelius's fangs appear, his ample hearing no doubt picking up the soft words. "Zy," he growls.

He might protest the idea of having sex with me, and I know why. He's afraid of losing control again. He ripped into me and that was even without doing more than kissing.

But that's precisely why I need him to go through with this. He needs to see what he's capable of. It's not just manifestation spirits who use the magic created by willpower.

All creatures do, in some form. Shifters often come into their powers when hit by a wave of anger or other intense forms of energy.

As do humans when they touch one of the portals dotting our world. The potent magic combines with their hidden desires, sprouting power when there was little else than a wish before.

"I'd like that," I whisper.

Zy's fingers have gone between my legs and he touches me. His gentle strokes go over the fabric of my underwear, enticing my body to instantly soak them with my desire.

Kornelius's nostrils flare in response.

A pained look enters his amber eyes as he speaks, his words accentuated by the size of his fangs that have only grown with his arousal. "Please, Issy. I don't want to hurt you."

"You mean you don't want to lose control," I counter. "You won't."

I can't say he won't hurt me, because my true desires are dark.

A little pain in the mix is what I need if he's going to satisfy me.

"He can warm you up," Zy suggests as he pulls my underwear up toward my abdomen, creating intense pressure on my clit. I squirm when he licks the edge of my ear. "He might not lose control, but I certainly would like for *you* to, baby girl."

"Yes," I agree. "I want that."

"Tell us exactly *how* you want it," Zy says.

I'm not one for words, at least not out loud, but I'm learning to find my voice, thanks to my mates.

My gaze dips to Kor's impressive girth again, then up to his face.

His fangs excite me just as much as the thought of him impaling me with his cock does.

"I... I like blood play," I decide aloud. "And some pain with the pleasure."

"There's been plenty of pain," Zy chides. "Plenty of blood, too."

"You asked what I want," I explain, but my words come out weak. I know he's right. The point of this is to show my mates they can control themselves, that they can trust themselves, and that we can act as the unit we need to be in order to defeat our enemies.

But now that I have them, I want more than that.

I want to bond with them as fate intended. I want to be *complete*.

"Then we will give you what you want," Kornelius says, making me lick my lips with anticipation. "But it's going to be on our terms."

What does that mean? I think.

Kornelius looks determined as he finally crawls onto the bed, going on his knees first, then lowers his mouth to the inside of my thigh.

His kiss comes with a graze of his fangs. I want him to bite me, but I don't ask him to go that far.

I know he's not ready for that, even if I am.

His kisses continue, going upward and skipping over the place where I want him. He resumes on the other leg, making me go mad with anticipation.

When I try to remove my underwear, both he and Zy stop me.

Kornelius nuzzles my sex with his nose. "These will stay on," he informs me. "For now."

"But—" My protest is cut short when he runs his tongue over the same spot, shooting pleasure through my core.

It's nice, but not enough.

"Distract her, Zy," Kor instructs before doing it again.

I'm displeased with the route this torment has taken when Zy reaches around me to pinch one of my nipples.

I squeak, but I'm silenced when he places his other

hand over my mouth. "Your voice is distracting my brother from his work," Zy teases.

I don't like to be silenced, but I understand this is a new game meant to stoke my desire.

Squirming, I moan with frustration when Kornelius laps at me three times in strong succession, then stops.

I make a sound against Zy's hand and try to bite him. He chuckles as he lifts the restraint away. "You think we don't know what turns you on, baby girl? You like danger and you like pain, and we're not going to cut you, or physically hurt you, so this is how we're going to play."

My stomach drops when I realize what he must mean. I've read enough smutty books to guess.

They're going to edge me.

My eyes widen when Kornelius gives me a rare grin. "And it'll keep things slow and safe." He nuzzles my sex again. "Plus, you smell fucking amazing. I could live between your legs for the rest of my life."

"That'll have to wait," Zy says with a sense of amusement. "There are beads in the drawer," Zy tells Kornelius with a jerk of his chin. "You get them. I'll put them on her."

Kor sighs, then rummages in the drawer, pulling out a few boxes.

He opens one and takes out the beads. "Here we are. New ones?"

"Of course," Zy says.

A spike of excitement mixed with fear hits my system when Kornelius approaches.

Fear because I have no experience with any of this.

I'm not sure if I can survive their combined efforts.

He and Zy slip my underwear off of me but don't give me time to adjust when the beads fall down my slit.

Zy secures something behind me, and then there's pressure right on my clit.

But not friction... not what I *need*.

Zy smiles against my cheek. "Let the fun begin."

Chapter 34

Zyran

S*o fucking beautiful.*

We've moved to the shower. Just like the bed, it's an oversized and luxurious place. Issy is as comfortable as we can make her while restrained and desperate.

She's on a cushioned bench, her wrists secured to chains on the wall that I've never used before and her knees spread open, her ankles bound just underneath her ass.

I never had a female in my life who truly wanted something like this.

And I never knew it could be so *fucking amazing*.

"Again," Kor says, stroking himself as he indulges in the view.

It's a spectacular sight, one that only gets better when I comply with Kor's request.

Our witch squirms as I press the button on a remote that controls the object inside of her. The beads are still in place, taut against her clit, and now the vibration gives them a little edge she's clearly enjoying.

"Please," she begs, then goes silent when I stop the vibration feature. The dildo inside continues to swirl, but she's lost the hope of climaxing without the extra stimulation. A little whimper comes from her, making my cock ache to fill her up like she wants us to do. We're both bigger than the object inside of her.

This is just as much of a torment for us as it is for her, but it's the only way to safely complete our bond. I know that's what she wants—it's what I want, too.

More than fucking anything.

But she asked us for pain with her pleasure—it wasn't just a request to satisfy her. It's what her soul needs to feel complete.

It's what we all need to get through what happened.

We've spent two hours taking turns with Issy, learning exactly what she likes.

The nipple clamps were fun, but I discovered that she prefers hot wax. Kor figured out her favorite type of dildo is the swirling one.

However, when it became evident that she liked to be bound, the setup in my shower made the most sense to move to the next step.

Kor wields one of the mobile showerheads and sets the temperature on scalding hot. *Good work-around,* I think. We can't really use wax here, so hot water will do.

"Do you remember your safe word?" Kor asks when he turns the water on, pointing it down at the drain while it reaches temperature.

Steam fills the shower.

Issy nods emphatically. "Yes, of course."

"You'll use it if you need to?" he presses.

I know he wants to make sure we don't have a repeat of last time. If she so much as utters her sister's name, both of us are going to respect it.

She growls. "Take these damn beads off," she says instead of answering the question.

I grin because that's the fire that means she's almost ready.

"Ramp up the setting," Kor instructs.

Issy opens her mouth to protest, but I set it on the next level and turn on the vibration.

She makes a strangled sound, and then Kor directs the wave of hot water directly onto her clit.

She screams as he rips the beads away. The heat and the pressure of the water make her entire body spasm.

Oh, fuck, I think, my cock jumping at the sight of her throbbing, swollen pussy turning red against the hot water.

"Maximum," Kor tells me.

I eagerly set the level on the top setting, nearly losing it when Issy unravels before us. The culmination of two hours of edging makes her fucking explode.

Her scream hits me with her magic, making me slip into a desperate state of lust.

Mine, a voice shouts in my head. The sense of control I have by making her finally come on our command—*my* command—is driving me mad.

The dildo inside of her is held in place by the bench, and she thrashes against the chains as a powerful orgasm wrecks her.

Fuck. Fuck!

I can hardly force myself to stay still, but I've had my turn with Issy.

I know Kor needs this more than I do, so I find the strength to stay put.

A snarl rips from my throat when he pulls the dildo out of her. She's crying, *begging*, and it flops onto the floor, still rolling in circles when he slams into her.

Oh, Goddess.

I didn't know I could enjoy watching my brother fuck our mate, but it's beautiful. It makes me feel wrong and right all at the same time.

Magic saturates the room, exploding in visible waves that transcend reality.

Issy is going to change the world, I realize, in awe of her power.

It also terrifies me, because the Houses will never let up once they learn the threat she poses.

Kor's gift has always been more of a curse for him, limiting him to where he can travel and threatening to yank him across the world without notice. Yet now he's in his element, giving Issy everything as he thrusts into her, shoving his cock deep into her swollen folds as she throws her head back and takes it like the good fucking girl she is.

She loves it. A smile crests her lips and then they're moving, whispering a spell that calls all of us to her.

A cold rush of air enters the room when the door opens, revealing Jasper and his nostrils flaring.

I'm impressed his restraint has lasted this long.

"All of you," she demands, magic lacing her words. "I need all of you, *now*."

Chapter 35

Issy

My mates have destroyed me.

Now I'm nothing more than a wallowing puddle of lust and need.

And something else.

A new wave of magic threatens to consume me. Perhaps it comes from fate, or maybe it's my true potential seeping through, but I know it's dangerous.

As Kor fucks me, sending my walls spasming around him, I don't *care*.

One orgasm has rolled into the next. I've gone from being a girl who has difficulty achieving orgasm to one who can't make them stop.

Kornelius has replaced the beads and vibration with his cock and his hips, rolling his strength through me and over my mound as he fucks me.

Magic cracks through my chains, breaking my binds, and I'm hanging on to him for dear life.

Jasper and Zy are both watching me with hungry looks.

Fangs bared.

Clothes gone.

I don't know how to take three men at the same time, but hopefully they can figure that part out for me.

"I need you all," I repeat. "*Please.*"

My demand has turned into begging again, but I don't care.

"Mine," Kor says as he rips the binds from my ankles, then lifts me onto his hips, fucking me while still standing.

I wrap my legs around him on instinct and hold on to his neck. All my pain is gone and now there are only waves of pleasure.

My skin tingles when I feel Jasper behind me. His hands cup my ass and Kor goes still.

Then Kornelius is kissing me while Jasper is *preparing* me.

Zy is beside me, whispering in my ear. "You're going to take all three of us," he says. "Don't forget your safe word, because at first, it's going to hurt." His cock edges at my already full entrance, making my eyes go wide. "You let us know if it's too much, baby girl."

That's not going to fit, I think, remembering that Zy is the largest of the three of them.

But the pressure at my entrance suggests he thinks I'm capable of it. Kornelius remains still, holding me against him while Zy struggles to make room.

My legs are straddled around Kornelius, Zy is beside us, his cock underneath my ass and edging around my entrance, while Jasper prepares me from behind.

Jasper is going to take my ass and Zy intends to share my pussy with Kor.

This can't work. It can't.

Yet all of my mates are slowly introducing me to the possibility. Zy pushes, sending pressure through me and I tense.

"Relax, sweetling," Kor says against my mouth. "You can do this."

"I can't," I say, fear lacing my words.

"We believe you can," Jasper counters. He places his hand on my shoulder and moves his cock to where his fingers are still working inside, forcing my muscles to loosen.

Belief is a powerful thing, I remind myself.

Maybe I don't believe in myself, but my mates do.

It's the lesson I was trying to teach them. Yet, it seems they're the ones intent on teaching *me*.

"Slow, deep breaths," Zy instructs when he moves in another inch.

They're doing it, I marvel. My breath has gone into quick, short pants and I try to obey his instruction.

Zy goes still while Jasper works himself in next.

They didn't lie to me. There's pain, but they're going slow enough to allow me time to adjust.

"Stay still," Kor instructs his brothers. He seems to be the leader, knowing how to read my body best.

I fucking love that.

He appears to know when I'm ready before I do and digs his fingers into my hips. "A little more," he tells them. "Zy first."

My body screams when his brother complies, going in a little bit farther until I decide the head of his cock must be all the way inside.

My safe word tingles on the edge of my tongue when the burn increases, but I swallow it down.

"Jas," Kornelius instructs next.

My muscles protest when there's pressure from behind.

Then I'm full. So. Fucking. Full.

"I-I..." I try to speak, but now I'm struggling to form words.

Or even think.

They all hold still as magic swarms between the four of us, growing and mounting into something unique.

Something that'll bond all of us permanently.

In this life... and the next.

I know this is rare. I know that other mates don't get to extend their bonds into the afterlife—and that sort of privilege both thrills and terrifies me.

Any thoughts I have are shut out when Kor gives his final order.

"She's ready."

Then they're all moving, slowly at first, and I groan as they fuck me.

Together.

All three of them.

Kornelius barely angles his hips, keeping steady while Zy works himself in all the way, then pulls out only half-way. I expect to keep things secure.

Then he does it again.

Jasper fucks me deepest, going all the way in until my body feels like I can't take them all. Until the burn is mixing with the intense pleasure slowly overtaking my mind. He's grinding against the thin barrier between Zy and Kor on the other side, driving me mad.

Pleasure blows behind my eyelids when I squeeze my eyes shut.

"Look at us, beautiful," Zy says.

And I obey, opening my eyes as Kornelius kisses my neck.

He doesn't bite. This isn't about blood-sharing today.

It's about bonding.

Zy's gaze douses me with magic, but it's his expression full of emotion that fills me with hope.

It's not just lust.

He's falling in love with me.

"We all are," Kor says against my neck, and I realize that they heard that.

They can hear my thoughts... which is proof that our bond is being secured to new levels.

I'm... falling in love, too.

I'm already in love. These are the first men to ever believe in me.

Maybe the first people in the world.

My sister loves me, but I'll always be *little* Issy. Sweet, delicate Issy who can't talk to anyone without killing them.

To these vampires, I'm a goddess.

And we want to worship you, Kor says in my mind.

Praise you, Zy adds.

And kill anyone outside of this mate circle who harms you, Jasper growls.

And then their magic rushes over me, making me come with them as dark bliss drags me under.

I might never want to see the light again.

"We're never doing that again," I groan against the pillow.

Zy chuckles as he hugs me to his chest.

Kornelius is snuggled between my breasts, his slow breathing suggesting he's asleep, and Jasper rests on a pillow with his hands behind his head.

And he's smiling at me like a lunatic.

"We are definitely doing that again," Jasper says with a gleam in his eye. His voice is soft, but husky with satisfaction. "Except next time, I'll join Zy in the front and feel you come around both our dicks."

"I want the back, though," Zy says, nudging himself against my butt cheeks in expectation. "That looked fun."

Jas chuckles again when I make a face, then settles into the pillow and closes his eyes. "Kor looked like he wasn't giving up his spot. Good luck convincing him to swap."

My men continue their banter of who is going to take me hardest and whose name I'll scream.

Spirits, is this my life now?

My body is very much not ready for another experience like the one they gave me, but I can't deny that everything has changed.

I'm complete.

Issy? Fallon's voice trickles into my mind, and I realize I've finally let my walls down.

Once again, it wasn't intentional to reach out to my twin, but it's a good time to talk to her.

Hey, I say in response.

Whoa, she replies. *You sound... Did you just have sex? Like, real fated-mate sex?*

A blush rushes up my chest and over my cheeks. Jasper keeps his eyes closed, but Zy whispers in my ear. "Tell her you had nasty vampire sex."

My heart skips a beat.

Can they hear her, too?

Issy? Fallon presses, likely waiting for a response.

Sorry. Um, no. Yes?

No, yes? she repeats.

Zy playfully growls. "Nasty vampire sex in all your holes," he adds. "Well, we did miss one. Maybe we can remedy that in a few hours."

I sigh, choosing to ignore him. *I mean yes. It's distracting now that my mates can hear you in my head.*

She goes quiet for a moment, then speaks again.

That's strange. My mates can't hear us when we talk.

Her voice has gone tense. She definitely doesn't like this development.

I snuggle against Zy's chest. "Can you try... not to

listen?" I ask him. "I'm able to put a wall around my mind. Just envision that and see if it works."

He chuckles again. "Sure thing, baby girl. I'll practice. Tell her to say something."

I direct my mind back to my sister. *Zy's listening right now. I'm not sure about the other two. I think Jas and Kor fell asleep.* Both of them are perfectly still and don't even seem to be breathing, but I'm growing used to their resting states. *But he's willing to practice the technique of walling us out. That'll make it where he can't listen in.*

Zy. Jas. Kor? Are those their names? Fallon asks, now with a hint of curiosity. *Or is that short for something?*

I kick myself that I haven't told Fallon more about my mates. I'd love nothing more than to gush about them like a teenager with her first crush—going over all the details and everything down to the curl of their long eyelashes.

But I'm not a teenager. I was denied youthful crushes. My parents can't be entirely blamed for that. When my powers manifested, it was clear that I would forever be alone.

Except, now I'm not. Now I'm in bed with my mates. My family.

"Did you hear her question?" I ask.

Zy nods. "Going to need more practice, love. I'm only able to mute it, but I'm trying to give you privacy since you asked for it. Just pretend I'm not listening and I'll distract myself by replaying in my head the sounds you made when we all fucked you."

Despite myself, a small smile tickles my lips. He's never had to control his power. His death sight is always switched on, so I believe him when he says he needs practice.

When his chest rumbles with a soft growl, I also believe that he's fully distracted by his own thoughts.

By memories of us—memories that will likely slip into fantasies of what he's going to do to me next.

Zyran Justi, I say in my mind, answering my sister's question before I get too caught up in the idea of fantasies. *Kornelius Justi. And Jasper Justi—you met him at the cottage.*

I can almost envision Fallon's piercing green eyes widening with shock. Probably because all their last names are the same. *They're related?*

They're triplets, I clarify, because that's actually an important point. *I met a manifestation spirit, Fallon. She helped create them so that they would be fated for a death witch capable of handling their combined power. So they would find me.*

I didn't add that she had cursed their blood and, by extension, me, so that I would be forced into the death plane.

Fallon is the only witch I know of who can physically walk in the death plane. She'd find Jewel and rip her to shreds.

The spirit hadn't intended to seek out my help, but rather use me as a medium for her power. Fallon would have been a better choice, but I know why fate chose me and not my sister for the triplets.

It wouldn't have been a good match. My inner darkness is something I've hidden, but Fallon is light and goodness. She's endured horrible darkness and is finally free of it.

I, on the other hand, am destined to remain in it forever.

And *thrive*.

So Jewel was stuck with me. I don't have magic to move in and out of the death plane like Fallon—but I can channel it. I understand how spells work and analyzing problems and mysteries is my forte.

This is something I can fix, if given the time. And after observing me in her library, I was glad to see she had changed her mind about destroying me to manipulate my power.

Instead, she let me go.

Which is exactly why I want to help her. She's a good person at heart. She's also a powerful woman caught up in the bullshit of the patriarchs and has been victimized just like the rest of us. With her help, perhaps the patriarchs can finally be dealt with permanently.

Fallon's quiet for a long time. I realize she's been talking to one of her mates when she finally answers me. *Kaspian says he's never heard of a manifestation spirit before. But if it can create a hybrid species and manipulate fate bonds before they even happen, it's dangerous. What does it want with you?*

I can tell my sister has gone into battle mode. She's going to want all the information and then she'll likely make up her mind in a matter of seconds.

If I can't convince her that Jewel is on our side, then that's going to put me in a horrible situation. Fallon is my world, my sister, my *twin*. She needs to be able to see my perspective on this, so I'm very careful with my words.

She wants my help, I say. *She was a witch trapped in the death plane before she became a manifestation spirit. That's how it works. It takes an incredible force of sheer will to create the magic that a manifestation spirit requires.*

From the ancient texts I remember, it's the only time a manifestation spirit will create something from nothing.

Even with the creation of the triplets, it wasn't from nothing. Their mother had found a way to connect with Jewel, providing her wish—and her will—to create the three vampires. Perhaps their mother could have become a manifestation spirit herself, but she chose to give up her chance to create *them*.

My heart twisted with the unexpected sorrow that gave me, because it was a sensation I shared.

My mother hadn't been strong enough to protect me throughout her life, but she did give me her death to help me defeat my father. She made the ultimate sacrifice for the love of her child.

Are you telling me she's already dead? Fallon asks.

It's a legitimate question, but I don't think Jewel is dead. *I said she's in the death plane,* I clarify. *She must have become a manifestation spirit before being trapped there, or maybe the process of trapping her there is when it happened. Regardless, she's made a library in the death plane and that's where she's holed up. She is keeping the patriarchs out, but it's a siege until we help her.*

Gods, Issy. That's how Daithi is doing this, isn't it? He's channeling her power.

Daithi had mentioned a fail-safe. I realize that Jewel must have been that safeguard in the event that he died.

Fallon breaking the headstone freed her mind, but her body is still trapped in a place Daithi can control her.

We have to get her out of there, I tell Fallon. *Without her, the patriarchs will be weak enough to be dealt with.*

It explains so much of their strength, their ability to manipulate my fate bonds, and my power.

The manifestation spirit is linked to me by blood and magic. Jewel is the key for Daithi to control me.

It's also the key to destroy him.

Okay, Fallon says and my heart lifts. *You want to help this spirit, then I will help you, too. But I have one condition, Issy, and it's nonnegotiable.*

What is it? I ask, ready to agree to almost anything.

You're coming to Reykjavík.

I can't, I protest. *Amala is waiting for the heat to die down before giving me the last piece of the puzzle I need. She can help me prove my innocence.*

Even if I defeat Daithi and the patriarchs, that's not going to solve my immediate problem in the land of the living.

Not to mention, I need Amala to teach me how to properly heal a wound with death magic because it keeps reopening—not something I dare share with Fallon. And that would be pretty hard to hide in person.

Then she's going to have to come here, or we'll portal wherever she wants. The heat is not dying down; it's getting worse. The Houses are all up in arms about the fallout in Lapland and the syndicates have made aggressive retaliatory strikes against a similar massacre in New York.

Several officials are dead and even the dukes had an assassination attempt. You cannot *be there when the Houses strike back.*

I wince. *I imagine that didn't go very well for the assassin.*

No, she agrees. *Tallis burned him beyond recognition, so we can't even confirm which syndicate is responsible. Which is why you need to come here. Kaspian has agreed to protect you.*

And my mates? I ask. Things have changed now that I'm fully mate-bonded to them. I'm also encouraged that we know more about Jewel and her connection to the patriarchs. Kaspian is going to be more interested in a manifestation spirit than my hybrid vampires.

Or at least, I hope Fallon can keep him interested in Jewel.

They'll be under the same protection, she says.

I need his vow, I demand. When Fallon sees my injury, I'm going to need a vow that can't be broken.

Is my word not enough? she asks, clearly ruffled by my demand. *You've changed, Issy.*

Perhaps I have.

His vow, I repeat.

There's a moment of silence, then Fallon finally answers. *He vows to protect you and all three of your mates. Now will you come to Reykjavík? I'll get Nolan.*

That won't be necessary, I say with a grin. I'm eager to test out my new ability with Kornelius. When I called him to me, it was a matter of channeling his power mixed with mine. But I decided where the tunnel he made went. It shouldn't be hard to form a portal anywhere I've been to before, just like Ayla does. That ability is tied to her spirit and can't be replicated, but I'm not replicating it. I'm doing something similar with Kor's ability that he already has.

Now that I have Kaspian's vow, going to my sister makes sense. Plus, I will need her for the next step in my plan.

The step that comes after killing Zane and Royce.

I'll be there tonight. See you soon, sis.

Chapter 37

Jasper

"I still don't like this plan," I say as I watch Issy get dressed.

Despite Zyran's attempts to convince our mate to indulge in our worship for at least a few more days, Issy seems determined to take action against her enemies.

I, for one, am eager to kill Zane. My brothers likely have more cause than I do to want him dead. But they're even more distracted by Issy's body than I am.

And that's saying something.

She slips a gauzy dress over her head and wiggles into it. It forms to her body and shows off her hips and her gorgeous breasts. Taking a look in the mirror, she frowns at it.

"That's because it's a plan where you have to trust me," she says, not looking away from herself. She murmurs a spell, making all of us flinch as she draws our magic into herself, and a blade appears in her hands.

It's like she's able to master our powers by instinct alone.

"I do trust you," I counter as she starts to shred the

fabric. My nostrils flare when she digs deep enough to graze her skin. "Is that necessary?" I ask.

Zy's threading his necklace through his fingers while Kornelius thumbs through a book. Given that Kornelius will be the one luring Royce, he's working on a spell to confirm their locations. But he pauses to look over the pages at our mate.

His expression glazes over with hunger.

"It needs to look realistic," she says. "I've run away and been attacked by Zane; that's what Royce needs to believe and how he needs to find me."

I know the plan. We've gone over it multiple times and brainstormed a hundred scenarios.

All of them put Issy in far too much danger.

But she's right that I don't have a better plan. Our timeline has been accelerated, given recent events. Even if we do seek asylum in Gold and Garnet, it's too much of a risk to leave Royce and Zane unchecked. They'll continue to stoke the fires between the syndicates and the Houses, leading the world into a war that'll burn the entire realm to the ground.

They need to die.

And to kill them, Issy has a brilliant plan, one that will pit them against each other.

I just can't accept the idea of using her as bait. Yet, I hadn't been able to accept Zyran or Kornelius ever touching her again after what happened, either. But here we are.

All permanently fate-bonded in this life and the next. I felt how deep the bond carved itself into my soul. I know what'll happen if Issy dies.

I'll go with her. There's no doubt about that. Strangely, I'm glad to know I wouldn't be left behind to slowly go mad.

Where she goes, I go.

Except for today—I have to watch her walk out that door with Zy as her escort. He'll leave her at an abandoned building and then the plan is set in place.

"Your scrying spell done yet, Kor?" Zy asks impatiently.

Kor seems to reluctantly glance back down at the pages. "I'll have to do them separately. One for vampire blood and another for warlock."

"Get on it," I snap, not hiding the edge to my voice.

I'm still pissed off at him. Issy might have forgiven him, but I won't.

Not anytime soon, anyway.

Issy ruffles at my tone. "Jasper, can I have a word with you? Alone?"

That doesn't sound good.

"Of course," I say, softer this time.

She nods. "Zy, stay with Kor and help him with the scrying spell. I'm going to talk to Jas about what we're trying to do here." She storms out of the room, her gauzy dress flowing in her wake.

Like a kicked puppy, I follow her.

When did I get so soft?

Chapter 38

Issy

I take Jasper out into the hall, glad to hear his footsteps behind me.

Zy and Kor have excellent hearing, so I head to the lower level that has a living area where we can talk.

I indicate one of the love seats and Jasper sighs, then sits. He leans back and looks me in the eyes. There's defiance there, but also desperation.

He's scared.

"I know what you're going to say," he says. The screams of the dead nearly drown him out, but I ignore the need to touch him.

"Do you?" I counter, crossing my arms. I don't take a seat. Instead, I stand before him just out of reach.

He nods. "You need my brothers and me on the same team—I get it. You already told me how your plan works." His jaw flexes. "Listen, Issy. It's a good plan. I'm not doubting that. I'm just saying—"

I don't let him finish. Inching my dress up, I straddle

him and press my hands against the head of the furniture. I'm wearing thin panties, allowing me to feel him when I relax onto his lap. "You're angry. You have every right to be. Your brothers broke your trust."

His throat bobs with a swallow as his gaze drops to my breasts, which are in his face. I had cut a line near one of them, meaning my blood is now tantalizingly close to him. He's still a vampire and I'm still a powerful witch designed to appeal to him.

Based on the flare of desire in his gaze, I more than appeal to him. He looks like he wants to devour me. "They broke *your* trust. I don't understand how you've forgiven them so easily."

He drags his gaze away from my breasts and to the raw wound I now have open on my neck. It's much better than it was before, but it's still bleeding. It just doesn't hurt as badly now that I've healed the more internal injuries and sent the muscles to knit back together. It looks a lot worse than it is.

He runs his fingers along the edge of my scarring skin. "Has fate blinded you to what they're capable of?"

"Zane and Royce are the enemies here," I remind him. "Daithi and the assholes trying to possess your bodies are the ones who are truly capable of evil things. Your brothers aren't evil." I glide my fingers over the stubble on his jaw, directing him to look at me. "*You* aren't evil."

He darkly chuckles. "Is that the lie you tell yourself to make all of this bearable, witchling?"

I lean down so I can graze his lips with mine while we

talk. His death touch is incredibly stimulating to my senses and I can't resist more contact. "Don't confuse darkness with evil, my love. We are dark creatures and to believe anything else is a lie. I'm far too damaged to ever believe I'll see the light again—and now that I've found you, Zy, and Kor, I realize that's okay. Sometimes the dark can be a peaceful place where we accept who and what we are."

I kiss him before he can reply. When he struggles against me and digs his fingers into my hip as if to remove me, I bite down on his tongue sharp enough to draw blood.

He snarls. "You want my darkness, Issy?"

"Yes," I whisper against him, putting my magic into the single word.

It unravels him, then he's clawing my underwear away and I'm working his zipper.

I can't get his pants off in this position, but it doesn't matter. The barrier of my panties is obliterated and he pushes himself inside me.

A groan escapes me, one of pain mixed with pleasure because I'm so sore. Having sex again was not on my mind, but it seems my mates and I can't keep our hands off each other.

He thrusts roughly into me, giving me what I had asked for.

"Bite me," I ask.

"No," he rumbles, driving up into me and holding me in place so it sends his dick deep inside.

My core burns with pleasure and he rolls my hips on

him, stimulating my clit against his hard muscles near the base of his groin. I whimper when he does it again. "It'll look more realistic with a fresh wound," I explain. "Please."

I really do need one of them to bite me. There's no way that Royce will buy my act if I don't have a vampire's mark.

Jasper utters a curse, then he pulls me into him. He grazes his fangs over the side of my neck that doesn't have a wound.

Zy had bitten me there, but those marks are long healed, leaving only small circles of pink skin.

Now Jasper reopens the skin with a delicate bite. He carefully sinks his fangs into my neck, but the bite is no less euphoric to my senses.

I'm designed for my mates in every way, just as they are designed for me.

My body responds to him, moving to sheathe him inside me as I ride him to my satisfaction.

"I love you, Jas," I whisper as his bite supplies me with the pain I need mixed with my pleasure.

It's the first time I've said those words out loud to any of them.

Only a few days have really passed since I met them, but it feels like I've known them for years. Too much has happened and my soul has recognized what is mine.

Jasper. Zyran. Kornelius.

They all belong to me.

Forever.

Jasper unlatches long enough to reply. "I love you, too, Issy," he whispers, his voice so low and growly I can hardly make out the words. He runs his tongue along the wounds he created. "Now be a good girl and come on my cock."

I smile when he pierces my skin again.

Because I'm eager to comply.

Chapter 39

Issy

"**S**o. Not. Fair," Zy complains as he takes a sharp corner onto yet another back road.

I roll my eyes. "You had me all to yourself just the other day. It's not like it's a contest."

Even if I want to touch Zy, I don't, mostly because I'm irritated. I'm wearing my collar because that's part of the plan. Kor put it on me before we left, and apparently, Zy can take it off, if needed. The plan makes sure at least one of the guys is with me at all times. When Zy leaves, Kor will replace him so when the time comes, someone can free me.

It still feels like a noose around my neck, though, pissing me off more. The collar is not something we've talked in depth about.

"But it *is* a contest," he retorts, taking another quick left and nearly sending me slamming against the car door. "Whoever gives you the most orgasms wins. I have some catching up to do."

I glance at him as worry tingles up my spine. "What

383

are you planning? Jas is tracking Zane, and Kor is meeting with Royce. We don't have much time."

And from experience, I know it takes me a while to get things going. I'm not one of those girls who can just come on command.

"I have a few tricks," he says, licking his lips. "Plus, your heart rate is accelerated. You're nervous. It'll calm you down."

"And it'll add another orgasm to your score," I guess.

He shrugs. "Win-win."

Such a sore loser, Jasper says in my head, but I realize he's talking to Zy. *Can't just leave it be, can you?*

Zy's eyes widen. "Oh, fuck no," he says. "You do not get to be in my head, you asshole." He holds up a finger. "I've been practicing walling techniques. Try talking to me *now*."

Zy's mental wall shoots up so hard I flinch. "Was that really necessary?" The fact that the triplets are now able to telepathically talk to each other is huge and should be celebrated. It'll make the plan that much easier to execute.

"Yes," he says with a grin, then adjusts his glasses. "Because Jasper is going to lose focus on tracking Zane once he hears you screaming *my* name. It's better if you shut him out until I'm done with you."

These three brothers are going to be a handful if they keep up this competition bullshit.

Despite my irritation, I'm curious as to what sort of tricks Zy has in mind.

What's going on, little witchling? Jasper says in my mind. *Zy was raging in my head and now he's gone. I can't say that's not an unnerving sensation—and knowing you're*

with him when he's behaving unstably has me nervous.
Especially when I'm not there.

I bite my lip and look out the window. We've moved outside of the populated area of Staten Island to the abandoned buildings dotting the outskirts.

It's a barrier between No Man's Land and what I used to call home. A place no one goes to without a desperate reason.

Being hunted by the Houses and tracked by a blood-thirsty vampire and Daithi's cousin definitely qualify as desperate reasons.

But I'm not hiding. I'm readying a trap that'll fix all of this.

Hopefully.

Maybe.

We're all going to die, aren't we? Jasper asks unhelp-fully in my mind—no doubt having heard my train of thought.

I frown. *No, we're not. Not if we stick to the plan. You let me handle Zy while you do your job, okay? Zane isn't going to lure himself into a trap where he's brutally dismembered.*

I can almost hear Jasper's murderous smile. *No, no, he's not.*

Do you trust me? I press, eager to move on with my plan.

Because Zy was right. I *am* nervous and I need my mates on board for this to work. Everything needs to go exactly as planned or we're done.

Of course, my love, he says, his voice softening. *I just wanted to add that even if we do die—*

We won't, I press. But he continues.

If we do, then I will die happy knowing I won't ever leave you. Because you're mine, sweetheart. In this life and the next.

Spirits. I don't know what I've done to earn mates like these, but my heart flutters at his words.

Be that as it may, I say, *if you trust me, then trust me. Trust me with Zyran. Trust me alone. And trust me even when you can't hear or feel me, okay?*

Issy, he says, *you're not going to shut me out like Zy suggested, are you?*

Jasper's words fade away as I do exactly that, and Zy's fingers thread through mine while I still look outside. The buildings have gone from modern townhomes to run-down slums.

"That's my good girl," he praises, making heat rush to my core.

"I hate it when you call me that," I whisper. I could choose to talk to him telepathically, but I'm already struggling to wall out so many minds from my own. It's easier to just speak aloud.

"Your blood pattern suggests otherwise," he says with confidence.

I raise a brow at him. "My blood pattern?"

He nods, then turns onto one last street before slowing down. From the map I memorized many years ago, we're in the unmarked area that'll fit perfectly for a trap. "My sight does more than kill people, baby girl. I can also see the path of your blood. And right now it's going right here." He slips his fingers lower, tickling between my thighs. "Which is a good thing because we only have about an hour, right?" He waggles his eyebrows when we come to a stop.

"Spirits," I curse before roughly yanking on the door handle, rushing out of the car before I fall for Zy's seduction.

I approach the rotten doorsteps to what must have been a beautiful mansion before Zy suddenly appears in front of me, using his vampire speed to his advantage. My surprised reflection looks back at me in his glasses.

He grins, showing a hint of his fangs that sends another annoying thrill through my body. "Are you ready for this, sweetheart?"

I frown. "I hope you mean the plan we're supposed to be focusing on. Because yes, I'm ready to kill my enemies and tear their souls from their bodies."

His grin widens. "Oh, I do love it when you're murderous, my mate. It's excellent foreplay." He holds out his hand and waits for me to accept it. "Shall we?"

I roll my eyes. "If you think you're going to distract me with your pretty looks, it's not going to work." My words deny him, but my body doesn't.

Placing my palm in his, my magic tingles with expectation. Which is probably a wise move. I expect that anything I touch in this ancient place will reek of death screams.

He seems amused as he slips off his glasses and pockets them. The hit of power from his green gaze makes my knees weak.

"As you say, baby girl." His grin remains in place as he escorts me inside.

The door is locked, but a simple spell gives us entry. A

hit of musty, stale air follows a current of history. The kind that has been lost for over fifty years since supernaturals took over this world.

I take a moment to gauge my surroundings. It's a nice entryway with an old painting—too bad it has too much dust on it for me to discern the image.

A chandelier boasts a thick array of cobwebs and the shadows stretch into a living area.

"Do your thing, little witch," Zy says, then removes my collar with a wink.

My magic resides in death—something that's of abundance here. These abandoned areas have been mired in the stillness of death for years.

I smile as my magic comes back to the surface, then utter the words of restoration that use that deathly power to turn back time of certain objects.

Because I don't mind showing off just a little bit.

My magic sweeps out with shadows, lighting the candles and sending the cobwebs curling, then heads to the living area. The furniture lightens in color and the fabric ripples with its original texture.

Even though I would like to see what this place looked like in its early days, I can't restore the whole place. The point is to make it believable and my magic is supposed to be limited to that of a single witch—not one with three powerful mates.

"Royce will think I've been hiding here," I say, satisfied as I summon empty dishes and ashes to the hearth. With a snap of my fingers, I add a log that's still burning. "I would have made myself comfortable for a few days while waiting for my sister to find me."

It's ironic that the plan includes making it look like I'd do exactly what I would have done had I not found my fated mates.

Fallon always came to my rescue and it wouldn't have been the first time I hid away in a quiet place, awaiting her strength to pull me from the mire.

It feels good to be able to handle myself for once.

"There she is," Zy says with pride. "My little witch ready for *fun*."

He guides me to the sofa and strips off his shirt, allowing me to see the silver chain with Jewel's emblem on it glinting over his skin.

He sits me down, then goes to his knees between my legs. I curl my fingers through his hair while I toy with the chain with my free hand. "Why do you have this?" I ask.

"It was my mother's," he says as he runs his strong hands over my thighs.

I know that he mentioned his mother had treated it like prayer beads, but that's not what I meant. "But where did *she* get it?"

"I wish I knew," he says with a guarded tone. I know it's a sensitive subject, but it's an important detail. I'd like to know if Jewel had planned all this or if it'd truly been instinct on her part. "My mother had a friend who watched us sometimes. She would stay the day, which was equivalent to overnight for a vamp, and get up just before the sun went down. My father is like most older vampires and he dislikes the sun, so it gave her a chance to talk to us."

I didn't have to read between the lines to know that this woman was likely one of Zane's mistresses.

Zy slips my dress up, inching it over my legs to reveal skin. He presses light kisses on the inside of my thigh when I talk. I continue to stroke my fingers through his silky hair. "And what would she tell you?"

"Stories," he says between kisses. He keeps his gaze on me, feeding me magic and truth all at the same time. "Such as the power of desire. My father desired my mother, and so fate gave her to him. My mother desired a child, and this necklace came into her life with the promise of a death goddess listening on the other side. It was a story she believed in, and so she made it true."

"That sounds like a nice story."

He trails his sharp fangs down my skin, leaving a pink line. The threat of his bite makes my heart skip a beat. "It was a lesson more than a story. She wanted me to know that I could have everything I want in life, but there will be a price. If my mother had really stopped to think about what it would cost her to have us, I wonder if I'd exist."

"You would," I say, gripping his hair at the roots and forcing him to look at me. "Because you're mine, Zyran Justi. I'd rip apart time itself to make sure you existed if I had to."

The melancholy of childhood memories leaves his brilliant gaze, replaced with adoration. "You would, wouldn't you? You'd find some old, dusty book that had dirty promises and it would get you all hot for the mates you were supposed to have."

I chuckle when he tugs against my grip and leans into me, running his tongue over the side of my breast where I had cut myself.

"Don't damage the look I'm going for," I chide, but seeing my blood on his tongue is doing darkly delicious things to me.

"But, I was thinking. Wouldn't a vampire go for thicker veins? Like these?" He goes between my legs and kisses the inside of my thigh again before swirling his tongue over one of the veins. "It's right here. I can see it throbbing for a bite."

"I did want to go for a realistic look," I agree on a short breath.

Zy is getting to me and he knows it.

He hums against my skin, pressing his lips to the spot as he makes me wait.

We don't have much time, but Zy seems confident that I'm going to melt for him long before we have to worry about Royce finding me.

Maybe he's right, if he keeps this up.

And I much prefer the idea of letting Zy distract me than waiting with my bundle of nerves for company.

"Have you heard of vampire kisses?" Zy asks, earning my attention.

"No. Should I have?" It's not something I've seen mentioned even in the smutty books I've read.

He growls against my skin. "It might be easier to show you. May I?"

He looks up at me, his green eyes glittering as he slides his fingers between my legs, rolling circles over my underwear.

"Y-yes," I agree, trying not to respond to his touch.

It's good, but I am far more curious about these vampire kisses.

He runs his tongue over one lengthy fang, then slowly moves to the spot he had indicated.

And bites—softly. But he pinches the skin with his mouth and *sucks*.

It's different from the long, hungry pulls that draw out blood. This doesn't seem to be an effective way for him to drink, but I realize he's not trying to drink.

When he lifts away, making me flinch when his fangs extract from my skin, a neat little heart-shaped bruise is left behind.

I laugh. "A vampire hickey?"

He's looking at his handiwork now rather than at me. "I prefer to call it a vampire kiss." He glances up at me. "Because three... two..."

One minute I'm laughing, the next I'm sucking in a gasp of air.

Spirits, what is that?

Pleasure rushes through me and my walls clench. I growl that I don't have anything filling me up. "Zy," I hiss. "What—"

"It's my magic, baby girl," he says with a grin. "It's in my blood, as well as my saliva. When I bite you like this, it'll make you horny as fuck. You're going to want to spread your pretty legs for me." He grins when I start to pant. "Hence, a *vampire kiss*."

Just as he said, I find myself widening my legs when he lowers to the other leg. "Do it again," I say.

"With pleasure, baby girl," he murmurs.

Then *bites*.

I throw my head back on the sofa when he begins the soft suction and I wait for the hit of pleasure.

It slams into me even harder than before.

Spirits.

Sparkles dance behind my vision and my blood rushes to all the places I want Zy's attention.

My nipples. My swollen breasts. And my nub of nerves that is now on fire.

He continues his slow work, biting me over and over again, injecting me with his magic until I'm writhing and begging him for release.

"As you wish," he murmurs.

Then pulls down my soaked underwear, exposing me. He runs his tongue over me, making me whimper before he bites.

There.

I scream when he sucks, each pull of his mouth driving me closer to the edge. He slips his fingers into me, giving me something to clench around.

Then his magic overrides all sensation, sending me careening off the edge.

He doesn't let up. He continues to suck, to mark, to extract every ounce of built-up pleasure that he's injected into me.

"Zyran!" I scream, not sure if I'm begging him to keep going or to stop, because my body is spasming around his fingers.

He pumps me, pushing his fingers into me up to his knuckles before pulling out, then he does it again.

He releases me and continues to massage me, drawing out my pleasure as I tremble and melt into the sofa.

"I told you that you'd be screaming my name, baby girl."

My eyes flutter closed. "Yes, Zy. You win."

He kisses my bruised thigh. "I sure have. I've won the most precious prize of all. You, Ishara Doyle. And no matter what happens when Royce gets here, know that you're not the only one who would claw through time and space for the love of a mate. Because I'm with you, my love. In this life and the next."

His words are reminiscent of Jasper's, but distinctly his own.

"In this life and the next," I agree.

It's a vow that feels an awful lot like a premonition.

But for the first time in my life, I'm not afraid to face my destiny.

I'm not afraid to stand on my own two feet.

Once they stop shaking, of course.

Chapter 10

Kornelius

I don't like it that Royce wants to meet me in a graveyard. Death witches and warlocks tend to be more powerful on unholy ground, especially in a graveyard of ancestors.

Sitting on one of the unreadable tombstones, I thump my heel against the ground. "Better not give that asshole any ammunition to work with," I growl, wondering if I'm sitting on one of the patriarchs' ancient graves.

The Outcast Coven has been around for a while, only making them stronger as the years go on.

They could be a formidable force, if they weren't so focused on infighting. The latest war resulted in a massacre very close to home—one I felt even behind my spelled walls.

I could be sitting on a land mine of power.

I don't like the thought of that, given the number of recent deaths. A chilled breeze rustles debris across the pale grass that has lost all its color. The stench of rot seeps up, burning my nostrils.

I scan the horizon, but Royce isn't here yet.

Perhaps I don't have anything to worry about and Royce is just trying to piss me off. He knows I don't like to be outside my room and my heightened sense of smell would obviously pick up any undecayed corpses.

Although, the recent graves would be those of the rapists I targeted, not patriarchs.

It made no difference. The death stone provided access to the spirits in the death plane—it's too bad I honestly still don't know where it has wound up.

My working theory wasn't too far from the truth I had given Royce to explain its absence. I said it had gone into hiding after so many deaths, "weighed" down by souls that flooded into the death plane after the massacres.

In truth, it had disappeared when I'd been spirited out of the airplane to the first massacre site in Lapland. But I don't believe it's a simple matter of death that sent it into hiding, or else prior massacres would have made it vanish, too.

No, the only time the death stone has ever pulled a disappearing act before was when Fallon's magic over-whelmed the death plane.

And that's not unlike what Issy did when she used Jasper as an amplifier and began her initial bond with him as her fated mate.

Which meant the death stone is no longer in two places at once. It's weak and seeking shelter.

It's in the death plane in a place where it feels safe.

If I were an ancient magical artifact tied to the power of death magic, where would I hide?

In a powerful source.

I frown.

Hmm, like a manifestation spirit?

That realization makes me want to seek out Issy, but I haven't quite figured out the new telepathic ability we apparently have. Whenever I attempt to reach out to her, it feels like I hit a wall.

Now, though, I realize she's in danger. Because if she's linked to the death stone in any way, that changes things.

I find the wall that feels like her, that smells like her floral, decadent tones that linger in her blood, and beat against it.

Issy!

Kornelius? she asks dreamily. *What's wrong? Are you okay?*

I'm about to answer when a voice interrupts my conversation with my mate.

"Kornelius, there you are," Royce says, far closer than I would have given him credit for.

I don't move, not eager to let him know that he snuck up on me.

No one surprises me.

"Royce," I say, not looking away from the horizon where I had been watching him.

Royce is here, I tell Issy.

A shadow slips over the cracked grass and I finally glance at him.

He appears quite smug, likely knowing that he caught me off guard. I know it's probably because we're in the center of a gravesite, one filled to the brim with his ancestral power, but that doesn't make me feel any better.

"You said you had an update for me?" he asks casually as he summons a chair of bones, showing off his magic.

He has a lot more than he should, even in the middle of a graveyard. "Yes," I say, keeping my tone relaxed despite my mind zipping through possibilities of what we might have missed.

I've been tracking Royce since he began the competition with Zane of hunting Issy. Although, neither of them had made any great strides in finding her.

Almost as if they were waiting for her to come to them.

Suddenly, this plan feels like it's the wrong one.

Issy, I think we made a mistake. We can't tell Royce where you are. Are you still with Zy? Tell him to get you out of—

"An update on the witch betrothed to my cousin?" Royce asks, his eyes glittering with cruelty as he once again interrupts my internal conversation with Issy. "Or an update on the death stone?"

Standing, I decide I need to change gears. Royce is up to something and I'm not going to fall for it. I'll have to explain the rest to Issy when I get a chance.

She won't like it, but I need something of value to distract Royce.

"There's been movement in the death plane. Something that doesn't belong there is causing trouble. Remember that death goddess that Zane is always going on about? It seems he was actually onto something."

Royce taps his chin. "Oh, not what I was expecting

you to say. A death goddess, hmm? Zane is a little off his nut, even if he is useful now and again with that phasing ability of his. But a deity hiding in the death plane? I'm going to need proof of that."

I shrug. "Take it or leave it. I'm just telling you what I've learned." It isn't uncommon for Zy and me to perform spells or scrying recon in the death plane. Given our hybrid nature, it makes us uniquely suited for riskier spells that might stop the caster's heart.

Ours already don't beat.

Royce grins and the sunlight flickers as if someone jiggled a switch. He vanishes, then appears right in front of me as shadows spiral around him with ominous waves. "I was hoping you were going to tell me what you've really been up to."

"And what is that?" I ask, keeping my voice steady.

Kor, are you okay? What's going on? Issy presses, but I can't reply to her with Royce distracting me.

He chuckles. "The truth, Kornelius. That you fucked that little witch of yours—prepared her tight pussy, am I right?" He leans in and lightly slaps my cheek, making me snarl. "How did it feel putting your cold, dead cock inside of her knowing that I'm next?"

I know he's goading me, but he's threatening Issy.

He's making me see *red*.

Snarling, I engage my vampiric speed that's comparable to Royce's strange power on this gravesite.

He doesn't even try to stop me.

Instead, he laughs when I rip into his throat and send his blood splattering over the thirsty, cracked grass.

I realize my mistake too late.

All this time we were planning a trap for Royce and Zane, unaware that the trap had already been placed.

We played right into their hands. My spirit screams as Royce engages the death stone link that has enslaved my soul for years. A graveyard is the perfect place to make the transition he was already planning when he arrived.

Maybe he's been planning it all along, just waiting for his chance.

The death stone is still a part of me, even if it has gone missing. And it is currently hiding inside of Jewel, a manifestation spirit with a direct link to my mate, to one of the most powerful death witches in the world that I am now permanently connected to.

Make room, Kornelius. It's time for you to fulfill your role as my vessel.

It's time to step aside.

It's time to wither and die.

Royce's voice shouts and rumbles through my mind like thunder, shoving me deeper into the depths of my psyche. Pain rakes through me as he tries to shove me out entirely, but I dig in and carve myself in place.

It leaves me helpless and completely immobile. I can't even hear more than an echo of Issy's questioning voice asking if I'm okay.

I watch in horror through my own eyes as Royce gains control of my limbs. He flexes my fingers, then tests out my fangs.

"Oh, this'll be fun," he murmurs using my voice, then steps over his spent body.

Kor? Issy presses again and I'm able to hear her.

But I can't reply.

To my horror, my voice responds to her, but it's not me saying the words. It's Royce.

I'm here, he says, using my voice. *I'm on my way.*

What about Royce? she asks.

A grin stretches across my face even though I didn't command my body to make the gesture. *Don't worry. He's coming, too.*

Chapter 11

Jasper

Zane's walking out in the open, in the middle of the day, and it's confusing the shit out of me.

Any news? I ask Zy.

There's no response, of course, because he's still walling me out like a dick.

It figures that the moment I obtain the skill to telepathically communicate with my brothers—brothers I had thought were long dead—they shut me out.

The last thing I heard from Zy was some lewd competition shit regarding our mate. Which could have been fun if we weren't in the middle of a life-or-death plan.

And now Zane is testing my stealth as he wanders past windows and earns looks from Outcast Coven members.

Some of them are likely matriarchs, and he ignores one when she tries to stop him.

"Vampire!" she snarls, tossing a magic rope at him like he's some loose bull in a herd of wildflowers. "You're coming with me!"

Zane phases straight through the restraint and keeps on going. "That's no way to treat one of your own. Mind your manners." He sends the rope phasing back at her, wrapping around her neck and choking her until she blacks out.

Zane keeps walking as if nothing of significance happened.

One of your own? I think. That's an odd thing for a vampire to say to a witch.

Something big is going down. My father wouldn't reveal his presence to the Outcast Coven unless he was untouchable.

Or was about to be.

What are you up to? I wonder as I stick to the minor shadows offered by one of the buildings. I stop at a crosswalk and patiently watch as he heads down a back road.

The direction where we've hidden Issy.

Zane is supposed to make his way there, eventually, but not until I receive the signal from Kor or Zy and lure him with her scent. I have a piece of her dress in my pocket in a zipped plastic bag. He can't smell it, and I'm not actively guiding him, so he shouldn't know where to go.

Yet, as I follow him through winding streets, it becomes apparent he knows precisely where Issy is holed up.

It's too early. No one has given me the signal that Royce is in place. The timing has to be perfect.

Royce has to find Issy, and then Zane needs to come in shortly after that. Not too long that Royce has a chance to go after our mate, and he certainly can't run into Royce before he sees Issy or it won't look so damning.

Royce is supposed to believe that Zane found Issy first and destroyed any chance for her to be suited for the living patriarchs as a mate. She will look half-dead, thanks to a little spell, and that has a short timeline for us to work with.

I'm about to stop him myself when I spot Kornelius waiting on the front steps of the run-down mansion where Issy is waiting inside.

What the hell?

Kornelius smirks when he sees Zane. "Took you long enough, old vamp."

Zane slaps Kor on the shoulder as if they're old friends. "It's my last day as a vampire. Has me a bit nostalgic, is all."

Last day as a vampire?

Kor chuckles and opens the door.

Zy is there waiting for them, which isn't part of the plan.

What the fuck are you doing, man?

He's staring at Kor. "You're not coming in here. I know what my brother smells like, and you are not my brother. Not anymore."

Kor chuckles. "Zane? Would you mind teaching *my brother* a lesson?"

If this is some new part of the plan, I'm left in the dark.

I expect this isn't the plan, though. Kornelius is

acting fucking strange and Zy is saying he isn't his brother. Did Kor do something to make him mad?

But why would he say he smelled different?

"Last warning, son," Zane says. "Let us through or you get to be a vessel earlier than planned. That would be a shame, because you're my favorite."

Zy's fingers flex, and it's the only warning before he rips his glasses from his face.

Kor steps between him and Zane. "Shut your eyes!"

Vessel, I repeat in my head. *Kor's a vessel!*

I'm not sure which patriarch has possessed him, but the last time this happened, it took Fallon's immense death magic to expel the spirit.

I'm not Fallon, but I also don't have any other recourse than to break from hiding and assault Kor and Zane from behind before they get into the mansion.

Issy is there, helpless.

Collared.

Silenced.

Zane must have known I was watching because he spins on me, raking his claws against my throat as he openly laughs. "You were right, Royce. This is fun."

"The fun has only just gotten started," Royce says with Kor's voice. He whispers a spell and it sends Zy flying overhead onto the street.

He's out cold while I'm left gasping for air, my open wound gushing blood onto the ground. His eyes are swollen shut as magic rips through him, jolting him awake and making him scream.

Royce and Zane are joking about who gets Issy first as they pass through the threshold.

"Shit," I curse when my wound finally closes, and I run for the open doorway.

But I slam into an invisible barrier, sending blood gushing from my nose. "Fuck! Issy! Kor!" I beat against it, fear gripping my dead heart. "*Get out of there!*"

Chapter 42

Issy

Footsteps sounding in the foyer make my heart skip a beat. I could have sworn I heard shouting outside, but it's difficult to hear over the screams of the dead.

I was right to worry that this ancient, abandoned place would be teeming with lost, miserable spirits. My thumb rolls over my temple as I struggle against the overlapping echoes in my mind.

Luckily, I shouldn't have to deal with it for too long. I'm expecting Kornelius any moment now. He's supposed to be leading Royce here for the next stage of the plan.

My collar is back in place, making me feel vulnerable even though I know Kor will be with me any minute to remove it when it's time.

I can't simply speak Royce dead—not when he would add to the patriarchs' ranks on the other side.

I need him to kill Zane, or at least injure him enough to allow my mates to finish the job, and then I need his blood while he's left alive.

Or partially alive.

It'll be the link I need to Daithi as an O'Neely blood relative.

Royce is going to see me bloodied, bitten, and disheveled. Then Kor will help him put two and two together.

As I lift the edge of my tattered dress, I'm both embarrassed and glad by the convincing touches that Zy added. He's gone to make sure Jas's part of the plan stays on track and will act as a decoy if needed. Because Jas is supposed to make sure Zane arrives when the shouting starts to get all the blame and hopefully spark a fight between the two of them.

It's a sound plan. Zane and Royce engaged in a competition to see who could hunt me down, so they're already pitted against one another. Royce thinks I'm his property because he's a patriarch-in-training and next in line. I'm his "reward" that Daithi will bless him with. If Zane ruins me, it should royally piss him off.

But when Kor walks in, I sense something has gone horribly wrong.

Especially when Zane enters right behind him.

Zane is grinning at me as if he's pleased by my ruined appearance. "Oh, aren't you beautiful covered in blood? That dress suits you too, little witch."

"You're going to have to share," Kor says, but his voice sounds off. He licks his lengthening fangs. "That smell is incredible. Is it always like this?"

Share? Smell? Is this some tactic to turn him against Royce because we've mixed up the order?

I'm lying on the sofa, leaning against the armrest with

my hand shading my gaze. I squint through the curtain of my eyelashes at them, not sure if I should break character.

I have suffered blood loss and fatigue pulls at me. It's not entirely an act, but adrenaline pumps through my rapidly beating heart.

Zy? Jas? I venture, hoping to reach out to my mates for information about what's going on.

I don't hear anything from either of them. Instead, the screams of the dead only seem to get louder as Kor and Zane approach.

My suspicions that something is horribly wrong are confirmed when Kor places his hand on my arm.

And the screams of the dead don't go silent. They *heighten*.

Zy! Jas! I shout in my head at my mates, but I can't get through.

"Kor?" I say when he wraps his fingers around my wrist and pulls me into his lap. I lean in and whisper. "My collar?"

"Is going to stay on," he says with a cruel grin. "Can't have you killing your new mates." He licks his lips when my eyes widen.

This isn't Kor.

I don't know how it's possible, but—

"*Royce?*" I hiss as I try to lurch away, but he has Kor's strength. I can't twist out of his grip.

"Aw," he murmurs, sounding disappointed. "I was hoping you wouldn't figure that out until I was already inside of you. Your vampires are nothing but body bags for the patriarchs. Don't you know that by now?"

Zane rolls his eyes. "You're no patriarch."

Kor—no, *Royce*—scoffs. "I believe I qualify for a promotion after dying for the cause. And the spell on Kornelius wouldn't have worked if I wasn't powerful enough to take over his body. So I'll take the title of patriarch now."

"Did you push out his spirit, too?" Zane presses.

Royce doesn't answer right away. "It doesn't matter. If he refuses to leave, he can stay as a prisoner in this body while he watches what I do to his witch."

While Royce's words terrify me, there's hope that flutters inside my chest.

Kor's still in there somewhere.

"And I'll be taking my prize, too." He growls as he presses his nose against my bruised throat. "Veins already opened for me, hmm? I do love the little act you were trying to pull—pitting Zane and me against each other. So cute to think we'd fall for that or that we don't have the penthouse bugged."

Shit. Of course the penthouse is bugged. The patriarchs must have let things fly just so Zy and Kor thought they could speak freely.

It was brilliant. It was a long-term game that the patriarchs are known for.

And I fell for it.

Zane blurs, yanking me out of Royce's lap. I screech from the rough jolt that nearly snaps my elbow as I stumble against the tall, blond-haired vampire. My mute collar prevents my voice from killing them like it should have.

You don't have any experience with feeding yet," Zane says to Royce. "You'll gnaw her head straight off without

414

learning control. And given that you chose one of the strongest of my sons, I'd appreciate not having to damage her to get her away from you when you fail."

Royce crosses his arms, making Kor's muscles bulge underneath his dress shirt. "And you propose to teach me control?"

"That was always the plan," Zane says with a grin.

My eyes widen. This is why Zane was kept around. The patriarchs needed a vampire to teach them how to function in the bodies of my mates.

Because even though they have death magic, they are vampires through and through.

Royce blurs across the room, placing a hand on me. "You'll have to teach me control after I get my first taste," he says, his eyes turning red with bloodlust.

Then he bites just above the edge of my collar.

The room explodes in chaos as I scream. Zane is shouting, clawing at Kor's body, and leaving deep gouges in his skin.

But Royce is oblivious. He sinks his fangs deep into my skin and starts to draw in long, suctioning pulls.

He begins to feed.

A single word tingles on the edge of my tongue. The only one that has any hope of saving me.

My sister's name.

And my safe word spelled to protect me if any of my mates go too far. Zy said the safe word spell applied to him and his brothers because we had bound it to his blood.

Blood he shares with Kor.

"Fallon!"

Magic snaps through me, crackling over my skin and making my collar burn like fire.

I claw at it as I scream. The sound only builds through the room, like pressing against a bubble that's about to burst.

I expect my sister's voice in my head, but she doesn't respond.

Which means either she's dead, or she can't hear me.

"Fucking bitch!" Zane growls, slapping me across the face. The force sends me sprawling across the floor. "Are you trying to kill my only shot at tasting a death goddess? This idiot might be pathetic, but he's my link to the death plane." He kicks me right in the ribs, making me grunt in pain as the wind is knocked out of me.

"Don't."

Kick.

"Fuck."

Kick.

"This up for me!"

Royce groans as he falls onto his back and clutches at his chest. "Holy shit. What was that?"

"A safe word that came in handy, even if it didn't work the first time," Zy says from the front door. He's bloody and hanging his arm around Jas, and his eyes are swollen shut.

Spirits, what did they do to you?

He looks like death warmed over, but he's alive. And he's *here*. They both are.

We all are, sweetheart, Kor's voice says inside my head.

Tears of relief prick my eyes.

Kor's in there, somewhere. His body flinches as Royce continues to grab at his chest.

His eyes change from red to silver and back to red again.

"Fuck! This asshole is trying to push me out!" Royce growls. There's an echo to his words now that wasn't there before.

Zane was rearing back to kick me again, but he's looking away from me now. "Damn idiot," he says, then spits. "You disgust me. I knew you were just a wannabe patriarch."

I claw my way across the splintered floorboards, ignoring the pain digging into my skin as I head toward Kor.

Follow my voice, I tell Kor. *You're in charge of your own body, not some asshole patriarch, you hear me?*

Keep talking, sweetheart, he replies. *Your voice is music to my ears.*

"Give me a blade," Zy says.

He's completely blind with his eyes swollen shut, so I'm not sure what he intends to do with a weapon. Dark veins spider out from his eyes, suggesting a spell is keeping him from healing.

Jasper doesn't question him. He produces two from the many he had stocked in his arsenal. "Take as many as you want, brother."

417

Zy takes a moment to compose himself, then swirls them both around using his wrists in a practiced motion.

A feral grin stretches over his lengthening fangs.

Jasper looks at me. "Turn the lights out, witchling."

I realize what my mates intend, but it takes faith in them to believe they can pull it off.

My lips move of their own accord, my spirit giving me all the faith I need.

And then the room goes dark, and the screams begin.

Chapter 13

Zyran

A rush of magic informs me that Issy has come through.

It's pitch black, leaving everyone else in the room just as helpless as me.

Although, *helpless* is a strong word. I'm never helpless, even temporarily blind.

"You underestimated me," I whisper, projecting my voice to the other side of the room with my magic.

An explosion of wood and cracked furniture tells me Zane has reacted, because I doubt that Royce is able to move right now.

And I know exactly where he is. Jasper whispered his precise location to me before Issy turned off the lights and blocked out any illumination coming in from the window.

As much as I'd enjoy going after our father, Jasper is the one who will get the honors.

I have a greater purpose.

Are you close, baby girl? I ask Issy through our shared mental connection.

I-I think so, she replies.

Good. Only move when I create a distraction.

"Damn it, Zyran!" my father shouts. "Quit being an ungrateful brat!"

"Ungrateful?" I ask with a lilt to my voice, this time sending it toward the fireplace.

A rush of heat tells me embers have been sent everywhere and my father hisses in pain. "When your mother, the most coveted vampire in generations, died giving birth to you three, do you think I wanted you? Three little death-mongers. Fuck no. I spared your lives!"

"How generous," I retort, sending my voice back toward the splintered wood. "I didn't know you loved our mother so much."

My father doesn't fall for it this time and rushes past me. If I had been a little to the left, he would have found me.

Careful, Zy, Jasper warns. *I'm close, but he's fast.*

I know our father is fast. That's why I'm playing dirty.

"Love?" he says with a cruel chuckle. "No. She was fucking useful. A *whore*. I sold her body and made a fucking fortune, and you assholes ruined it."

I freeze.

Don't let him goad you, Issy says in my mind. *My father was no better. Do you remember what I did to him? Do you remember what I showed you?*

The spelled dream memory sweeps through my mind.

Issy had been fearless, powerful, and bold.

When I think of my mother, I don't feel like any of those things.

A voice tickles the back of my neck. "Gotcha," Zane says, then slams into me. Pain explodes down my neck as he bites hard enough to snap my collarbone.

"Zy!" Issy screams. Her words are stunted by the damn mute collar that we should never have put on her. Now we're going to pay the price with our blood.

I don't have time to fight Zane. The plan hinges on Royce. We may not have his body, but we have the body he's possessing.

It's going to have to be enough.

"I got him, Zy!" Jasper shouts as my father growls against my neck, shredding muscle and sinew as I struggle forward.

I can't get to him with my blades, but that's okay. Jasper hits him, forcing him to unlatch from my neck long enough for me to lunge forward.

Brace yourself, Kor, I warn. It's the only heads-up he gets before two blades slam into his chest cavity.

Royce's spirit roars as he receives the full hit of pain that causes. It won't kill him, being in a vampire body, but it'll hurt like fuck.

Now, Issy! I tell my mate, and then I feel her hand on my wrist.

She leans into me and whispers a spell while I reach up and prepare to remove her collar.

She leans into Kor next, presumably licking the blood from his chest, and that's my moment.

Now, Zy, she tells me, still maintaining that confident, bold tone that she had when she killed her own father.

Ignoring the screams of pain stabbing down my neckline, I remove her collar, then I'm hit with the full, pent-up power of her voice.

"Get out, Royce O'Neely. Kornelius Justi is *mine.*"

Chapter 44

Issy

Т he plan doesn't include killing Royce so soon, but he's technically already dead.

The mark on my wrist burns as I absorb his spirit while he tries to escape. It's an alteration to the plan, but it works.

Fallon's voice cuts through a moment later, telling me that the barrier around the room has dropped. *Issy! I heard you call me. What the hell is going on? Where are you?*

Not now, Fallon, I hiss as I try to concentrate.

I'm weaving the most complex spell of my life. It's a combination of multiple spell books in various languages, and it's all from memory.

My sister blessedly remains silent as I utter the words one after another, looping them together with matching linguistics to write the spell.

One segment for binding Royce's bloodline to my command, similar to what the patriarchs did to all the females in the Outcast Coven. It weaves through his spirit like a needle with magical string.

He screams at every stitch. His spirit breaks apart, fraying at the edges until he's an emblem for me to wear on my heart.

Then Royce is no more—he's simply power for me to wield.

The next segment is for linking that power to Jewel through the mark on my wrist.

Zy's necklace responds to my words and lights up, providing illumination in the otherwise pitch-black room.

This part of the spell has accidentally linked him, too, because technically he also shares the mark. I curse myself for not thinking of that.

Because now all my mates are glowing—meaning they're coming with me.

To the death plane.

Shit.

The air vibrates as I continue the spell, unable to stop now. It could kill us all and likely punch a hole through Staten Island in the process. It wouldn't be a portal. It would be a vortex of death.

As much as I want to burn this place to the ground, a fragment of hope still remains. I saw all the headstones my sister had broken. I learned of all the women ultimately freed—the matriarchs who could finally retake control and make the Outcast Coven what it was meant to be.

Whatever that looks like, they deserve a chance.

Hope is the third segment, and I form the words as Jasper takes out his lifetime of anger on his father.

I speak of the future as Jasper slashes with a long blade, taking off an arm.

I speak of new generations as he removes a leg.

Blood coats the splintered floor by the time he's done, and I'm ready to move on to the final segment of my spell.

A low hum reverberates in my throat while I allow Jasper to complete his job. We don't need Zane anymore.

Now, Jas, I whisper into his mind.

He glances up at me, briefly, his dark eyes teeming with retribution and rage.

Zyran is holding on to the daggers in Kor's chest, while Kor struggles to breathe.

It's no matter. We'll all be transported to the death plane soon.

Jasper looks down at his father, a body with no limbs and bloody stumps. The vampire stares back at him with dark eyes filled with hate. "You should never have been born," he growls.

"Goodbye, Father," Jasper whispers, then cleanly slices off his head.

It rolls across the ground without ceremony as I speak the last part of the spell in my native tongue.

"Powers of death, accept this sacrifice. Take us to a goddess who's not a goddess—a spirit of hope and a spirit of light that burns in the dark. Bring to her the key to break chains and the medium of death to transform into life.

"Bring her our hope.
"Bring her our hate.
"Bring her our *souls*."
So it is done. So mote it be.

Chapter 45

Issy

I expected a trip to the death plane to be more painful in my corporeal form, but it's not.

My spell is effective, using Royce's spirit to weave a netting of protection over all of us as I step into the library that Jewel built.

She's waiting for me, sweating and weak as she leans against massive doors. They bump against her back, bulging with a weight coming from behind it.

"About time," she says with a frail laugh.

Her soft silver hair seems flat and wet ringlets cling to her face. Her eyes, once a light blue but now more of a soft gray, widen when my mates come up from behind me.

Jasper takes my hand. Zy loops his arm around my waist, and Kor takes his place at my back, resting a palm on my shoulder.

All of them are touching me, providing me with strength and magic.

But most of all, they remain at my side or behind me, letting me take the lead.

That is the power of their trust.

Their belief.

"So these are your mates, huh?" Jewel asks with a sense of awe. She leans away from the door, then a rough slam comes from the other side, making the reinforcement beam crack.

She curses and pushes back up against it again. She's clearly struggling when she shouldn't be. She's one of the most powerful supernatural species to exist.

"You're a manifestation spirit, Jewel," I tell her. My words roll out in waves of power. My spell is in full effect, and each lapping echo of energy rushes toward Jewel, seeping into her and putting color back into her face. "You can do anything that you believe you can do, so why are you holding up the door to this library looking like you're about to lose?"

Jewel blinks at me a few times. My magic has helped her to roll her shoulders back as she seems to think of her answer. "I-I don't know. I'm just tired."

"It's not strength that's been worn down," Kor offers from behind me. "It's your confidence." He presses a kiss to the back of my head. "My mate here believes in you, Jewel. Enough to bring us here to show you herself."

Another bulge at the reinforcement makes the entire door crack and Jewel squeaks with alarm. "I'm sorry, but I don't think that's going to do me much good. My magic doesn't work... that way, *oof.*"

Another slam sends her flying forward, but I don't move to help her.

Because she needs to see for herself what she's capable of.

"Let them in," I say, eager to face Daithi and his army. "You won't have to fight them alone."

Jewel scrambles to her feet as the door continues to crack, revealing dark gouges that allow us to see through to the other side into the native land of the death plane.

It's dark, gloomy, and rocky. The only thing that pleases me about it is knowing that Daithi must hate it here.

Jewel joins me as the door disintegrates, revealing the patriarchs just as I remember them.

They're wearing robes and Daithi is their lead. He has stubble as if he hasn't shaved, even though I know it's his spirit looking at me now. He gives me a cruel grin. "Issy, my dear. How sweet of you to bring our vessels to me."

Jasper moves as if to step in front of me, but I hold him back.

All of you need to keep your hands on me. Feed me as much of your magic as you can.

It'll weaken them, but we only have one shot at this.

Daithi approaches, then stops to regard Jewel. "And you, stubborn thing. I'm going to put you back in the tomb designed for you. You're important to me, dear."

She backs up far enough to brush against me. "You mean my *magic* is important to you. That's how you've done all this, right?" She starts counting off items on her fingers. "Made spells to use vampire hybrids for your vessels. Kept you and your buddies corporeal enough in the death plane to walk around and get into trouble. Oh, and don't get me started on the death stone shit."

Daithi frowns at the mention of the stone. "Yes, about that. I'd like it back now."

"It's been lost since the first massacre in Lapland," Kor says.

I grin because I know exactly where it went.

"Not lost," I say, glancing at Jewel. "*Hidden.*" I show her the mark on my wrist. "It's here, isn't it?"

Her eyes widen. "I... placed it in you?"

"You entrusted it to me," I correct her. "Now it's your turn to take it back. To destroy it for good."

"No!" Daithi shouts as the patriarchs corral around him, murmuring a spell.

An invisible weight presses down on me, but I know this spell. It's a suppression spell that'll put the victim in a coma if allowed to progress.

Always trying to make us go to sleep, I muse as I wave away the dark magic with a blast of energy. *Always trying to silence voices more powerful than your own.*

Jewel ignores the chaos. Instead, she's pressing her fingers against my skin, staring at the mark as her expression changes.

I smile when I see hope in her eyes.

The death stone glitters into existence as the mark she placed on me fades. It rises into the air.

Jewel glances at me, but I give her a nod. "All yours."

She's been locked in here for Gods know how long. This is her win to take.

She bites her lower lip, then reaches up to touch the stone. "I'm finally free," she breathes, her belief transforming into reality as the stone fractures.

She's gone in the next instant, but I remain. My spell

that's keeping us here is weakening. We'll be going soon, just like she did, but not right away.

Because I have a job to finish here.

The ground rumbles and shakes in response and the patriarchs are left without their lifeline.

I shrug off my mates, giving them each an encouraging caress before I approach Daithi, who is the last one holding on.

"So much turmoil, and for what?" I ask him as he crumples to the ground. Each word I utter now shreds his spirit like gauze caught in the heat of a flame.

His robes dig into him when he moves, turning into molten power that drips down to his translucent bones.

The patriarchs behind him are nothing but a rippling pond of death. Darkness sweeps through them and they fizzle like acid, the weak spell giving them form slowly fading.

They won't have a tombstone to go to.

They won't get to *stay*.

Glee fills me as I watch each patriarch puff out of existence as if he had never been born.

Daithi, though, will be the last. He's selfishly kept more of the stolen energy from Jewel to himself.

He'll die like the rest of them, but I'm going to make sure he suffers.

"This... is the order of things!" he growls in reply. "Men in charge. Women in their place! You would do foolish, useless things with your power if left unchecked!"

I run my finger over his chin, delighting when his skin tears.

He screams.

"Then I shall do this foolish thing, Daithi. I'll rip away everything you hold dear. I'll ensure the women of the Outcast Coven will thrive and I'll erase every impact of the patriarchs from the documentation of time." I glance around the library, watching as it melts away.

All the knowledge won't be lost, though. Jewel will hold on to it for me.

I lean into Daithi, hoping he can last long enough for everything I have to say. "You won't even be dust as far as history is concerned."

He wheezes as my words thrash around us, forming a storm. Through the rushing glimmers between the tempest, I can see my mates watching me.

Zyran's bright green eyes glow with power and approval.

Kornelius is pleased.

And Jasper looks like he wants to kiss me.

"Damn bitch in heat," Daithi growls. I'm impressed he still has the strength to form words. "You're my mate! Mine to fuck. Mine to own!"

I run my fingers around his disintegrating neck, forcing him to look up at me as he fades away. "Not anymore," I say, this time keeping my words barely above a whisper. "But you? You're mine... mine to *destroy*."

I push all of my power into each syllable. I rejoice when his spirit finally fractures. Darkness bleeds into his eyes and his skin melts away, leaving a screaming skull until even that is gone.

You're so fucking beautiful, Jasper says in my mind.

So ruthless, Zy adds with a pleased lilt to his voice.

And completely ours, Kor says.

I look up at them as I allow my spell to reach completion, to draw us back to the realm of the living.

Because my work here is done... and now all I want to do is revel in bliss with my mates.

Take me into your darkness, my loves. Take me so deep that I'll never want to see the light again.

Chapter 16

Issy

Three weeks later...

I'm woken up the same way I have been for roughly the past three weeks.

With a kiss on my lips. A kiss on my throat.

And a kiss on the inside of my thigh.

"Don't open your eyes yet," Zy whispers in my ear. "We're going to play the guessing game this morning."

My insides flip.

Because the *guessing game* means we're definitely going to be late for breakfast with my sister.

It's an important day. One that I want to spend with her, but my mates seem intent on keeping me to themselves.

"We don't have time," I protest, but a hand gently covers my eyes. I guess it's Kor's based on the strong but gentle touch of it.

"There's always time to love you," Zy tells me. His

441

voice has a playful tease to it, one that he gets when I know he's determined to have his way.

I usually wind up squeezed between the three of them, limp and useless and very, very satisfied by the time they're done with me.

Which sounds wonderful, but my mates have me for the rest of our lives. My sister, though, is a busy queen. She made special time for me today.

Another hand slips up my throat, putting weight on my collarbone, while a body rests against my hip.

That's definitely Jasper.

"Let me talk to her," I say, careful not to speak my sister's name aloud.

Her name is still considered a safe word and I don't know if the spell remains active. I haven't had to use it in the past three weeks.

My mates know my limits now and they don't cross them.

"You have thirty seconds," Zy whispers in my ear.

Fallon? I say, reaching out to her in my mind. If Zy says I have thirty seconds, then that's it.

I could push him if I wanted to, but I honestly enjoy his games. He would respect my boundaries if I established them.

But I'm weak for my mates, so I let them get away with far too much. Even if they've refused to feed on me while trapped in this cottage, they have no problem doing everything else to make my body sing.

Hey! my sister says. *I was just picking out what to wear. Do you think the blue dress or red dress would match what you're wearing?* She goes silent for a second. *Gods, I'm so insensitive. Pretend I didn't ask you that.*

I grin because today is my last day as a mortal witch.

The last day I'll have a heartbeat.

Because my mates are going to turn me into a hybrid like them.

I could wear red, I suggest. *Just because my mates have to drink all my blood doesn't mean I can't have a little dark humor about it.*

Fallon sighs on the other end. *Are you positive you want to go through with this? I mean... never mind. We can talk about it over breakfast. I made sure the chef prepared every delicious dish I could think of. Belgian waffles with strawberries and whipped cream, soft-boiled eggs in golden holders, ham and cheese croissants—*

I stop her before she makes me too hungry, because Zy is now nibbling impatiently at my ear, making me hungry for something else. *I'm going to miss breakfast,* I tell her mournfully. *My mates seem intent on distracting me.*

Fallon isn't mad. She chuckles as if she can relate, which she most assuredly can. Her phantoms especially have made her late for more than one visit with me. *I'm honestly not surprised. That's okay. We can meet for lunch or dinner instead. I'll tell the chef to get started. Oh! That means we can do steak and shrimp and lobster. There are these little beef pocket things, too, that I just discovered.*

There she goes, making me hungry again—but dinner does sound good now.

Showing off the fact that you have a royal chef? I muse. Although, I'm grateful for her efforts to make my last day eating food as a source of nutrition worthwhile. She has held off trying to change my mind. The only thing she said about it was that she felt it was too big a sacrifice to give up my birthright.

But what birthright do I really have? What does it bring me?

My mates are my world. I want them and nothing else.

That was a sentiment she understood, so she backed off. Luckily, she's been more supportive than I could have hoped and now she's trying to make sure I celebrate my last day.

I'm queen, might as well embrace it. She chuckles again. *Will you still be teleporting using Kornelius's ability? Or do you want me to talk to Amala? She is supplying Nolan with some more portal potions—but she sure does charge an arm and a leg for them. They're pretty rare. And probably illegal.*

I giggle. *No need to waste expenses on me, sister. We'll be there by dinner.*

I don't even suggest lunch because I know that won't be happening.

I'll see you then, Issy. Have fuuuuuun.

I can practically see her eyebrows waggling.

"Time's up," Zy whispers in my ear. "Let the guessing game begin. You have a fifty-fifty chance to guess correctly and receive your reward."

The hand on my throat and the one over my eyes disappear. I've opened my eyes, but the room is pitch black even though it's morning.

My mates have picked up a few tricks in the past three

weeks. I can't see a thing as strong arms spread my legs and a thumb prepares me, rolling on my clit and making me bow off the bed. I'm always naked and ready for them, per their request.

And often rewarded for it.

Spirits...

This never gets old. I expected to tire of sex after the initial honeymoon period with my mates. After destroying Daithi and the patriarchs for good, I returned to the abandoned house with all my mates and I fully healed.

A blessing from Jewel.

She joined us when we portaled back to my sister's and explained everything that had happened to her. Now we're in my cottage in Lapland and almost done with restorations while Jewel seeks asylum in Reykjavík.

The matter of the Houses wanting me dead is still an issue. Tensions have run high, and while I'm under the protection of the dukes, it's only a temporary situation.

We talked about solutions to appease the Houses. A permanent mute collar was one of them, but I couldn't stomach that idea.

Telling the Houses to fuck off was another, but Kaspian convinced me that would result in more death than my conscience could bear.

I already have a thousand murders to atone for, and it feels fitting that the punishment will be sacrificing my life.

But I won't die, even though my heart will stop.

I will become something new.

Reborn.

"Guess who," Zy whispers in my ear when one of my mates enters me.

I draw in a deep breath as the fullness stretches me. My mind goes completely blank and I'm unable to even think for a moment.

Kornelius and Jasper are similar in size, but their methods are different.

They like to trick me, though. They are able to talk telepathically and give each other tips about what the other might do.

The mate entering me pulls me into him by wrapping strong hands around my thighs so that he goes deep. Then he leans over me and glides his fingers down my ass, not stopping even when he reaches my back entrance.

He slips two fingers in, giving me a full feeling that has me panting while he slowly thrusts, keeping his hips secured on my clit to supply the pressure I need.

It's a move Jasper would do. Kor likes to look at my body while one of his brothers stimulates my nipples. Jasper is still the worst when it comes to sharing, but it could all be a trick.

My mate pauses when I haven't spoken, leaving me full with his fingers and his cock.

"Fifty-fifty," Zy says.

"I'm not sure," I admit.

Zy clicks his tongue in my ear. "Then guess—that's the game, baby girl."

I *want* to guess correctly. My reward is the orgasm my mates are pushing me toward.

If I'm wrong, I'll be edged until I'm a begging, wallowing mess.

Which, in all honesty, is also fun, but I don't know if I can handle delayed gratification right now.

But then the mate inside of me gives me a little hint.

He uses his magic, sending a throbbing wave of pleasure through me by touch alone. It nearly makes me climax as it gathers at my core.

That's something only Jasper can do.

Cheat, Kor says to him, allowing me to hear their conversation in my head.

"It's Jasper," I say, pleased.

"Very good, little witchling," Jasper says, moving his body again, sending sensation rolling through me.

His magic coaxes me.

His fingers fill me.

And his cock touches that deep part inside of me that threatens to make me explode.

Zy chuckles in my ear, then kisses my neck while Kor joins in, taking my mouth with his.

"You win, baby girl," Zy whispers, and that's all the encouragement Jasper needs.

I let pleasure take me under while still surrounded by darkness.

All my mates work in tandem to bring me bliss, and I greedily take it. It's the last day I'll be Ishara Doyle, the death witch with the deadly voice.

It's the last day the world will fear me as uncontrollable.

Amala has told us what'll happen when my mates turn me.

I will be banished from the death plane. I'll lose my

447

connection to it entirely and be left with only the ability to access magic in the realm of the living.

I will still be able to cast spells and manipulate death magic, but I'll be immortal and denied my headstone.

It's a sacrifice—but it also means I'll never risk losing my mates.

Because when I die, I'll go where they go.

As immortals, our deaths will hopefully be nonexistent, or a very long time from now. And I won't have to worry about the issue of aging while they remain forever young.

As euphoria overtakes me, I know I've made the right decision, because I'll always be with my mates just as we are now.

You are mine.

All of you.

Forevermore.

Epilogue: Issy

Two days later...

"**W**hat the fuck happened to our cottage?" Ayla asks as she stands in the doorway, completely stunned. She's sporting a heavy backpack and lets it fall to the ground.

Putting the book I'm reading in my lap, I respond with sign language out of habit, even though I don't need to. *I redecorated.*

That's an understatement, really. The cottage was practically falling in on itself by the time Daithi's army was done with it, then the forest tried to reclaim it while I was gone.

While my mates were helping me fix it back up, I might have gotten a little carried away.

"Redecorated?" she says incredulously, entering the living area to wander through the new leather couches and polished oak end tables until she arrives at the new bar Zy installed. He had to pop out the entire cottage wall to fit it in, but there's nothing a little magic and shirtless, manly labor can't fix.

She stares at the various liquors, at the painted cabinets that Kor and I picked out colors for, and then blinks at a new espresso machine that Jasper bought for me when he found out I like coffee.

"How did you afford all this? Did you finally ask Fallon for money?"

I smile but make sure not to laugh. "Not exactly," I say aloud. "Let's just say I've come into contact with rare supernatural blood that buys anything I want."

Ayla freezes, not from what I said but because I said the words out loud. Fear flashes over her face before curiosity takes over when her spirit isn't ripped from her body.

I know it's rude to frighten her, but I can't resist the surprise.

You guys can come out now, I mentally think to my mates waiting patiently in the bedroom.

They knew that my cousin and roommate would finally be coming home today. She has been on a mission of her own, traveling the world, and as expected, she's out of touch when it comes to the latest news regarding me. Usually, there's not too much going on. My life has been uneventful since Fallon saved me.

And then that changed pretty quickly.

I have no doubt she heard about the massacres, but Fallon told her that I was safe and left it at that so I could have my fun.

Ayla produces a knife and twirls it. "I assume your

miraculous ability to speak without killing everyone around you has something to do with your new mates?"

I frown. "Hey, that was supposed to be a surprise."

Ayla gives me a flat stare. "Fallon told me. Otherwise, I would have sensed their auras and come in here and killed them, thinking someone else had forcibly mated you."

"Oh," I said sheepishly. "I didn't think of that."

She points the knife at the doorway. "Are they going to come out now or stand there all night?"

Ayla's magic hums around her with threatening waves when Zy, Jas, and Kor enter the room. Her power resides in soul magic, allowing her many gifts that would make most people envious.

Her looks are one of her best features, though, and I can't help but glance at my mates to see their reactions. She's gorgeous. Because she's adopted, she doesn't share my ethnicity. Where my hair is blonde, hers is black as midnight, with dark, almond-shaped eyes to match. Her olive skin is different from my own and looks silky to the touch.

It doesn't matter that she's been traveling. She's beautiful.

And untrusting. She was forcibly mated just like most witches in the Outcast Coven and she has no interest in taking a mate again.

Although, I have a feeling she will soon. There's something about her that seems compatible with darkness.

But she can't have my mates, my darkness. Possessive

instinct makes me evaluate their reactions to the unmated beauty that is my cousin.

Luckily, they only boast looks of intrigue and curiosity.

Zy gives me a look as if he knows what I'm thinking and his expression changes to one of devious sensuality when he meets my gaze. He's wearing his glasses, but his slight grin tells me that he's already planning activities for tonight.

Spirits, I need to move. Even though Ayla travels a lot, I do not want to be sharing a wall with her when she's home, not when Zy has that look.

"Ayla, meet my mates," I say, hoping an introduction will be a good place to start before I throw ideas about moving at her, because I have no idea where I'll go. I like it here.

Maybe my mates will build me a new cottage farther in the woods, I think to myself, although I haven't walled my thoughts off from my mates, so Zy responds.

You mean a secluded place where no one can hear you scream? Of course, baby girl. I'd love to build a new house for you.

I roll my eyes, but it sounds kind of wonderful.

Especially because my mates love to make me scream, even if my voice doesn't hold the same power it used to.

I'm absolutely adding a sex basement, too, Zy adds, making me blush.

Zy heads to the bar and begins making drinks. "What's your poison, Ayla?"

Ayla frowns, ignoring Zy while Jasper flops onto the

new sofa and Kornelius crosses his arms and leans against the mantel, looking amused by the situation.

It takes a few hours to explain the whole background to Ayla, but she listens intently while sipping the drink Zy made for her. After convincing her to drink it, she admitted it was good.

"A vampire," she says while coddling her glass that's more ice than drink now. The fireplace cheerfully burns while my mates have made themselves scarce.

There's not a lot of room in the cottage, so they left to tend to their hobbies. Zy likes to work in my garden. He's done a great job restoring it. Kornelius and Jasper headed into town, looking for trouble.

They always come back with a story and a new book for me to read.

And sometimes, blood.

"A vampire," I confirm, grinning to show off my fangs. I've learned how to control them, to a degree.

Ayla's eyes widen. "Wow. And where do you get... you know, the stuff you need to drink?"

"My mates," I say simply. "I feed on them and they mix in blood with Zy's drinks, too. Just... don't open the new freezer."

The blood bags in our freezer are a gift from my sister. It's one of the few expenses I've accepted from her, because I didn't want to risk myself or my mates getting too hungry and causing trouble. While I haven't been able to stomach drinking blood straight, drinking from my mates is a pastime I thoroughly enjoy and sustains me as long as they're drinking enough blood for all of us.

Ayla nods. "Noted." She sighs, then leans back in her

chair. "Well, I brought you a present, but I don't know if you'll want it now."

I raise an eyebrow. "A present? I always like presents."

She chuckles. "When I crossed into populated areas, mostly Gold and Garnet territory across the map, I picked up a few smut books that you like in other languages." She glances at the door. "Not sure if you need them now."

Doubling over, I laugh my first belly laugh in a while. "Oh, Ayla! Did you think I read those because I wasn't getting any?"

She smirks. "Well, *yeah*."

I wipe away cheerful tears. "No! I enjoy the romance and the story. The excitement and the thrill. It's not... it's not like that."

Ayla pulls the books out of her bag. She's packed them with her clothing to keep them from being damaged. "Uh-huh, whatever you say." She unwraps them, then hands them to me. "Maybe have your mates buddy-read with you. There's one in there about *knotting*."

I make a little "O" shape with my mouth. "Knotting? What's that?"

I know what it is, but Ayla has already made enough fun of me for tonight.

She grins. "I guess you'll have to read them to find out. I guarantee, though, your mates won't be able to replicate that one."

"A shame," I say. Although, given what knotting is, I'm glad they're not capable of it. They sensually torture me enough.

I flip open the first book and read the passage aloud.

Ayla leans back into her chair and smiles, clearly enjoying me reading to her.

Because I'm using my voice. I'm able to speak and be heard.

And for the first time in my life... I'm free.

The End

Need even more? Check out these IVV Universe Standalone Books with Shared Characters in Taste Me:

What happens when Ayla meets her knotty mate? Find out in Chase Me by Lexi C. Foss

Read Fallon's story that takes place before Issy finds her voice in Claim Me by Lexi C. Foss

Read about the sexy dukes in Mark Me by Mila Young

Jewel's story is coming up next in Treasure Me by J.R. Thorn in the next IVV season—see you there!

Author's Note

Thank you for reading *Taste Me*! I'm exhausted, thrilled, and on a coffee and adrenaline high as I write this closing note after finishing one of the most challenging and rewarding books of my author career.

Issy is such a complex character and one I feel very close to. She has her sister, Fallon, and all the feelings that come with their unique relationship make the story rich, emotional, and rounded.

Finding herself seemed like an impossible struggle, at least in her mind. And watching Issy grow throughout the book to the badass woman she becomes is mesmerizing.

Although, I wasn't sure if I was going to get through it a few times. Not because of anything Issy did, but because her guys would not stop trying to bone her!

Fated-mate sex, as Fallon called it, is seriously no joke.

It was hilarious how many times I texted my coauthor and editor, complaining about how the guys would not let up, to everyone's amusement. But, at the end of the day, I realize that even the safe word Zy developed was a vital part of the plot. Without it, would Issy have been able to overcome Royce's hold on Kor?

Maybe not.

I hope you enjoyed this complex tale. I look forward to writing Jewel's story next in *Treasure Me*! This story will be under my "Jennifer Thorn" pen name because it's MF. For clarification, any book that's solely "J.R. Thorn" will be reverse harem paranormal romance, but if it says "J.R. Thorn writing as Jennifer Thorn" or simply "Jennifer Thorn," then you can expect MF PNR.

Why MF? Because I might die if I write another standalone with three mates in it again. Too many peens. So much math. (And yes, I looked up questionable internet content to confirm that the explicit scenes in *Taste Me* were biologically possible and accurate. You're welcome.)

FOR THE CAUSE.

On that closing note, I hope you find me on social media so you don't miss my next release. See you on the other side!

XOXO

Jen

- J.R. Thorn

J.R. Thorn

Reverse Harem Paranormal Romance - Never Choose.

J.R. Thorn is a Reverse Harem Paranormal Romance Author who loves coffee, stormy weather, and heated discussions with her inner muse. She can often be found scribing her steamy stories in her writing cave far away from the prying eyes of her toddler, husband, two vocal cats, and canine pack!

www.AuthorJRThorn.com

Recommended Reading Order

All Books are Standalone Series listed by their sequential order of events

Elemental Fae Universe Reading List

Elemental Fae Academy: Books 1-3

Midnight Fae Academy

Fortune Fae Academy

Fortune Fae M/M Steamy Episodes

Candela

Winter Fae Queen

Hell Fae

Blood Stone Series Universe Reading List
Recommended Reading Order is Below

Seven Sins (Books 1-3)

Book 1: Succubus Sins

Book 2: Siren Sins

Book 3: Vampire Sins

The Vampire Curse: Royal Covens (Books 1-3)

Book 1: Her Vampire Mentors

Book Three: Moon Queen

Book Four: Moon Kissed

Dark Arts Academy (Vella)

Ongoing serial

Book One (KU)

Book Two (KU)

Unicorn Shifter Academy

• *Book One*

• *Book Two*

• *Book Three*

Non-RH Books (J.R. Thorn writing as Jennifer Thorn)

Noir Reformatory Universe Reading List

Noir Reformatory: The Beginning (Standalone)

Noir Reformatory: First Offense

Noir Reformatory: Second Offense

Noir Reformatory Turns RH from this point with the addition of a third mate

Noir Reformatory: Third Offense

Sins of the Fae King Universe Reading List

(Book 1) Captured by the Fae King

(Book 2) Betrayed by the Fae King

Learn More at www.AuthorJRThorn.com

JUST A TASTE, BABY GIRL...

Made in the USA
Columbia, SC
19 July 2024

38942154R00290